Bashert

HERB FREED

Bashert

BELLROCK PRESS LOS ANGELES

Bashert by Herb Freed
Published by Bellrock Press, Los Angeles, CA

To reach the author or Bellrock Press email: bellrockpress@aol.com

ISBN: 978-0-9985339-0-2

Other available versions:
Digital Distribution
ISBN: 978-0-9985339-1-9

Manufactured in the United States of America

First Edition

Cover and book design by John Lotte

The hands are the hands of Esau, but the voice is the voice of Marion.

All biography is fiction. And all fiction is biography.

—MARION S. FREED

Bashert

In every generation,

God follows two people He ordained at the beginning of time,

Urging them to observe His first commandment to Adam and Eve,

To unite body and soul and become one flesh,

For this is the purpose of Creation.

—FROM THE *BAAL SHEM TOV*

{ Chapter One }

1983

"My God!" Dan laughed out loud. He lay on his bed, his long body entwined with Marion's, his heart bursting with joy. They had just made love for the first time and he couldn't stop laughing. Marion laughed with him and gazed searchingly into his eyes.

"Are you okay?" she asked, tenderly.

"I don't know what's happening to me. I am happier than I ever have been, but it's so new. I'm not sure how to process it."

"I know we've just met," Marion said, "and this may be premature, but I want you to know that I have no plans to trap you or limit you in any way. If you ever want to make love to another woman, that's not a problem. Just tell me who she is and I'll be her."

Dan howled. "Marion, Marion! You are not trapping me. I want you. You're funny, you're smart, you're so . . . how did I ever find you?"

DAN AND MARION found one another four days earlier and they both knew the instant their eyes met that it was preordained. The morning after they met at a Writers Guild reading, he called. "Dear beautiful lady, this is Dan, as in the guy you met in the Zanuck Theater last night."

He invited Marion to his house in Hancock Park for dinner that evening. She came with Sheldon Keller, her writing partner and escort to the writer's event, but didn't leave with him. The next night, Dan stayed at Marion's house in Century City and the following morning she made a startling announcement to her therapist.

"I met the man I'm going to spend the rest of my life with."

"The man you met . . . two days ago?"

"Four."

"Do you realize how nutty that sounds?"

"It doesn't feel nutty at all. Thrilling, new, but definitely not crazy."

"We have to talk about this."

"I don't want to talk anymore. I've talked too much for too long. I'm happy, Larry, happier than I have ever been so I won't be needing therapy any longer."

"I'm afraid you're a lot sicker than I thought, Marion."

"Not sick. *Bashert.*"

"I'm sorry, I don't understand Hebrew. What does that mean, exactly?"

"My lover-hyphen-rabbi told me it's a Yiddish word that describes an important event for which there is no explanation other than destiny or the Divine Plan. The simple meaning is preordained."

"And you feel you were preordained to . . . ?"

"Be with this man for all eternity."

"I see, and you were preordained by . . . ?"

LATER THAT NIGHT, while Dan and Marion were dancing naked in her bedroom to "Carnival," the theme from *Black Orpheus. "Manhã, tão bonita manhã . . . ,"* Marion asked, "Do you believe we were preordained by God?"

With his arms wrapped around her, eyes closed, Dan said, "I believe we are one soul divided at birth by God, the cosmos and some indefinable mystical power and our mission in life was to find our other half. *Bashert.*"

Marion stopped dancing. "Then, you do believe our meeting was preordained by God?"

"I do," he said and caressed her neck. "Speaking of heavenly wonders, what is that divine fragrance?"

"Me, Marion . . . and the slightest whiff of Yves St. Laurent, Paris."

"Absolutely divine," Dan said and dropped to his knees.

"What are you doing?"

"Exploring parts of our body I didn't know we had before our souls were reunited."

"TALK TO ME," SHE SAID, sprawled on her soft linen sheets with her head on his chest and feeling happier and more alive than at any time she could remember. "How *did* we find one another? How does any preordained couple come together?"

"It's a mystery."

"Come on Dan, we're both screenwriters. If you can't do

better than that, I'm reporting you to the Guild . . . and the rabbis' union. They have one, don't they?"

"They do, but my membership expired. The concept of *bashert* lovers derives from the Kabbalah and I could dazzle you with a bunch of arcane sources, but the best description of the process is in a Polish movie made by Karl Levi in the mid-Fifties. The film is in Yiddish and titled—not surprisingly—*Bashert*."

"You're serious?"

"I take it you didn't see the film?"

Marion didn't know if he was teasing, but the way Dan told stories made her feel peaceful, like a little girl sitting on her father's lap when he brought home books from the library before she was able to read. She loved the way her father sounded and smelled. She memorized every word, even the ones she didn't understand.

"The film reveals in agonizing detail how complicated the procedure is and how hard God has to work to bring together a designated couple."

"I like it already," Marion said. "This Levi guy apparently shares my theological conviction, namely that God is a lazy son of a bitch. He works a total of six days and expects to free load for the rest of eternity? I'm glad He has something to keep him busy other than making floods and destroying cities of the wicked, some of which didn't seem all that bad to me, by the way, but go on."

Dan gave Marion a huge smile.

"The film opens in Europe a century ago. Several generations of Jewish families have to be divinely manipulated in order that a single preordained couple—divided at birth—could find one another in this life. One family leaves Kiev to escape the pogroms while the other is driven from Minsk by an edict of the Czar. They both settle in Warsaw, where the two families live within walking distance of one another, but no matter how hard He works, everything goes wrong. Both fathers go into the same business—*shmatas*—and become bitter competitors. The families despise one another to the point where any contact is unthinkable. It looks as if the preordained plan won't work out . . ."

"I love you, Dan."

That stopped him short. He loved her, too, but he didn't think they were ready to say *the word*.

"Go on with the story. I'm loving this movie."

"Right . . . yes, the movie. The plot jumps to the present day and goes from black and white to color. Descendants of the Warsaw families are now in Paris. One gives birth to a handsome boy and the other, a beautiful daughter, but the children grow up with divergent interests. She is a talented dancer who becomes a fashion model. He's a Yeshiva student who everybody believes will become an important rabbi, but just before he is ordained, he reveals that his true passion is photography. As *fate* would have it, he becomes a world-renowned fashion photographer. If they met, they would immediately recognize their essence in the other, but almost as if they were on separate conveyer belts moving in opposite directions, they keep passing—and never noticing—their preordained other."

"So what happens?"

"In the climactic scene, the model and photographer get out of different taxis at the same airport within minutes of one another. Cameras follow them on a split screen as they enter the airport . . . and board the same plane but sit in different sections. When the plane arrives at their destination, they disembark and we follow their luggage, merging as it offloads to the terminal chute and rolls down to the baggage claim area together. Great tracking shot. Okay, here comes the meeting, yes? No. The man is engrossed in a phone call and by the time he claims his luggage, she's gone. Just when you thought it was safe to despair, he hails a cab that he has to share with . . . her! Fade out. Closing credits roll over blue sky, and end just as the lovers are lifted up to the clouds followed by bright letters in Yiddish that spell *Bashert*."

Marion kissed Dan's cheek and laid her head back on his chest.

{ Chapter Two }

Four days earlier

"WHY IN THE WORLD would I want to go to a script reading?"

Marion was already furious with Sheldon. They were collaborating on a screenplay and as usual, he arrived an hour late, laden with lox, cream cheese, bialys, herring and a variety of side dishes she couldn't stand to look at. To top it off, rather than start work on the difficult scene that stumped them yesterday, he was more excited about the plans he made for that evening.

"On the Fox lot? At the Zanuck Theater, no less!" Marion could barely contain her anger. "Why, so I can run into all the producers and directors I entertained in my home for the past twenty years and now avoid me like the plague? What's the point? Those readings are strictly for studio hacks and junior agents blowing smoke up each other's asses about multiple picture deals that don't exist."

"When was the last time anybody who's anybody in this town saw you?"

"I go out a lot."

"Yeah, with losers, *schnorrers* and hangers-on who can't get arrested. For them, being seen with the ex-wife of Terry Gladstone is a big plus, and you always end up paying the tab. It's time you got back with the A-crowd. All the beautiful people, the great and near-great will be there tonight and that's where you belong. Once they see how dazzling you look, believe me, your dance card will fill up."

"My dance card went up in flames when I divorced Terry. Do you think anybody in this town will give me the time of day? All my friends, people I respected and loved, treat me like a leper."

"Not all," he said. Sheldon Keller was a respected TV comedy writer and one of the few friends that remained loyal to her after the divorce. In Tinsel Town that takes guts because the narrative created by the trades, publicists, and studios is that the star, studio exec, mogul, whatever . . . is always the victim despite the fact that everyone knows he is an abusive philanderer.

"Face it, Marion," Sheldon said as he made the biggest bagel, lox and cream cheese sandwich Marion had ever seen, with a thick slice of onion and half a tomato oozing out of the edges.

"You're dripping," she said pointing to the tomato seeds on his chin.

Rather than wipe it off, he pushed it into his mouth, swallowed and continued. "Remember where we are. This is Hollywood. Our moral codes are similar in many ways to the more remote villages of Afghanistan. When the wife of a sultan or mullah is banished, she becomes an object of derision and everyone is obliged to spit on her. Hence, you dear Marion, banished wife of a powerful agent, gets spat upon regularly. Standup comics and talk show hosts toss zingers at you every day. My question to you is: how long do you intend to take it lying down? As your best friend and staunchest supporter, I must remind you that you're a talented writer and brilliant film editor, not to mention a very desirable sex object, and if you don't fight back your career is over and that would be a damn shame."

"If it were just the clowns I wouldn't care," Marion said, "but my manager, my lawyer, my closest friends, even my yogi won't return my calls. What can I do about that?"

"You can take the offensive. I started yesterday." Sheldon unfolded the morning copy of *Daily Variety* he extracted from one of the bags overflowing with small white cartons of delicious deli. The entire last page was filled with a smiling picture of Marion's ex with the caption: 'Terry Gladstone can *kush mir in tochus.* For the seven people in this town who don't understand Yiddish: He can kiss me where the sun don't shine.' The signatures underneath were: Sheldon Keller, Gore Vidal, Robert Altman, Gil Cates, Leonard Stern and twelve other highly respected directors, producers and writers who remained loyal to Marion.

She stared at the signatures, fought back tears and hugged Sheldon.

"We have to be at the Zanuck Theater at seven," he said. "Starting tonight, Marion is back!"

"What should I wear?"

"As little as possible."

6.1 miles across town

"WHY? I NEVER GO TO SCRIPT READINGS. It's like looking at an X-ray and trying to read a person's soul. No way."

"Whoa, Dan. There is a very good reason to attend this particular reading," Glen said.

"What's that?" Dan was definitely not enthusiastic about sitting through an analysis of someone else's screenplay.

"One word: Klein."

"Klein . . . as in Sally?"

"Okay, two words. Sally Klein is moderating the Writers Guild reading at the Fox Theater.

"Have you ever met her?"

"No, but I will tonight."

Dan warmed to the idea. Dan and his friend, Glen Taylor, had co-authored a screenplay that was on the verge of being green-lighted, but the studio was holding out for a strong female lead . . . like Sally Klein! "You know, her agent nixed it."

"Charlie Magnum?" Glen said. "Forget him! He won't read a script unless he gets a firm offer up front, which no one is giving these days. If I can corner Sally for five minutes, I'm sure I can convince her to read *The Sisters O'Rourke.*"

"Brilliant."

THE ZANUCK THEATER on the Fox lot was packed with writers, agents, a sprinkling of studio execs, actors looking to break in and a large number eager to get back. On stage, six actors sharing three microphones sat on stools with scripts on their laps.

Sally Klein, in her signature Motorcycle jacket and Brando cap raked sharply to one side, stood center stage and introduced the writer and lead cast. "Tonight's screenplay is a work in progress," she announced. "There will be a Q and A at the end of the reading. Gloria Marx, the writer, and the cast, welcome your constructive and hopefully brief comments."

The reading was predictable. The question-and-answer period was not.

"Mickey Rooney and Donald O'Connor wouldn't have done a piece of *drek* like this forty years ago," was the first comment from the audience.

"It would be helpful if you could provide some constructive format for your observations . . . and perhaps from this decade," Sally scolded.

Unfortunately, no one warned her that the most ferocious critics at these readings are other writers, resentful that this screenplay was selected and theirs was not.

"A farrago of undulating mischief," was one of the more eloquent blows to the midsection.

"Pretentious . . . unfunny . . ."

"This is a blood fest," Dan whispered to Glen. "Why would any writer subject himself to this kind of flagellation?"

"Publicity."

"But it's bad publicity."

"In this town, there's no such thing."

"Remind me never to come to one of these readings again."

"Eyes on the prize. Remember why we're here."

Dan had never seen such a hostile audience. He was not sure he could sit still. The questions were more like taunts but rising to one's feet to criticize a competitor's work provided a moment of attention to writers who were traditionally ignored. So, despite elegantly phrased hyperbolic flashes of wit, pre-planned puns and flowery literary allusions, the crowd was out for blood.

Marion was appalled. The cruel nature of this public flogging was too reminiscent of her mother's constant tongue thrashings and she began to feel uneasy when suddenly, a hush settled over the auditorium and a soft but commanding voice emerged from across the room. The audience had to quiet down in order to hear.

"I'd like to talk about some of the good things we heard tonight and there were many, if we allowed ourselves to view this work for what it is and not for what some people wish it wasn't."

All Marion saw was a tall, slender man, whose face was surrounded by dark curls and a neatly trimmed beard. Silhouetted by stage lights, his features were hard to make out, but the voice . . . she couldn't place it immediately, but it was familiar.

"I don't know the writer," the man continued, "and I am not involved in this project in any way, but I respect the work she and the actors put into this reading. Many of the lines were hysterical, but I have a thought you might consider. The plot is fascinating—three people engaged in the same infidelity—but it is revealed too casually. Where is the explosive tension that should emerge from three separate voices in conflict? Don't let the actors tell us about the fire, make us feel their heat. You've created a plot that works, but I'd like to get to know each of your characters better. If you let me hear specific voices, I'll know who to root for."

Sally Klein and half the audience applauded the practical suggestion from the tall, slender man, but Marion heard something else.

AT THE CHEESE AND WINE BUFFET, Dan stood alone as hungry writers filled paper plates with a variety of chips, dips and cheese cubes . . . when someone tapped him on the shoulder.

"Excuse me."

Dan turned around and found himself face to face with a slim, dark-haired beauty who took his breath away. He wanted to say something, but no words seemed right, so he just stared.

"Are you the one who complimented the author for the good points and talked about unique voices?" Her voice was as captivating as her face.

"I guess I did. I hope I didn't offend."

"God, no," she laughed. "I loved what you said and the way you said it."

"How was that?"

"Kindly. The sort of thing you don't find in this town."

Dan needed to say something ... something funny or wise, but the only thing that came out was "You have beautiful eyes."

Marion suddenly recognized it, her father's voice! He always made her feel like the most special girl in the world. It was his calm demeanor and predictable kindness that saved her from complete mental annihilation at the hands of her beastly mother. Every time he walked through the front door, she would jump into his waiting arms and plant kisses on every part of his face.

"I'm Marion," she finally said.

Dan studied her enchanting face, the intensity of her gaze, the way she carried herself . . . *I know her.*

"And you are?" Marion asked.

"I'm sorry. Dan. Dan Sobol."

"Are you a writer, Dan?"

"I do write, but only as a last resort. I'm a director. If a piece of dialogue has to be rewritten or if a scene is missing, I'll do it, but facing a blank page is as enjoyable for me as a root canal."

"What kind of films do you direct?" she asked.

"Whatever I can get. I'm independent but I have a production deal with E.S.I."

"Steve Weisman?"

"Do you know Steve?" Dan raised an eyebrow, and wondered how much to tell her about Steve. For another time, Dan decided.

"I submitted a script to him a couple of years ago."

"Did he make the film?"

"No. He said he liked my writing, but it wasn't his genre. What he meant was 'not enough slashing.'"

"So you're a writer?"

"I am and I guess my skin is thicker than yours because I don't find writing all that painful. In fact, I can't think of a better high."

"Please explain that to me. What is it about grinding words together to find *le mot juste* that gives you such pleasure?"

"I love stories. The first words I learned to speak were, 'tell me a story, daddy.' When I finally learned to read, I couldn't get enough. I lived in an endless variety of exciting worlds with each book I read. I still do."

"But that's reading," Dan said, "not writing."

"For me, it's both. Some of my most enjoyable reading pops right out of my typewriter. When I finish a page, I can't wait to read what I've written."

Dan clapped his hands. "Brilliant. I envy you. So you spend your days happily writing and reading?"

"My day job is film editing, but I am writing with a partner."

"Writing *and* editing? So you get to create the story and edit the final version? The only thing missing is directing. Have you considered that?"

She laughed. "My favorite *New Yorker* cartoon is the seal balancing a ball on its nose and the caption reads, 'What I really want to do is direct.' No, Dan. Unlike everyone else in the western world, directing is not for me."

They talked and talked. That is to say, Marion talked and Dan listened. He was captivated by her quick wit. She's so funny and smart, he thought. He should say something, but what? That he's overwhelmed? He was still in mourning, sort of, but he knew Anne wouldn't want him to be alone for the rest of his life. Besides, where can this possibly lead, anyway? Conflicting thoughts swirled through his brain, but one thing he knew for certain. He didn't want this to end.

Marion ran out of nervous conversation and they both stood quietly, shyly looking at one another when a portly man in a three piece suit with an antique watch and fob draped over his expansive belly, approached them and put his arm around Marion.

"So, nu? Wasn't that the liveliest funeral you ever attended?"

"More like an assassination," Marion said.

Dan recognized him as one of the more vituperative critics.

"When you find yourself in the middle of a firing squad, which side do you want to be on?" Sheldon quipped.

"Sorry, I'm not buying that," she said. "Dan, this is Sheldon Keller, my writing partner."

Sheldon took his hand. "I'm sorry we couldn't meet at a happier occasion. Dan, is it?"

"Yes. Dan . . . Dan Sobol. I'm here as a guest . . . I don't normally . . ."

"Too much information," Sheldon said. "I see you sniffing around my friend, but it's okay, she blew me off years ago and not in a nice way. Listen, Dan Sobol-the-guest-who-doesn't-normally, we're going out for a bite, *eppes tzum esssen.* Why don't you come along?"

"Sheldon," Marion whispered, "Dan is probably here with his wife or girlfriend, so don't push. I just met the guy. Go easy."

"I am going easy," Sheldon whispered back. "I see you like him, so what's the problem?" Turning to Dan, he said in his best stentorian projection, "We're going to Junior's Deli. Please join us and bring both your wife *and* your girlfriend."

"I'm a widower," Dan said, "but I am here with someone." At which point Glen came over and was introduced to Marion and Sheldon. He said to Sheldon in perfect Litvak-accented Yiddish, *"Vos Machst du landesman?"*

"Retzt Yiddish?" Sheldon said, surprised that Glen, an African-American, spoke Yiddish with the same intonation as his grandmother from Plotzk. Sheldon put his arm around Glen and said, "Pastrami on rye with new pickles, it is."

AT THE DELI, Sheldon sat next to Glen and regaled him with one joke after another. "A priest, minister and rabbi . . ."

"Sheldon, please," Glen said. "I've heard every priest, minister and rabbi joke . . . ."

"Not this one. I just wrote it for Jack Carter."

"Go ahead."

"A priest, minister and rabbi go into a bar. The bartender looks at them and says, 'Is this a joke?'"

Glen groaned. "Okay, okay. I've got one for you . . ."

Across the table, oblivious to the comedy duo, Marion and Dan devoured each revelation about the other.

"You went to Barnard? When?"

"A long time ago," Marion said coyly.

"I was at Columbia from '55 to '59."

"That's when I was at Barnard!"

"Did you ever go to the Friday night concerts at Julliard?"

"I rarely missed one."

"How is it we never met?"

"If I remember what you said tonight, I would have to conclude that we were hearing different voices at the time."

My God, Dan thought. This woman is . . . she is . . . who is she?

Marion took a sip of her tea. "Why did you leave Struthers, Ohio, wherever that is, and move to New York? There are friendlier places."

"I wasn't looking for friends. I wanted to find the Elysian Fields."

"And you found them in Manhattan?"

"Absolutely. Coming to New York was like a coronation. Every morning when I climbed out of the subway on 125th, I was greeted by the rapturous sounds of Handel's *Messiah* wafting out of the rehearsal halls at Juilliard and I joined in." Dan began to sing in full voice. *". . . arise, arise, for thy light is come!"*

People in the surrounding booths looked to see if Mel Brooks or one of the other celebrities who frequent the deli was singing aloud, but when they saw it was "nobody" they turned back to their food.

Dan's enthusiasm was awakening something in Marion that had been dormant for a long time. She felt her heart beat faster and she knew . . . she knew, but did he?

To break the silence, she asked, "Did you always want to direct?"

"No. To be perfectly honest, I was a rabbi for eight years before I made the switch."

Marion's jaw dropped. "How did you go from being a rabbi to directing movies? And why?"

"*How* is a long story but *why* is easier. The life was too limiting for me. The calling was real and the work was satisfying up to a point, but I derive as much satisfaction from film, theater, and dance as I do from studying the classics. If I lived in Da Vinci's time, I might have remained a rabbi. Then it was okay to be a polymath, but it isn't anymore."

"So . . ." Marion teased, "in addition to being a rabbi, you wanted to be a painter, an architect, *and* a sculptor? Maybe build flying machines with catapults on the side?"

"Da Vinci was one kind of polymath. We had others. In the twelfth century, it was not unusual to be a rabbi, physician, poet *and* the most powerful general in Saladin's army."

"I agree it would be awkward to be a rabbi these days and a senior officer in any Arab army."

"I never intended to go that far," Dan said, "but neither my teachers nor I believed our society was ready for a flamenco dancing rabbi."

"Are you a flamenco dancer?"

"Among other things."

Marion's heart was racing. "So you're a rabbi! Are you still religious?"

"Not in the traditional sense, but I do study Torah, Talmud, the classics."

"Will you teach me the Kabbalah?" Marion asked eagerly.

"I would be happy to, but of all the sources to choose from, why the Kabbalah?"

"I heard Professor Abrams' lecture at the 92nd Street Y on the power of unspoken words and it changed my life. 'The Kabbalah,' he said, 'teaches that earthly voices describe feelings, ideas, thoughts, and these sounds enlightened. But there are celestial voices that transcend sound and when one trains himself to receive, they not only enlighten the brain, they ennoble the spirit.' In that moment, a world opened up for me. I always felt compelled to write but nothing was completely satisfying until I started to edit film. Juxtaposing images taught me to hear voices that transcend sound, and that was how I decided to become a hyphenate: writer-film editor."

"That was Professor Joshua Abrams?"

"You must have heard of him."

"He was my mentor at the Seminary."

"You *know* Joshua Abrams?"

"The most influential man in my life. I took his undergrad classes at the Seminary while I was at Columbia and when I applied to rabbinical school, he was on the acceptance committee. Before any questions were asked, Professor Abrams stood up and said, 'I know this young man. He will make a fine rabbi.' He shook my hand and I was accepted without answering one question."

"What did he think about your leaving to make movies?"

"When I was struggling with that, he was the first person I consulted."

"Did he try to change your mind?"

"No. He listened. I told him I had spent eight years preaching, comforting the sick, consoling the bereaved and counseling a congregation of over six hundred souls in the Pacific Palisades. At the end of every day, I asked myself two questions. Did I give everything I possibly could to the people I served *and* was it gratifying for me?"

Marion stared at this gentle man's face. "Two good questions. What were your answers?"

"I wasn't sure how to phrase what I *wanted* to say, so I quoted a line from Tagore. 'God respects us when we work, but He loves us when we sing.' Professor Abrams gave me a pained look. He knew what was coming next. I said, 'I know God respects me for my work, but I haven't been singing for a very long time.'"

"How did he respond?"

"He puffed on his pipe for what seemed like a long time. Then he said, 'Each of us is born to a mystical refrain. Throughout our lives, we search for that one melody that brings harmony to our soul. Some hear it early, some not at all. You are one of the lucky ones, Daniel. Sing your song joyously. I pray you find blessing in your labors.'"

WHEN THEY LEFT THE DELI, Marion and Dan were walking on the same cloud, not holding hands, but aching to. Sheldon and Glen traded cards and handed their tickets to the parking attendants. Marion and Dan stood by, conspicuously silent. Sheldon's Mercedes and Glen's Audi came and they left. The attendants took Marion and Dan's tickets and sprinted off again.

Marion looked at Dan, then, dropped her eyes when he looked at her. Neither of them knew how to prolong the evening without sounding awkward, so they didn't speak. When their cars came, Dan offered a friendly embrace. She submitted, both of them hoping to appear casual. It started out as a friendly enough hug, but she held on and he wasn't going to let go. Dan hadn't felt this way in a long time and as their bodies pressed together, he was engulfed in a rising tide of heat. He heard her breathing faster and it excited him. Still holding on, he pulled back slightly because he wanted to look at her face again. He couldn't believe how beautiful she was. Marion looked at him and they kissed. It was a daring, passionate kiss and that familiar feeling Dan had earlier when he first looked at her, returned to inform him that something wondrous was happening. *I know you . . . I know you . . .*

THE DAY AFTER THEIR MEETING, Marion and Sheldon were working together. More precisely, Sheldon worked his way across a huge plate of gefilte fish while Marion nervously paced the floor, looking at the phone every few minutes.

"Do you think he'll call? He said he would, but why should he? He's a director . . . and a widower! You should have heard how he talked about his wife, how he suffered and wept for her. It was heartbreaking. He is the most sensitive man I ever met. Every woman in the world is probably after him. What would he want with me, a forty-five-year-old divorced loser?"

"What would he want with you? Look at yourself. You're a magnificent piece of womanhood. As for age, those streaks of gray over his ears tell me he's at least five years older than you, but who cares? You're a knockout. When you walk down the red carpet, the paparazzi pop their razzis."

"But Dan isn't looking for glamour. He's a man of depth. He was a rabbi. I barely went to Hebrew School. And he's funny. You heard him last night. He's got a great sense of humor and he doesn't beg for laughs by impersonating paraplegics like Terry. He is so sweet, I want to kiss him."

"You said you did, as I recall."

"That was a mistake, wasn't it? He must think I'm so desperate I'll crush him. That's why he'll never call. He's too gentle for me, isn't he?"

"If he survives in this business, he's can't be all that gentle. Directors are a ruthless lot."

"Do you think he would hire me?"

"Before he marries you or after?"

"Stop making fun!"

The phone on her desk rang. She let it ring several times, nervously waiting for the right moment to pick up.

"Answer the damn phone!" Sheldon barked.

"Hi Dan . . . of course I remember you. Nice of you to call . . . yeah . . . me too." She listened and nodded. "I'm working with Sheldon right now. Can I call you back in five minutes?" She wrote down his number and hung up.

"Dan wants you and me to come to his house for dinner tonight. I don't want to sound too desperate. Should I call back and say no, I'm booked up all week?"

"Marion!" Sheldon roared.

PART TWO

29 years later

Rough Landing

{ Chapter Three }

DAN LOOKED OUT at the vast emptiness thirty thousand feet below and his mind went blank. He turned to the mess on his tray table: remnants of the *New York Times Book Review,* a semi-damp cloth, folded boarding pass, gum wrappers, a few empty miniature liquor bottles . . .

Where is the flight attendant? He looked around and saw rows of passengers, sleeping, reading and typing on laptops, but no flight attendants. He noticed that some of the passengers were resting peacefully, wearing headphones.

Dan foraged through the seat pocket in front of him and found his headphones. Lying back, he touched the start button and . . . *Mi chiamano, Mimi* from *La Boheme* wafted into his gin-soaked brain.

Vivo sola, soletta. I live all alone in a white room and stare at the sky . . . when will the thaw come that melts the ice in my heart?

A sad grimace settled on Dan's face. *Mi chiamano, Mimi.*

The first time he heard that aria was during one of the most blissful—and miserable—times of his life.

". . . suo prima il bacio . . . her kiss was like the sun . . ."

By then, he and Marion had been able to travel around the U.S. and to three continents, making small but successful movies together. Marion wrote and edited and he directed, but in reality, they interchanged roles on the set and in the editing room every day. They made movies like they danced: together. They never had too much money, but enough to enjoy small hotels, local cuisine, and a life of love and art intertwined . . .

Dan couldn't remember how often he had read and reread the *La Boheme* portion of his diary. It was always heartbreaking, but also sustaining, especially during these last two and a half years. He rummaged through the debris on his tray table once again. Somewhere past the empty bottles and under the tiny damp towel, he found a blue notebook with a hand drawn title: *Remembrances of Things Past—Dan Sobol's Diary.*

He slowly opened the diary to a page that read *July 18, 2004, Paris. Opera Bastille. La Boheme.* Ten years ago today! Tears appeared in the corners of his eyes as the words rose from the page, carrying him back to that exquisitely happy and unbearably painful time.

> To go or not to go? La Boheme was Marion's favorite opera but from the time she awoke, she suffered from a severe Lupus flare. Shooting pains raced through her ankles and wrists. Clogged sinuses made simple breathing difficult. I called the Opera Bastille and ordered a wheelchair. That didn't do much for her spirits. Marion was always one of the most elegant women in Paris and being reduced to getting around in a wheelchair was just too depressing. I knew very little about opera and Marion assured me that if I ever

saw a really good performance of La Boheme, I would understand what it was that had so captivated her.

She thought a nap might provide the energy she needed to go out, so I gave her as many pain killers as she could take and applied compresses to her wrists and ankles. When the spams passed, I read her to sleep.

"I love you, Dan," she said as she drifted off, and despite the anxieties that plagued me all day, I suddenly felt hopeful and buoyant.

When we arrived at the Opera Bastille that evening, we discovered there was a lift to the Parterre, so Marion opted out of the wheelchair. Leaning on my arm, she walked slowly to the gate where the usherette led us down the ramp to the fifteenth row, just the right distance from the stage, with a large walking aisle in front so Marion could sit with her legs outstretched.

The set was austere: A dark, windowless room with a rumpled bed, a single chair and small wooden table.

Rodolfo the poet was perfectly cast as the handsome tenor lead and when he hit the high notes, easily, brazenly, it was as though there were fireworks on stage.

Mimi looked appropriately waifish, small and slender with an angelic voice and sweet, vulnerable face. The power of their love was palpable, tender but foreboding.

In the last act, Mimi had become cadaverously thin and could no longer suppress the consumptive cough as she pleaded with her lover to stand by her. I felt myself drawn into their pain. Rodolfo revealed the reason he had stayed away. It was not because he suspected she was unfaithful, but he was frightened because he knew how sick she was and he couldn't bear to expose himself to that kind of grief. NO! I said to myself and only I understood the dread that filled my heart at that moment, but there I was, transfixed by horror. *"O Mimi, tu piu non torni?*

"O Mimi, will you never return?"

The death scene struck such an intimate chord that I felt the actors spoke directly to me in a voice that was eerily familiar. Experiencing this with the one I love, and whose illness cast a pall over every dream we had of a future, made it one of the most heart-rending moments of my life. I am so in love with her. It grows with every moment we share, every time we talk, make love, read or laugh together. The truth is I'm terrified that the day is rapidly approaching when she will leave me. Marion, *tu piu no torni* . . . and I will be left to drift in unbearable aloneness. I couldn't take that again. Not this time. Not this time!!!

When the opera ended, we held one another's hands, unable to utter a word, until we were the only ones left in the theater.

There was a light drizzle when we crossed the Place de la Bastille, so we went into the first bistro we could find. The décor was hospitable and the food turned out to be superb. We had a delicious sole muniere with a bottle of vintage Pouilly-Fuisse, followed by the most sublime cherry sabayon. The evening that had filled me with so much dread, became enchanting. The rain stopped, Marion felt happy and the full moon gave me permission to hope. We walked back to the hotel, across the Pont Marie, the lovers bridge, made the same wish and kissed . . . long, sweet . . . divine.

Dan felt his heart burst as he closed his diary.

"God, how I cherished life with Marion, my basherte . . ." Tears flowed down his face and it took all his strength to keep from wailing aloud.

An amplified voice burst through the cabin. *"The Captain has turned off the fasten seat belt sign. Please feel free . . ."*

Dan felt someone rudely tugging at his sleeve. Through his tears, he saw a little girl of about five or six with twines of licorice colored curls hovering around her perfect face, staring at him. In one hand, she held a furry little yellow doll with a ring in its belly. With the other hand, she tugged at Dan's sleeve.

"Don't cry," she said.

Dan looked at the little munchkin and didn't know what to say. He wiped his eyes with a napkin from the tray.

"Are you sad?"

"Am I . . . ?"

"Sad."

"Yes, dear. I'm afraid I am. What's your name?"

"Abbie. Do you want to be happy?"

"Yes Abbie, I would like that very much."

She held her furry little doll close to Dan's face and when she pulled the ring in its belly, a loud, electronic laugh burst forth. HAHAHA.

Abbie laughed and looked at Dan. Despite the tears, he couldn't help smiling. Abbie pulled the ring again. HAHAHA. The sound was as silly and disarming as before.

When the laughter stopped, Abbie looked at Dan seriously and said, "Don't be sad anymore, okay?"

"Abbie!" A handsome young woman with the same halo of curls approached. She looked on with pride, fully aware of the joy her daughter brought wherever she went. Still, she chastised the little girl lovingly. "You know you're not supposed to bother other passengers." Taking Abbie's hand, she led her back up the aisle of the plane. Dan watched as the little girl waved to him and pulled the string on the doll's belly letting loose another round of HAHAHA and disappeared amid the packed rows of distant faces.

Dan eventually fell back asleep.

"HOW CAN ANYBODY *not* love little girls?" Marion asked when she took Dan to the playground in Rancho Park, a few weeks after they met. They strolled past the busy children and proud watchful parents. "Look!" Marion said. "None of the little girls are wearing shoes. They love the feel of grass under their feet." She laughed aloud and watched the joyful children on swings whose mothers and fathers pushed them high into the air.

"Over there," Marion said, pointing to a little girl with golden ringlets standing on her daddy's feet as he waltzed her around the playground. The girl's eyes were closed and her smile was radiant. "That's me!" Marion said. "That's how my father taught me to dance. The happiest times of my life were when I stood on his feet and we danced together. We were Fred and Ginger at all the family occasions. Of course that only enflamed my jealous mother, who never stopped nagging my father. 'Aaron!' I can still hear that shrill scream. 'You're spoiling that child rotten and I won't have it!'"

"Your mother made you stop dancing?"

"Are you kidding? She tried, but dancing was the most important thing in my life and I found plenty of ways to deceive her. My father, who I adored, enrolled me in every dance class he could, from tap to ballet to ballroom. Me, stop dancing? I'd sooner stop breathing."

Watching the father and daughter waltz by, Marion's face glowed.

On a nearby bench, a mother sat with her newborn resting on her bent knees, inches from her face, silently gazing into the huge eyes of her blessed gift.

"That bond is so palpable," Marion said. "I can feel it. Can't you?"

"Why didn't you ever have children? You obviously love them."

The jubilant expression faded. "My ovaries burst when I was nineteen."

"Marion, I am so sorry! How . . . ?"

"It's called adnexal torsion and it's pretty rare. I was one of the unlucky victims," she said and retreated into silence. Dan put his arm through hers and they continued to walk.

"I felt the first rumblings when I was in my sophomore year at Barnard. I thought it was my usual nervous stomach preparing for midterms, but the pain never went away. It only got worse. The spasms in my stomach became sharper and lasted longer but the serious ruptures didn't start until after *the call.*"

"The call?"

"About six months after the first attack, I got a call from my mother. I haven't told you much about her, have I?"

"Very little."

Marion sat down on a bench facing the swings. Dan sat next to her and put his hand on hers.

"The phone rang as I was rushing out of my dorm room. I was late for my class with Marc van Doren, who I loved. I thought for a moment I should let it go, but it rang incessantly so I picked up.

"'Your father's dead!' My mother screamed at the top of

her voice. Before I could catch my breath, she unleashed a barrage of venom. 'You killed him, dancing and rolling around in gutters with those college boys every night! I hope you're satisfied.'"

"Your mother said that? What terrible things to say!"

Marion could offer nothing more than a sad frown. "I don't know if I fainted or just thought I did, but the next thing I remember, I was standing on a mound of mud in a cemetery on Long Island."

She became silent for a long while. Dan's gentle grip on her hand tightened.

"The rabbi said a lot of words, but I couldn't make them out. The circling crows angrily flapped their wings, making it hard to hear anything else. The people standing around a hole in the ground kept saying 'amen' and seemed to agree that my father was in that wooden box, dead. I knew that was a despicable lie! What about all our years of magical dreams and dancing and laughter and happy hugs? The screeching crows above my head became so loud I thought it was my mother, screaming again at my father. 'You're a loser, Aaron. Look at Ceil with her new mink . . . and Roz, who is going to Cannes this summer . . . and . . . why can't you find new clients? You're just a loser . . . ' I felt my insides start to churn. When the funeral attendant nudged me and offered a shovel full of dirt, I looked at the coffin in the hole below and all I remember was an explosion in every part of my body and the most excruciating pain. When I awoke, I was in a hospital room with tubes, plastic bags, and beeping machines all around me. My mother sat in the chair next to my bed reading *Vogue*. I remember trying to speak, but no words came. When she saw I was awake, she let me have it. 'Look at you. They took out your ovaries. You're an empty vessel. No one will ever want to marry you now. Who's going to support me?' She kept talking but what I heard was the hiss of a cobra and I thought of only one thing: flight. I had to get away from that witch before she killed me."

"So what did you do?"

"I married the first guy who asked me."

"Who was that?"

"His name is Terry Gladstone. You probably know him."

"The agent? I never met him but I've heard stories."

"What have you heard?"

"Tough, power hungry, unscrupulous like every other agent in this town. I can't imagine the two of you together."

"When I met Terry, he wasn't all that tough and he certainly wasn't powerful. He was just another hustler who drove a cab at night, but he was always funny and that was important to me at the time."

"You married him because he was funny?"

"It was just after my father died. I was living with my mother and all I could think about was either killing myself or throwing her down a flight of stairs. When I found a boy who could make me laugh *and* was willing to take me out of that hellhole, I jumped at the chance."

"How did you meet him?"

"I was eating lunch one afternoon at Chockfull O'Nuts when Terry came in, looked around, couldn't find an empty stool so he asked if he could sit on my lap. I didn't know what to say. Before I could think of anything, he went into a Jerry Lewis imitation. *'Dean, Dean, Dean! You say you love me. You don't even know . . . I'm livin?'"* He grinned and I noticed that everyone around me was laughing. I started to laugh, too. It was such a silly, clownish thing to do. He picked up my tab and sang aloud *'you don't have to say you love me, just let me sit on your lap.'* I hadn't laughed in so long, I didn't want to stop.

I don't have much good to say about Terry, but he was funny in the beginning."

"When did it turn sour?"

"It started about five years into the marriage, when the hustler-slash-comedian suddenly struck gold. One night, Mabel Schuster got into his cab and he had her laughing so hard, she insisted he hang out with her while she was in New York."

"Mable Schuster, the agent who screams at actors on the red carpet that their careers are in the toilet unless they sign with her? I've heard those stories, too."

"That's her. Mabel was crazy about Terry. Nobody else could make her laugh the way he did. She said if he ever thought of moving to L.A., she would find a place for him in the agency. We took her up on it and Mable set him up as her personal assistant, where he not only made her laugh all day; he had her star clients and even her competitors, howling. When she died, her clients moved over to Terry and that's when his career blossomed . . . together with his ego. Terry's publicist made sure we showed up at all the red carpet affairs and soon we became part of the Hollywood elite."

"Every girl's dream," Dan said.

"Nightmare is more like it. My life became an endless series of humiliations. It wasn't just the regular *consultations* with aspiring starlets in his office that made me furious. Every other day the tabloids had pictures of him and his latest bimbo smooching it up at some club."

"Did you ever love him?"

"In the beginning I thought I did, but once he became a Hollywood power broker, I realized there was no way the marriage could work. We were both in love with the same person, him."

"What did you do?"

"Nothing. He stopped being funny and I stopped laughing. Then he got into serious drugs and became physically abusive. I knew I was sinking into a bottomless pit, but what could I do?"

"Why didn't you leave?"

"Good question. I didn't think I had the strength to do that on my own. My father, the only person who would stand up for me, was dead. What alternative did I have? Go back to my mother? So, I did nothing. I left it up to him to deal the final blow."

"Did he?"

"If you look just below my left ear, you'll see a small residual scar; my going away present. That punch was literally my Zen slap." She looked at Dan for a long silent moment. "So, that's the story of my life. Still want to hang around?"

"Do you still like to dance?"

"I do."

He stood up and reached for her hands. "Kick your shoes off."

She kicked them off and climbed onto Dan's feet. He kissed her while they twirled around the playground. She threw her head back and laughed. Dancing in the playground yard surrounded by happy, happy children, Marion was alive.

"Dance me, Dan," she said. "Dance me to the end of time."

"THIS IS YOUR CAPTAIN AGAIN. In approximately thirty minutes we'll be landing in Kingston, Jamaica."

Gurgling sounds crept out of Dan's stomach. As long as he was able to distract himself from the reason for this trip, he could push his anger and sadness to a back burner, but *La Boheme* had long since ended and the happy children were gone.

Dancing Marion was gone.

{ Chapter Four }

Ten Days Earlier

OUT OF THE BLUE, Dan received an unwelcome phone message from a friend who had drifted away. His best friend! Dan was upset that Steve Weisman, an older brother-like figure, had been virtually out of touch since Marion's death over two years ago.

"We have to have lunch, Dan. To talk. It's important." That was the entire message. Steve's voice was as distinct as ever. Clear, baritone, persuasive.

The phone call sent Dan into a spiral. He was alternately open to reconnecting with Steve and furious at having been abandoned. He decided to let Steve wait.

That night, Dan couldn't sleep. He turned over everything in his head about his relationship with Steve . . . about Marion . . . about his first wife, Anne . . . about love and loss . . . about life and death.

DAN'S INTRODUCTION TO DEATH came at the age of seven. His parents took him and his big brother, Art, on a trip to Akron. He recalled that his mom was uncharacteristically silent, even when he and Art got bored counting cows and started to jump around in the back seat. After an hour of riding in the old Dodge, they expected to leap out of the car and play kick-the-can with their cousins, but that didn't happen. When they arrived, everybody was strangely solemn. As soon as his mother got out of the car, Aunt Esther embraced her. For some reason Dan didn't understand, his mother burst into tears and wept uncontrollably. He and Art were both shocked. They heard the adults talking about their cousin Rosie and they were going to leave the kids at the house while they went to the you-know-where. Mom couldn't stop crying. Somebody said she was so sorry Rosie . . . but Aunt Esther quickly silenced her. "Don't use that word in front of the children."

When he was eleven, Dan's paternal grandmother, who lived with them and read racy stories aloud from the Yiddish newspapers was rushed to the hospital and placed in an oxygen tent. The word he had learned by that time—death—reappeared but was still a hushed whisper when the kids were around. At the cemetery, his father wept for the mother who rescued him from a Red Army firing squad by bribing the local commissar.

When speaking of how the righteous are called to their eternal rest, the rabbi used the phrase "the angel of death." What kind of angels do Jews have, young Dan thought. Christian angels are cute little cherubs. Jews have the worst angels!

Two years later, Dan's father was in the hospital on life support. His mother, Bertha, was dutiful and strong, but Dan's older brother and protector, was in the hallway facing the wall, weeping. "Please God, don't let him die," his brother pleaded, but apparently the "angel" wasn't moved.

Years later, when he was a rabbinical student, Dan was asked to officiate at the funeral of a young man who was killed in an accident on the Long Island Expressway. At the funeral, the bereft mother wailed, pleading with Dan to explain this horrible tragedy.

"Why, Rabbi, why? Jerry was so young and beautiful. Why him and not me? The pain . . . the pain. I can't stand it!"

Somehow, Dan found comforting words. "There is no way to escape the pain, but know that Jerry will be with you forever. His enthusiasm, his humor, his love surrounds you. You see that. I know you do because I can feel it and that is what will sustain you even in your darkest hours . . ."

Dan was better able to deal with the pain of loss when consoling strangers, but when it hit home, the pro-forma consolation didn't work. When he answered a call from his sister-in-law Marge, who told him that his brother Art had died on takeoff in a military training exercise crash, he collapsed. The question he had been asked so many times—"Why?"—thundered through his fractured heart and there were no words of comfort. Dan fell to the floor and wept until he realized that it was going to get worse. He would have to break the news to his mother. When Dan knocked on her door, Bertha was surprised. At first, she was happy to see him, but in a second, she turned white. She looked into the grief-stricken eyes of her beloved son and saw the Angel of Death.

DAN MET ANNE two months after his brother died when his interest in remaining a rabbi was already in decline. When they were introduced at a midtown Manhattan party, Dan was beside himself. "You're Anne Marisse! I saw you in *Gypsy* on opening night. You were fantastic. *I used to be a shleppa,"* he started to sing. Anne looked a little embarrassed but happy to meet such an enthusiastic fan. "*. . . but now I'm Miss Mazeppa."* Dan couldn't hide his enthusiasm. "I don't know if you noticed, but when you came out for the curtain call, I kept applauding long after everybody else stopped."

"That was you?"

Dan called Anne several times and each conversation was better than the last. He was a funny guy and she loved to laugh. He fantasized about her and wanted more than anything to go on a real date, but Anne was reluctant and he didn't understand why. Dan pushed hard because he felt he just might have met *the* girl. She was good looking, smart, a gifted actress and he was admittedly stage struck. In addition—and not unimportant—she was the daughter of a rabbi, unfortunately, an ultra-orthodox fanatic.

"Why won't you go out with me?" Dan asked her one evening on the phone.

"Don't take this personally. I don't know you very well, but I do know a lot of rabbis and I despise all of them."

"You won't despise me. I'm not a fanatic. I live in the twentieth century. I love the theater. I don't spit on the floor to deflect the evil eye and I have no problem touching women."

They both loved classic old films and Dan convinced her to join him for a retrospective at The Thalia on the upper West Side. The feature was *Casablanca*. Later at the Carnegie delicatessen, the irritated middle-aged waitress in space shoes tapped her pad while Dan scrutinized the menu. He pretended to be in an awful funk. Then, he slammed down his menu and screamed at the waitress in perfect Bogie, "Go ahead Sam, play it! If she can take it so can I."

The waitress shrugged. "I get all kinds," she mumbled, but Anne howled! "That was the best Bogie I ever heard! Do you do any others?"

"Impressions? I got a million of 'em." He pushed up his chest, curled his lip and Mae West came out. *"When ah'm good, ah'm really good, but when I'm bad, I'm bettah!"*

Anne couldn't stop laughing and Dan couldn't be happier. From then on, every phone call opened with a different voice, from Cary Grant to Tiny Tim. Anne took him to parties where he met her friends, most of whom were working actors and always ready to sing or dance. He was smitten and fell right in with her crowd. A natural mimic, Dan often entertained them with his impersonations. Their response was precisely what he longed to hear: "You ought to be an actor."

Between shows, Anne worked at Titra Sound, a studio that produced English sound tracks for foreign films. At the time, she was dubbing voices for Anna Magnani and Sophia Loren. When a new set of films came in from Japan, the director went in search of male actors who could do a convincing Japanese accent. Anne arranged an audition for Dan. He faked a bio and was hired on the spot. The result was that Dan became the voice of three characters in *Godzilla*. Even better, he got his SAG card. That set his mind spinning and the joy he found performing—however minimally—started to take over his life. Anne convinced him to take acting lessons in addition to dance classes. Her lust for life energized him and provided the drive he needed to transform himself. He was propelled by a new vision. They would marry, and Dan and Anne Sobol would become the next "first couple of the American Stage."

THEY WERE MARRIED for just over three years when Anne went on tour as Dulcinea in *Man of Le Mancha*. When she returned, complaining of abdominal pains, Dan took her to the hospital. The Angel of Death was back, only more fiercely than before.

Colon cancer. Undergoing radiation and chemo, Anne became weaker by the day. She was a strong believer in Edgar Cayce's teachings about self-healing and there was no doubt in her mind that she could cure herself. In the hospital, lugubrious doctors told her that nothing short of a miracle could save her. Anne responded by wearing a badge boldly proclaiming, "I *Am* a Miracle."

Dan's mother came from Ohio to be with him. One night, when he returned from the hospital, he cried in her arms. "We have to pray, *mine zun,*" she said in Yiddish. "*Gott vet helfen.*"

"*Tateh muss betten Gott fare ir. Zie is krank, mama, zeir krank.* God isn't listening to me, Mama!"

When he left that night, he didn't really believe that God would respond to him or his mother or even his dead father, but a Jew has to pray.

One afternoon, a small group of nuns paraded through the oncology floor hoping to comfort the afflicted, singing as they walked. "*Sleep my child and peace attend thee all through the night . . .*" They waved cheerfully at patients as they strolled down the long corridor. "*. . . guardian angels God will send thee . . .*"

Dan went to the door to greet them when he suddenly heard BEEP BEEP BEEP BEEP. The unmistakable sounds of Anne's IVAC monitor cut through the singing. Nurses rushed in and rushed out pulling her bed as they raced down the hall. The code-blue alert rang through the ward and Dan, barely able to breathe, ran alongside them to the O.R.

He waited outside for what seemed like an eternity, afraid to think or feel anything. When the doctor came out, he nodded. "She's intubated, but she's breathing," and walked away quickly. When they allowed Dan to enter, he stood beside her bed, trying with all his might not to burst into tears. With the tube in her throat, Anne looked at him for a long time. A wide-open stare he would never forget. Then, she wrote on a pad: "Is this the end?"

"NO! It can't be," he said. It won't be." But of course, it was.

Anne's death was devastating. All the hopes and dreams of their new life together painfully evaporated. Where would he go? What could he do without his best friend? How did he survive when other members of his family were taken by the ghastly angel? He recalled the words of the Yiddish Poet, Leivick, author of the long, agonizing elegy, "Fumes of Treblinka." *"So what does a Jew do when the sun disappears? He cries until there are no tears left, then he picks himself up, curses his God and continues to wander in darkness."*

YEARS LATER, when Marion died, he tried to recall Leivick's poem, but it sounded obscene. Continue to wander? Where? Why? Without her, there was no reason to go, to do or to be anywhere. Everyone loses family and even best friends, but Marion wasn't just family or best friend. Marion and Dan were two halves of the same soul! Is it possible to survive in any recognizable form with half a body? Half a brain? Half a heart? No more than it is to live with half a soul. For the first time, Dan fully understood Beckett's play. There comes a time when there is no pleasure, nothing means anything and all that is left is to wait for Godot.

{ Chapter Five }

THE DAY FINALLY ARRIVED for Dan to lunch with his old friend Steve Weisman, the meeting he'd been dreading but also longed for. Steve, a successful producer, had made enough money to buy a swanky, popular LA restaurant, the Paladin Club. The back corner table was exclusively his.

After a restrained embrace, Steve asked Dan, "How long has it been?"

"Since our last lunch?"

"I was referring to . . ."

"Two years, seven months, six days," Dan replied softly.

Steve nodded and felt the regret to his core. He had let his friend, his former rabbi, a good man down. Steve had a producer's heart of stone, except when it came to Dan and Marion.

Dan was upset with himself, too. What the hell kind of answer was that? Obviously a subconscious request for continued sympathy, but he couldn't restrain himself. He was hurting, dammit, still hurting after two years, seven months and six days. He didn't want to dissolve into a puddle of tears either, but this was Marion and her death was the total eclipse of the sun.

They both quietly slid into either side of the leather-upholstered booth, and Steve poured from a bottle of wine already at tableside in a silver ice bucket. He raised his glass.

"To Marion," Steve said. They toasted then retreated into silence.

Dan wasn't sure he could avoid a discussion of death and the horrors of surviving, but he was determined to try. "So, how's the film business these days?"

"Different," Steve said. "It doesn't pay to make films anymore. It's all distribution. With TV, cable, computers and foreign paying top dollar for our library, I can't complain, but the business as we knew it is dead."

The last thing Dan cared about at that point in his life was the film business, but even that was dead. There was no escaping the grim reaper.

"The special today is your favorite, Mr. Weisman," the waiter graciously interrupted.

"Branzino?" Steve was delighted. "Bring it on, Danny," he said and handed the waiter his menu, while Dan clawed his way back to the present.

The waiter looked at Dan.

"The same."

"So," Steve said. "How *are* you getting on, Dan?"

"As best I can." What more could he say? *How do I explain what it is like to live without oxygen?*

Switching gears, Dan asked: "And what have you been up to, Steve?"

"This place takes up a lot of my time now. Otherwise, not much, other than the divorce."

"Divorce?"

"Simone and I are finally breaking up. I didn't want to burden you with my problems considering what you've been through."

"I'm sorry to hear that." The truth is Dan never liked Simone, Steve's vapid wife, whose interests in life were shopping for haute couture clothes and hanging Teutonic wall tapestries that were as out of place in an oceanfront house as was the full suit of armor that greeted guests in the foyer.

"Nothing to be sorry about," Steve said. "The marriage was never right. Great in bed, in the beginning anyway, but that got old. I always had enough freedom to pursue other interests so I made peace with it."

"So, why now?"

"For my ex-rabbi's ears only, I've been seeing someone."

"Someone special, I hope."

"Special enough to cost me an arm and a leg and possibly more."

"How is Simone handling it?"

"It was awful in the beginning but once her lawyers decided that she deserves two thirds of everything I own, her tears magically dried up. Naturally, I'm fighting it but I may end up spending more than that on an endless legal battle. It's a nightmare, but I've had a few in my life. I'll get through it."

"I don't know what to say. I wish you only happiness. It was no secret that Simone was never very fond of me . . . or Marion."

"Well, you have to admit, it was quite a strange set of circumstances, Dan. *Our* daughter, Molly, essentially left home after a fight with Simone and went to live with you and Marion. I was okay with it because I knew she'd be happier out of Simone's grasp and there was nobody I trusted more than you and Marion. Yes, Simone hated you both, but Marion in particular. There was no way for her not to. Molly not only rejected Simone but drove in the nail by making a point of calling Marion, Mama, and Simone, Simone, to her face. I'm sorry it also drove a wedge between us, over time."

Dan wasn't ready to address his feelings about Steve's abandonment of him. "Sadly, I haven't heard from Molly in a while. Where is she now?"

"Jamaica," Steve said. "She met someone down there and stayed. You and Marion made a film in Jamaica a while back, didn't you?"

"Yes, *Sunsplash*. As I recall, you financed it."

"Right. Why do I always forget that one? Where did you stay?"

"The Poseidon in Montego Bay. Marion loved it. Why do you ask?"

Steve smiled. "I bought it last year. Changed the name. It's now called Moonlight Bay Resort, but they still have the peacocks and bungalows that open onto private beaches. I love it, too. I go there whenever I can get away."

"How does Molly like it?"

"Since I own the place, she won't go near it. Vintage Molly, but I don't have to tell you. How well do you remember her?"

"I was there the day Molly was born, so I guess we go back a way. And there were her teen years with us. But the day of her birth . . . that was a day I'll never forget."

"As I remember it," Steve said. "You came to the hospital stoned out of your skull."

What a day it was, Dan thought. He reached back to that afternoon in January so many years ago.

HE AND MARION had been celebrating their fifth anniversary during one of the worst storms in California history. They danced in their bedroom, thrilling to the touch of each other's bodies as winds howled and lightning flashed outside the large picture window. The rolling thunder provided a steady beat for Joe Cocker's broken voice as it growled out of the cassette recorder. *"What do you see when you turn out the light . . ."*

Dan remembered exactly how his body felt at that moment, the pulsating touch of Marion's warm sweet-scented skin. He sang aloud, drowning out the tape.

"What do you see when you turn out the light . . ."

Dan waited for Marion to join in, but she didn't.

"The next line . . . ." Dan coaxed. "Go on, you know it."

Marion's mind was adrift.

"Come on, we've sung it a dozen times," Dan pleaded, doing his best Joe Cocker. *". . . ah cain't say . . ."*

Emerging from another world, Marion sang softly. *"I can't say . . . but I know it's mine."*

"Right," Dan said.

Her eyes moistened.

"What's wrong?"

"I don't know," she said. "I feel like crying. Just happy, I guess."

He pressed his body against hers and they continued to dance in rhythm with the storm.

Slowly, imperceptibly at first, they felt their world being infiltrated by an irritating ring.

Marion stopped dancing. "Didn't you turn off the phones?"

"I thought I did."

Marion looked at the flashing white phone on Dan's night table.

"Don't answer it," he said.

"It's your private line."

"Who calls me on that line beside you?"

"I don't know but it might be important."

Reluctantly, Dan picked up the receiver. "What?!" He barked.

"She's here! I can't believe it!"

"Who is this?"

"The happiest man in the world," the man half cried and half laughed.

"I don't know any such person."

"It's me. Steve!"

"My God, Steve. What happened to you?"

"I never believed in God until now, but I just saw her face!"

"Slow down. Where are you?"

"Cedars-Sinai and I'm looking at my Molly, the most beautiful baby on God's earth . . ."

On the drive to the hospital, the windshield wipers barely kept up with the lashing downpour. "I completely forgot Simone was pregnant," Dan said. "We never see her. Steve and I played golf two weeks ago and he never even mentioned it. Did he say anything to you?"

Marion shook her head.

When they entered the posh hospital suite, Simone was completely sedated. Steve was so excited he embraced Dan before he could drop his umbrella. The nurse rocked the screaming infant in her arms, but was unable to calm her. Marion's eyes locked onto her gaze and she immediately stopped crying. As if in a dream, Marion dropped her wet coat to the floor and reached for the baby. Dan had never seen her like that. As she picked up the child and placed it next to her bosom, the song they had been dancing to all afternoon, lodged in his brain and he couldn't stop thinking about it. *What do you see when you turn out the light? I can't say, but I know it's mine.*

Marion's face was radiant and her heart was pounding. She didn't know whether to scream or laugh out loud but she heard the child in her arms, inches from her face say, "I'm here, Mama!"

PART THREE

Molly

1989

{ Chapter Six }

MARION PRACTICALLY LIVED at Steve's house during the following weeks and months. She sat at Molly's crib and stared at the infant for hours, riveted to every motion, every sound. If a day went by without seeing little Molly, Marion was distraught.

Simone not only didn't mind, she didn't notice. She never wanted a child. She had married a very rich man with a private jet that took her to parties in London, celebrations in Cannes and new friends all over the world that provided her with the kind of life she dreamed of. Having a child was a compromise because Steve, who grew up in an orphanage, had fantasies about how he would give a baby of his everything he never had. Unfortunately, he had no innate parenting skills and the result was that he was never able to bond with his daughter in any meaningful way. Simone had no interest in mothering. As far as she was concerned, Molly was a pest and the less time she had to devote to her, the better.

Marion, on the other hand saw the introduction of Molly into her life as a gift from God and she couldn't be happier or more fulfilled.

During those first few years, the child became increasingly precious and Marion had to be pried loose from her at the end of her daily visits.

"Don't go, Mamie!" Little Molly pleaded as she stood at the door, trying to block Marion's exit.

Marion's heart broke every time she had to leave and she managed to delay her departure by agreeing to tell one more story, watch one more episode of *Shrek*, during which Molly chatted away and never even looked at the TV. She loved cuddling in Marion's arms and talking and talking and talking and Marion couldn't get enough. It took so long for her to leave Molly that Dan jokingly but affectionately suggested she start to say goodbye the minute she walked in the door.

Marion happily provided all the love her perfect Molly craved, the love she never received from her self-centered mother, professional nannies or even her father, who loved her but lacked even the basic instincts of parenting. Having grown up in an orphanage, Steve never learned how to express affection. Luckily, at this time Marion was writing at home most days. If she had to go to the studio for a meeting or to supervise cutting on a difficult scene, she'd race home and run down the block to see her daughter—yes, she used the possessive—laden with all manner of gifts that were greeted with the most exuberant laughter, hugs and kisses only a child can bestow.

Marion taught Molly how to make little earrings that she pasted on her ears and rings for every finger. The gift she brought Molly for her third birthday was the pièce de résistance for the child, but caused both of her nannies to quit: a pair of tap shoes from Denmark that lit up and made resonant honking sounds with every step. Molly danced around the house for weeks, happy, happy, happy. The only unpleasant times were when, despite the many delays, Marion had to leave. Molly was upset and Marion's heart was heavy. Leaving to go home—just down the block—was painful for both of them.

By the time she was ten, Molly's relationship with Simone became increasingly hostile and on her eleventh birthday, she staged a full-fledged rebellion. At dinner, Molly dismissed the help and made an announcement. "This is not working."

"What's not working?" Steve asked.

"Everything. This house sucks. This so-called family is totally dysfunctional and we have to make some serious changes." She had just watched an episode of *Night Court* on TV. "I'd like to settle this amical . . . amically, whatever, but if we have to go to court, so be it."

Simone laughed, but Steve was shocked.

"I'm sorry, Dad. I know you try really hard, but let's face facts. Being born to Simone was a mistake and it's not too late to correct it. I want to live with Marion, who, I happen to know is my true mother and if you don't let me, I'll run away and you'll never see me again."

"Good riddance to bad rubbish," was Simone's maternal blessing. Molly burst into tears and ran to her room. Steve was traumatized. A nightmare from his childhood returned to haunt him. Tibor, his only friend at the orphanage, was eleven, the same age as Molly, when he ran away. Steve didn't remember the exact details, but Tibor was in the director's office being paddled mercilessly for some minor infraction. When he refused to apologize, the punishment increased. Tibor picked up a bronze trophy and hit the director in the face. They called the police but Tibor ran away. When his body was finally discovered, he had been savagely brutalized and fear of what happens to runaway children was permanently seared into Steve's consciousness. He shuddered to think what would happen to his Molly if she actually did run away. She was spoiled and independent but so very vulnerable. If anything happened to her, he could never forgive himself.

Steve knocked on her door. She didn't answer. It wasn't locked, so he opened it. "May I come in?" He wanted to hold her, caress her, but he didn't know how. Instead, he lifted her, awkwardly, like he did when she was a toddler.

"Please put me down, Dad." She wasn't crying anymore, but her face was red with anger. She turned away from him and took her backpack down from the closet.

"I have an idea," Steve said. "How would you like a stable and horses? I can have one built for you right here on the grounds."

Molly looked at him, exasperated. "I am allergic to animal hair, Dad!" She shook her head in disbelief.

"I'm sorry, I forgot. How about coming to Egypt with us this summer? You always said you would like to see the pyramids."

"Yes, but not with Simone. That woman hates me and I can't live another day with her," she said, opening her backpack. "I'm leaving, one way or another."

Watching his baby stuff her clothes, books and dolls into her backpack was heartbreaking. "Maybe I could arrange with Dan and Marion for you to stay overnight with them once or twice a week. How about that?"

"NO. NO. NO. I've had it with Simone. It's over! I am Marion's daughter and either you let me go to live with her or I will run away and you'll never see me again and I mean it."

Steve was desperate. He didn't really think Molly would run away, but he was shocked to hear his daughter use those words. What if she does run away? He paced the room, holding back tears as he watched his little girl preparing to separate from him. *Why can't I show her how much I love her? Why can't I be a father like other fathers?*

"I'm sorry, Dad, I really am," she said and hugged him. "It's not your fault, but that's the way it is. Look, it's not the end of the world. I'll be right down the block, for God's sake. We can see each other whenever you want."

Like a slap in the face, Steve finally realized what was happening and despite his wealth and power, there was nothing he could do to prevent it. Trying to find a way to accept the harsh reality, he negotiated with himself. *She's right. I can always drop in to visit Dan and Marion to see how my little girl is getting on . . . still . . . God, this hurts!*

It was a severe blow, but like everything else in his life, Steve made himself deal with it. He was always grateful to Dan and Marion for raising Molly, but there was a mountain-size *shtuch* of failure in his heart that he couldn't do it himself.

{ Chapter Seven }

EVERYTHING MOLLY wanted to know about life, she learned by studying Marion's every word, every move and the questions never ended. She sat on the floor in Marion's bathroom for hours, watching her apply eye make-up and lipstick. She learned what blouse goes with what pants and when to wear a skirt or dress and what colors emphasize her best features. One night as Marion was dressing to attend a formal dinner, Molly sat on her perch next to the sink, watching intently.

"Why are you wearing your hair up, Mama? You have such pretty, long, wavy hair."

"Come here and clip my necklace in the back, dear, you'll see."

Looking over Marion's shoulder into the mirror, Molly smiled. "By putting your hair up, the eye goes immediately to the necklace. Cool."

Marion and Molly became inseparable. They cooked together, played Scrabble, and did homework. Molly's favorite movie was *The Red Shoes* and when Marion bought her a tutu and toe shoes, she danced around the house, playing all the roles.

"Vy do you vant to dance?" Molly had a great ear for dialects, a skill she picked up from Dan, and mimicked Lermontov.

"Why do you want to live?" Molly switched to Victoria Page, the main character in *The Red Shoes*.

"Vell, I don't know exactly vy, but I must."

"That's my answer, too," Molly said, "I don't know vy exactly, but I must so long as I have Mama." She put her arm around Marion's waist and they twirled around the house together.

Dan was happy to see his *basherte* so totally fulfilled in her new role. His life with Marion was blissful and he was glad she could derive so much satisfaction from being a mother. Watching Marion glow with every accomplishment of her daughter warmed his heart and he recalled a rabbinic maxim: *Even more than the calf needs to suckle, the mother needs to give milk.*

WITH MOLLY IN THEIR LIVES, Marion curtailed her movie work. Sixteen years on the Hollywood treadmill, even the travel around the world, could not match her new joy: Molly. She drove Molly to school, worked on the lot or at home until early afternoon, and then picked Molly up. If Dan wasn't away on a shoot, dinnertime was a joyous event for the three of them. Anytime Dan came home from a trip, a special dinner and dessert awaited him. Dan's heart soared when he pulled into the driveway.

Years before Molly moved in, Marion studied with a yogi who taught her how to master the power of visualization. She revised it and called her version *mind-travel*.

Sitting cross-legged on the floor with hands resting on their thighs, eyes closed and facing one another, Marion taught Molly her special meditation. "Breathe deeply . . . in and out.. . slower with each number as you count backwards . . . ten . . . nine . . . eight . . . How do you feel?"

"Relaxed," Molly said. "Light as a feather, actually."

"Good. Now we're going to visualize all the colors of the spectrum because that will provide a bridge of light that will enable us to mind travel through multiple universes together."

"I don't know what you mean."

"That's okay. You won't understand it all at once, but over time, as we go through the exercises, your body will actually feel the sensations that accompany the images you call up along the way. Let's begin with something real easy. Keep your eyes closed and concentrate on visualizing the color red . . . red . . . what pops into your mind when you focus on the color?"

"I see a fat Santa Claus in a red sleigh."

"Hah. Good one. All right then. By listening to your voice with my eyes closed, I can see the images you are seeing, a jolly Santa in a red coat and red sleigh. Now let's slowly advance to the color orange. I am visualizing lush orange rays of the early morning sun. Breathe deeply, in and out and tell me if you can see it."

"I do! It feels like I'm getting up early when the sun just begins to peek through my window."

"Now, let's see ourselves holding hands and flying out of your bedroom window to visit our own private Disneyland . . ."

"I'm holding on to you, Mama."

"We've arrived at the park, but in order to get in, we must skip across a bridge of colors," Marion said, "yellow, green, blue and finally violet. Let me know how it feels when you get there."

"I just hop-scotched over violet and I feel great!"

"Where do you want to go from here?"

"How about Hawaii? I saw a picture in Dan's magazine."

"Look down. We're flying over the Big Island right now."

That meditative technique brought them into a secret world of virtual journeys and they always emerged with an elevated sense of their inseparable union.

ONE THING MOLLY was unprepared for were the lupus attacks that assaulted Marion without warning. The first time it happened, Molly was petrified. Helplessly watching her mother writhe in pain, Molly felt her world slip away and she couldn't stop crying.

Ultimately, the symptoms passed but Molly was a nervous wreck.

"Don't be afraid," Marion murmured. I get these from time to time, but they go away.

"What if they don't? What if you die?"

"Everyone dies but even then, I won't abandon you. We'll be together forever."

"What do you mean?"

"People whose souls are interwoven, like ours, are capable of remaining connected, even in future incarnations."

"Is that true?"

"Yes, darling, it is true."

"Where did you learn that?"

"The first inklings came to me when I began to meditate in a serious way, but the full picture didn't become clear until I met Dan's mother, Bertha."

"My grandmother?"

"Yes, dear Molly. Your grandmother."

"Do I call her Bertha or Grandma?"

"Whatever you call her, she will answer . . . as will I."

THE STORIES Dan had told Marion about his mother's fight for survival touched her deeply. Born in the Ukraine, Bertha and her sister, Ida, fled after a pogrom killed both their parents and every Jew in the village who couldn't find a place to hide. The teenage girls spent two years travelling from one far flung *shtetl* to the next until they got to Turkey and from there, steerage to the U.S. where they were sheltered by remnants of a once large family.

Shortly after Marion and Dan moved in together, she said, "I want to meet your mother."

"Do you want to travel twenty-five hundred miles to spend a glorious weekend in gloomy Struthers, Ohio?"

"Why don't we bring her here?"

"I have offered any number of times, but she won't hear of it."

"I'd like to try."

Dan couldn't hide the frown. He was a caring son, but he wasn't at all enthusiastic about that idea. Bertha was a dear woman and a loving mother but she was from a different generation, one that was accustomed to talking incessantly about everything and nothing.

"She's not a very sophisticated woman," Dan said. "I don't' know if you'd find much common ground."

"Who are you protecting, your mother or me? Do you think I can't connect with someone who didn't go to Barnard? You call her at least once a week. What do you talk about?"

"I tell her what I'm doing and she asks me what I'm eating and am I dressing warmly because she heard on TV that we're having a cold spell in L.A."

"Sounds like you two are communicating. If I'm going to share your life, I'd like her to know what I'm eating and thinking . . . and that I have warm sweaters."

Dan smiled and surrounded Marion with his arms.

DAN'S FATHER DIED nearly fifteen years ago. Since that time, Bertha's life had been shrinking. Most of her friends and relatives were dead or dying so Marion decided they should go to Ohio to convince her to move to Los Angeles. There she would be near her son and his *basherte* instead of sitting alone in her small apartment, staring at the walls.

When they arrived, Bertha was sitting alone in her dark apartment staring at the walls. After the introductions, there were hugs, tears, blessings, and endless sighs.

"I want you to know, dear Miriam . . ." Bertha said.

"It's Marion, mom," Dan gently reminded.

"I love that name, Miriam. Remember, it was cousin Miriam's name, may she rest in peace, but I love your new name just as much. Miriam, isn't it?"

"Marion, Mom."

"Marion, of course. You said that. I'm such a stupid. It takes time for me to catch on. My hearing isn't so good."

"You got it just right, Bertha," Marion said.

Dan took his familiar place on the Barcalounger while Marion sat next to Bertha on the small sofa. "Such a beauty," Bertha said. "You're a good man, Danele, and a good son and you suffered plenty, God knows. You deserve a beauty like Marion."

"Tell me, Bertha," Marion asked, "How do you do it? I mean, living alone all these years?"

Dan heard that story far too many times. He reached for

the TV remote, but the look Marion shot at him blocked that thought.

"It's lonesome. I won't kid you," Bertha said, "but I've got no complaints. After all, I had my Solly for thirty-eight years. A loving husband like that, they don't make anymore. Plus two accomplished children who made from my dreary life a palace of memories. What right do I have to complain?" Her mind seemed to go blank and she became silent.

Marion moved closer. "Go on, Mom."

"It's hard," she said, "not to have somebody you can talk out the heart with."

"What's in your heart, Mama? I want to know."

In no particular order, Bertha proceeded to talk about the dead, the dying, and the ones in intensive care, then stopped suddenly. "I almost forgot. Dinner is ready an hour ago already. I hope it's not all dried out." She got up and made her way to the kitchen.

It was Friday night and Bertha had prepared a huge Shabbos dinner with homemade gefilte fish. "I should buy the ready-made garbage, excuse me, they try to sell you for a fortune in the kosher deli?" There was also chopped liver, chicken soup with matzo balls, chicken, brisket, kugel, and more. Bertha lit the Sabbath candles and Dan stood up to recite *kiddush* over the wine. When he was finished, Marion kissed Dan's mother and said, "Bertha, I am in love with your son." Bertha's eyes filled with tears.

After dinner, they talked and laughed. "Mom," Marion finally said, "the reason we came is because we would like you to move to Los Angeles to be near us."

"Darling," Bertha said, "you are so lovely and I would be thrilled to live nearby you and Danele, but how can I? My husband Solly is buried twenty minutes by bus. I visit his grave whenever I have to talk out the heart. A week from Sunday, April twenty-fifth, is his *Yortzeit,* the anniversary of his death. In the olden days, we used to go by the Hebrew calendar, but who can remember all that? So, we celebrate by the regular date. Let me explain you darling, a *Yortzeit* by us is like an anniversary party, but because the person is dead you don't bake a cake, you light a candle."

"I know, Mom," Marion said. "I light a *Yortzeit* candle for my father every year."

Bertha smiled, put her hand to her heart and sighed as only a Jewish mother can when she discovers that her son is marrying within the faith. "God bless you, darling," she said as she wiped away the tears. "Danele, don't forget, a week from this coming Sunday. Not this Sunday, the one after, April twenty-fifth to light a *Yortzeit* candle."

"Every year on the twenty-fifth of April, I light a candle *and* recite both the *Kaddish* and the *El Moleh Rachmim*. I have never missed one."

"Is that a beautiful son, or what?" Bertha looked at him and *kvelled*. "Anyhow, what was I saying? So, I will go to the cemetery a week from Sunday and talk out my heart with Solly. What would I do if I was so far away? I could never visit him."

"Don't you think he would want you to be near Dan and me rather than sitting here alone?"

"How can a person know what a husband wants after he passes away?"

"The Kabbalah, I learned, tells us that our severed soul—that is, our loved one who passed on—sends us messages all the time, but we're often too busy and distracted to hear them."

"Wouldn't a person recognize the voice?"

"It doesn't always come that directly. The message might be in what you hear someone say on TV or from a person you're talking to about something totally different. It may seem to have nothing to do with what's been on your mind, but if you learn to listen, you will hear what you need to hear."

The doorbell tingled. When Dan opened the door, Mrs. Bevilaqua, Bertha's new neighbor stood in the entranceway carrying a tray overflowing with cookies, cake, fruit, and thinly sliced Sicilian delicacies. It seemed pointless to mention that they had just finished a nine-course meal. Obviously Bertha had boasted to her new friend that her son and fiancée were coming to visit and she was invited to come over to bask in the glory of the son she had heard so much about—and who comes to visit a neighbor empty-handed?

"Please call me Josephine. Such a pleasure to meet you, Father Sobol. You're even handsomer than the pictures and you look so young and so casual. I never seen a priest dressed so casual."

"He's not a rabbi anymore," Bertha corrected her.

"And what a stunning wife. Our priests don't marry, of course, but I never seen such beauty in my whole life as your daughter-in-law, I swear to God."

"We're not married yet," Dan said "but I'm hopeful."

After the introductions they sat in Bertha's small living room where the two neighbors smiled and kvelled at Dan and Marion.

"She's so gorgeous and he's so handsome," the nice Italian neighbor said as Bertha glowed, "When I look at them, I feel like Christ has risen and he's back in the arms of Mother Mary." Then to everyone's surprise, Josephine started to cry uncontrollably.

"I'm sorry," she said several times but continued to cry until she stopped. "You see, Bertha, your children are so beautiful they remind me . . . of my dog."

"Your dog?" Bertha was confused.

"You remember I told you about my little Alfredo? I named him after my favorite pasta. I loved him more than life. He died just a year ago." She crossed herself and wiped away the tears. "I loved that dog so much. We lived in the country then, with a big backyard. I couldn't wait to get up in the morning to kiss my little sweetheart, pet him, feed him, and take him out so he could do his business in the yard where nobody would step in it. I wanted him to sleep in our bed but my dead husband, Ugo, God rest his soul, was so mean, he never let Alfredo sleep with us. I always hated him for that."

"You never told me about that," Bertha said.

"Don't get me started on Ugo, that miserable sumna bitch, excuse me, may he rest in peace. I hope he drowns in hell. Anyway, after he died, Alfredo slept with me every night. I thanked my Saint Philomena every day for that beautiful dog. I know she sent him to me as a reward for all the shit, excuse me, I took all those years from that sumna bitch of a husband. Anyway, when my little dog died, it will be exactly a year ago one week from Sunday . . . where was I?"

"A week from . . . Sunday?" Bertha asked.

Marion moved closer to Bertha and held her hand.

"That's right. When my Alfredo died, it will be exactly a year, one week from next Sunday, did I tell you that?"

"Yes, you did," Bertha answered in a strange voice.

"I swear to God, I thought I was going to have a mental breakdown. If it wasn't for my Patron Saint Philomena telling me my dog's in heaven waiting for me, I would have gone off my mind. Maybe I did. I'm so nervous all the time it's hard to know for sure. So, anyway, why am I telling you this? It's something I'm feeling now that I haven't felt in a whole year and I don't know why I can't stop crying. It's just that when

I look into your children's saintly faces, all I can think about is the one thing in this life I loved most," and she started to cry again. "My Saint Philomena has been telling me all along Alfredo's at peace with the angels. But now, I'm looking at your children and I feel like she's telling me something different, like something's wrong here."

"What is she telling you?" Marion asked.

"I feel like she's telling me it's time to go away, to leave Struthers. Leave Struthers? And go where? Am I going crazy or what?"

Bertha turned white.

"You say your dog died last year, a week from this coming Sunday," Marion said. 'What was the date, exactly?"

"April twenty-fifth. I'll never forget that day as long as I live."

Bertha stared at her nice Italian neighbor who was sobbing, then turned to Marion. "I recognized the voice," she said softly.

BERTHA LEFT OHIO for California on April twenty-sixth, one day after Sol's *Yortzeit*.

To Molly, these events were not scrapbook reminiscences.

They were the *Gospel According to Molly:*

Chapter the first: The magical meeting of the *bashert* couple, Marion and Dan.

Chapter the second: The transcendent bond that joined Molly's soul with Marion minutes after she was delivered from the womb.

Chapter the third: Bertha's awakening to the call of the cosmos.

{ Chapter Eight }

AT HER BAT MITZVAH, Molly looked positively radiant in the *kippa* and *talit* from Israel with gold trim to match her dress.

Steve's social and business relations were intermingled and he wanted to make this affair the event of the season. That morning, the synagogue was packed with celebrities, politicians, and CEOs. When Molly was called to the Torah, she chanted her portion brilliantly. People don't normally applaud in a synagogue, but when Molly finished the nuanced Hebrew chant, Steve's guests cheered and whooped. It was a triumphant moment and he couldn't have been prouder. Even Simone grudgingly appreciated the accomplishment of the child she never connected with.

Marion was nervous, but excited. This was her daughter coming of age and her heart was on that pulpit guiding every glance, every move Molly made.

After the crowd quieted down, Dan, who was officiating

for the first time in many years, introduced the Bat Mitzvah and asked her to deliver her message to the congregation. He was eager to hear what Molly was going to say because although he offered to help with the speech, she refused. She got everything she needed from Marion.

"The topic I have chosen," she began, her voice brimming with confidence, "is from the Book of Ruth. It's about two amazing women and how they turned each other's suffering into triumph and their misery into redemption." Dan's eyes were focused on Marion as Molly was speaking. Tears flowed down her cheeks as she mouthed every word. When he looked back at Molly, Dan saw that she was not reading her speech. She was speaking by heart, from the heart, and staring directly at Marion.

"Wither thou goest, I will go and where thou liest, I will lie. Even death cannot separate us. As you die, I will die and our souls will be joined together for all eternity."

When Molly finished her speech, she kissed Dan's cheek and came down from the pulpit. She walked to the pew where Marion was sitting and embraced her. Marion was bawling. Steve was unnerved and looked at Dan to do something. Without even hazarding a look at Simone, Dan rose immediately and said, "I'd like to ask Steve and Simone to stand and recite the parental prayer of gratitude with me. Molly, would you come back to the pulpit, please?"

"I'm good," Molly said defiantly.

"FLAN FOR MR. WEISMAN," the waiter smiled and turned to Dan. "And for Mr. Sobol?"

Dan tried to hold onto the image of Marion and Molly embracing, but they drifted away.

"Dessert for Mr. Sobol" The waiter asked again. Dan shook his head. The waiter left. After a brief, uncomfortable silence, Steve put down his glass and without looking at Dan, asked, "When was the last time you spoke to Molly?"

"At least a year ago, maybe longer. How is she?"

Steve reached into his jacket pocket and took out his phone. He flicked it open and showed the picture of a pretty young woman whose face was not all that different from the little girl of three that Dan fell in love with, but with wild hair, straddling a Harley-Davidson. This was vintage Molly, full of adolescent rebellion.

"Beautiful," Dan said, "I've seen that picture. No surprise about the motorcycle. Molly always wore badges of defiance."

"It's an old picture, but it's my favorite. She hates it. Maybe that's why I like it." Hesitatingly, Steve said, "When did you say you spoke to her?"

"Sometime after the funeral. She called. I can't remember exactly when. Why?"

"Just curious. What did you talk about?"

"Not much. She was clearly shaken, but promised to stay in touch with me because that's what Marion tells her she must do. Those were her exact words, present tense. I didn't know how to respond so I didn't say anything. Then, a year or so later, she sent me a card from the San Mateo County Jail for Women. 'Have you spoken to Marion lately?' That was the entire card. I called the jail to see if she needed help, but she had already been released. It was some overnight disturbing-the-peace thing. I didn't know what she was protesting or how to reach her. The sergeant I spoke to didn't have much information either so I didn't pursue it. I meant to call you, but I didn't. I don't know why."

"It doesn't matter. Shortly after the arrest in San

Mateo—naturally I paid her bail—she went to Israel. Did you know that?"

"No. Why? Did she become a Zionist all of a sudden?"

"I doubt it because after Israel there was Nepal and then back to Israel, but you never know with Molly. The trip began with a tour of the Sinai. Then, there was Nepal and back to Israel and finally, Jamaica. She never told me anything about those trips and I never asked. She just kept sending the bills and I kept paying them. Why, I asked myself a hundred times? What kind of shmuck am I? To be perfectly honest, I always had this fantasy that someday she and I would be able to get along. I would give anything for that to happen, but whenever I suggested a trip or vacation together, even without Simone, she always refused. Then suddenly, wonder of wonders, miracle of miracles she called last week to tell me her life had completely turned around. She even had the tattoo on her ass removed."

"Give me her number," Dan said. "I'll give her a call."

"You can do more than that." Steve took an envelope out of his pocket and placed it on the table next to Dan. It was an airline ticket.

"Molly says she wants to get married and she insists you conduct the ceremony," Steve said hesitatingly. "The pisser is if I can't convince you go to Jamaica to do it, I'm not invited to the wedding. That would be a major blow to me, Dan. Really major."

Dan was trying to comprehend this completely out-of-the-blue news. Was Molly to be back in his life? "Wow, Steve . . . but why Jamaica?"

"My son-in-law-to-be works there. More specifically, he's stationed there. She emailed me the latest this morning."

He picked up his phone again and swiped to another picture. Molly looked totally different from the one on the motorcycle. Her hair was long and wavy and her face was that of a woman, not a child, and a familiar woman at that. She smiled broadly, with both arms wrapped tightly around the chest of an incredibly handsome young black man.

"Aren't you going to say the obvious?" Steve teased.

"After you, Groucho."

"He doesn't look Jewish, right? Well he's not only Jewish, he's Israeli, born in Ethiopia, can track his ancestry back to King Solomon and the Queen of Sheba. He came to Israel as a kid on that famous airlift in the Eighties. You must have heard about that."

"Fourteen thousand Ethiopian Jews airlifted to Israel in thirty-six hours," Dan said proudly. "Nothing short of miraculous."

"Rocky . . . some name for a Jew, huh? Rocky and his folks became the ideal Israeli family. His father is a cardiologist and his mother, a professor of something at the Hebrew University in Jerusalem. He joined an elite unit of the IDF and became a war hero. The reason they're in Jamaica is because Rocky, a.k.a. Colonel Rachmiel ben-Solomon is the military attaché to the Israeli Consulate in Kingston." Steve put away his phone while Dan looked pensively at the airline reservation.

"I've never asked anyone for a favor in my life," Steve said solemnly. "I can't tell you how hard it is for me now. Believe me, buddy, I can imagine what your life has been these last few years . . . but I don't think I can handle not being at my baby's wedding." His face took on the same penitential sadness that was seared into his flesh after Molly moved out. "Will you do this for me?"

How could Dan refuse? But go to Jamaica without Marion? Jamaica, where they celebrated their honeymoon, made their first film together and shared so many idyllic memories? And go back alone? How painful would that be?

I'm sorry, Steve. I would do it if I could, but I can't. I just can't . . . is what he wanted to say but the words he heard coming out of his mouth were, "Of course."

PART FOUR

Moonlight Bay

{ Chapter Nine }

DAN'S EARDRUMS FELT the descent of the plane as the first glimpse of Kingston appeared through the window in the next seat. Dan looked at his tray table. Anything left? The first three miniature gin bottles were empty but the fourth was still sealed. He unscrewed the tiny top and poured the liquid down his throat in one long guzzle; the flavor of charred oak with a hint of cherry seared his palate.

How long has it been since I was on a plane? Having flown all over the world for so many years, it occurred to him that he and Marion hadn't been on a plane in . . . how long? All those trips together—Rome, Madrid, Tel Aviv, Paris, London, Guatemala—and how many times back and forth to Jamaica? Flying had always been exciting. On their way to a location it was the anticipation. How would they pull this one off? On the way home, there was the exhilaration of completing another film. Even flying was part of the stimulation. The ever present danger that is part of air travel added yet another romantic ingredient. "If we go down, we go together" and they clinked glasses. At thirty thousand feet, they were precisely where they wanted to be—together. That's what gave life meaning and rendered death irrelevant.

Above the clouds, we drank until we couldn't think in words. I had everything I wanted in life just looking at her, inhaling her, embracing her and when her radiant face beckoned, kissing her.

Dan looked at Marion in the window seat next to him. "Hiya, gorgeous," he said, smiling broadly.

"Excuse me?" The woman next to him, who had been staring out the window, looked at him quizzically. It wasn't Marion.

"Wha . . . ! I'm so sorry, Miss. Forgive me, I was in some distant place . . ." He had never done that before.

"No problem," the woman said, half smiling, as the plane hit the tarmac.

What's happening to me?

Bumpy landing. Depressing. Horrible. At home, whenever Dan was in this kind of mood, he got quiet and sullen. Without a word, Marion would pick up her ukulele and softly sing, *Nobody knows you when you're down and out* . . . It worked every time. Despite himself, he felt the gloom slip away. *When you get back on your feet again, everybody's gonna want to be your long-lost friend.*

Marion's comforting voice drowned out the static as he deplaned and walked down the long passageway, but began to fade as he reached the luggage carousel. By the time he went through customs, it was gone. Customs? What the hell does anyone bring *into* Jamaica?

"Dan Sobol, passenger on flight 352 from Los Angeles, kindly approach the Imperial Caribbean Air Welcome Desk. Dan Sobol, passenger . . ." Fortunately the announcement was repeated

over and over. The distortion was so great Dan didn't recognize his name at first.

Following signs to the Welcome Desk, everything felt wrong. Colliding voices blared through loud speakers. The brash, incomprehensible words welcoming tourists to the "I-land in the Sun" sounded hostile.

Where in hell am I? This is not the Jamaica I remember. This is a circus. What happened to the tropical paradise it used to be? The radiant vision of Marion, singing with David ben David, to the cheers and applause of the entire crew filled his heart. Joy and laughter was everywhere.

But that was in another life.

"Welcome to Jamaica, Mr. Sobol," the overly solicitous attendant at the Welcome Desk said. "I am fortunate indeed to make your acquaintance. We received a call directly from Mr. Fishburne himself, head manager of Moonlight Bay Resort. He said you were a V.I.P. and were to be treated as an honored guest."

"So, where's my car?"

"The manager of the hotel called personally."

"You said that."

"Of course," he laughed. "Moonlight Bay Resort is the most prestigious hotel on the Island. I'm sure you will be most comfortably ensconced."

"Where can I find my driver!?"

"Ah yes. Mr. Fishburne, the hotel manager apologized effusively but their driver did not come to work today. He begs your indulgence."

"What does that mean?"

"Mr. Fishburne felt very bad indeed, but you arrived just as festivities are getting underway and the whole Island is in celebration mode. Jubilation Day, you know."

Dan took a deep breath. No point arguing. "So how do I get to the hotel?"

"Mr. Fishburne asked if you would be so kind as to take a taxi. He will gleefully reimburse your expenses, in addition to a complimentary cocktail."

Without a word, Dan reached for his cell phone.

"I'm sorry, sir. Cell phones aren't operating at the moment. Overload due to the many festivities. Jubilation Day, you know. However, there is a taxi stand right out front or you can call from any phone booth with a token." The attendant reached into a drawer and drew out a wad of tokens. "Please accept these as a gift from Imperial Caribbean Air."

Outside the terminal, clusters of musicians in colorful costumes strolled through the broad square followed by men in high hats and sandwich boards that read "Happy Jubilation Day." Dan looked in all directions. Not the slightest hint of a cab. A local ambled by.

"Excuse me," Dan called out. "Can you tell me where I can find a taxi?"

"Taxi?" The man thought, scratching his chin, and then exclaimed, "At de taxi stand, mon! Where you tink?"

Dan looked. No taxi stands. No cabs and no buses. He thought his brain would explode. It didn't. It just stopped.

Think rationally. Should I go back in and grab that obsequious Welcome Desk attendant by the throat and make him find one?

Furious as he was, Dan knew he wouldn't do that and if he did, all he would get would be more flowery bullshit. Feeling totally abandoned, Dan was clearly a stranger in a strange land. Standing alone, not knowing what to do, a gaily attired woman stopped, pointed across the road and gently said, "de taxi stand is just down dat block. Happy Jubilation Day." That gesture brought Dan the whiff of humanity he needed.

He dragged his suitcase behind him until he found a clearly marked taxi stand, but of course there were no cabs there, either. What did he expect? Jamaica had always been the most disorganized, chaotic place on earth, but it was charming—then. Now it only added to his feeling of alienation.

Grumbling, bitching, and exhausted from all the schlepping, he finally found a phone booth across the square from the terminal. Luckily he had tokens that were generously provided by the airline. The phone box *gleefully* swallowed all his tokens but never delivered a dial tone. Dan hit the phone box. Nothing. He hit it again and again with both hands then pounded angrily. There was a tinkling sound and a gush of tokens poured onto the pavement, but no dial tone. Dan's mind went blank again. He'd been in situations like this before, but he couldn't remember what he did about it so he just stood, befuddled. *I've got to get out of here,* he said to himself. The thought raged through his brain but crashed into a wall of reality. He remembered checking on return flights when he wasn't sure he would be able to go through with this, but there weren't any until next Tuesday. *Next Tuesday? I'm stuck!*

After a few minutes of standing around like a *putz,* he sat on the ground like a *putz.* Dan leaned against his suitcase without a thought in his head. The cheerful groups that crisscrossed the streets, smiling and waving happy Jubilation Day wishes, depressed him beyond words. Goddamn Steve! Goddamn Molly! Goddamn me!

He closed his eyes. What would Marion do? If she were here now, what would she say?

Silence. More silence. Then, "Welcome." It's hard to know exactly how long Dan sat on the ground across from the terminal before the word registered. That gentle greeting came from someone standing in front of him, backlit by the sun. Dan shielded his eyes from the glare and saw a man of indeterminate age with piercing eyes and an immensely handsome face, leaning on a walking stick shaped like the Lion of Judah.

He smiled broadly and extended his hand to Dan, who was still squatting on the ground. "I welcome you, my brother, in de name of de twelve tribes of Isr'al who were lost and scattered abroad but now are founded in our little island, Jamaica. I also welcome you in de name of de prophet Ja, who has revealed himself in the personality of His Imper'al Majesty, Emperor Haile Selassie, De First." He placed his hand on his heart and said, "Selassiyai! Rastafarai!"

Dan stood up slowly and shook the man's hand. "Thank you, all of you and a special thanks to ten of the lost tribes of Israel," he said. "Fortunately, I've been in touch with the other two."

"Me too," the man said, and laughed and laughed.

Dan couldn't understand why this stranger continued to laugh so exuberantly at his lame joke.

"My brother appears to be experiencin' difficulties."

"This *ba-kakte* phone doesn't work."

"Your first time in Jamaica?"

"I was here twenty-seven years ago."

"Well, dat phone ain't been operative for the last twenty-six, but if you tell me who you want to talk to, maybe I can help."

"Moonlight Bay Resort was supposed to arrange transportation, but their driver didn't come to work today so I am supposed to call a cab, but the phones don't work and the taxi stand is completely empty."

"Nobody come to work today, mon! It's Jubilation Day, de most important holiday in Jamaica. Come only once every fifty years."

"Jubilation Day?"

"Straight from de Holy Book. Every fifty years when de Jubilee come, slaves were freed and everybody rejoiced. When slavery ends, it's time to celebrate, right?"

"Right."

"So why would a person go to work when he can celebrate?" He started to laugh again.

Inexplicably, Dan felt himself smiling. *Can't argue with that.*

"If all my brother needs is a ride to Moonlight Bay Resort, his prayer has been answered. Praise Ja," the man said and pointed to a junk heap of a car parked behind him.

Dan looked at the pile of scrap strung together from an incongruous combination of Ford, Chevrolet and Dodge parts. He had never seen a more bizarre looking automobile outside of an amusement park.

The man smiled proudly. "Never seen anyting like dis, I'll bet."

"You're right," Dan said. He looked at the car listing to one side, mounted on four different type tires. "Will this car make it to Montego Bay?"

The man laughed again. "Dis car will carry Abednego's new friend wherever he need to go."

"Abednego, as in . . . ?" Dan was momentarily transported back to his childhood in Ohio and the sounds that rocked Prospect Street from the church on the corner every Sunday morning. *There were three children from the land of Israel, Shadrach, Meshach, Abednego . . ."*

"De Bible? Correct. Me and me brudders, we all tree of us was in de fiery furnace and we wuz all saved by de grace of God. My predecessor, Abednego de first was de one who showed Nebuchadnezzar de light and I, his humble descendant, continue his good works to dis very day. Yes, me and me great ancestor share many of de same attributes, except one," he winked. "He did not know how to drive a car." He laughed again.

Dan looked over the junk heap and wondered in that brief moment if it was better to wait. Wait? For what? He couldn't even find a working phone.

"Thank you," he said. "I would be very grateful if you would . . ."

"No need to tank de servant. Give tanks to de Master who provided Moses wid a staff, Joshua wid a chorus of trumpets, David, a sling, and humble Abednego wid de appropriate mechanism to deliver his brother to Moonlight Bay Resort." He laughed and laughed.

Dan heard himself laughing too. He was no longer stuck! He had a way out and the sludge that kept his brain in a vise began to drain off.

"What dey call you, brother?"

"Dan."

"Daniel?" Abednego let out a howl. "Daniel! We was in de lion's den togeder, mon. Don you remember? Daniel and Abednego. It say so right dere in de Holy Book. Praise Ja! I knew dere was a reason I was sent here today but I didn't know what it was. Don you see, mon? You and me, we're *bashert.*"

"How do you know that word?"

"Everybody in Jamaica know *bashert.*" Abednego smiled broadly and sang: *"Ja make de woman basherte, an de mon bashert and he place dem bot in de garden of love."* He laughed and said "*Bashert* was de mos popular song on de I-land long time ago. Did you ever hear it?"

"Yes, I did . . . a long time ago."

MARION AND DAN were boarding the plane home after a blissful honeymoon in Jamaica. "This is where we have to make our first film together," Marion said. "The music, the air, the rhythm of life on this island are all part of the drama. It's opera, Dan. It's ballet. What better way to tell the story of eternal love?"

The music . . . the rhythms, Reggae? A light went on in the business side of Dan's brain. *Worldwide music rights!* "Let's pitch it to Steve as soon as we get home."

Dan was keenly aware of Steve's taste in films and Marion's love story didn't come anywhere close. When Steve brought Dan into the company, he spelled out his philosophy of film-making in graphic terms. "Why is E.S.I. the most profitable independent studio in the country? Because I pay close attention to my ass. Every pitch consists of fifty to sixty words. If my ass begins to squirm before the pitch is over, I know it's a loser and I pass. If I hear a sixty-word pitch and my ass doesn't move once, I know it's a winner and I'll make the film."

"So how can we impact Steve's ass?"

"You tell him what's in your heart and I'll do the rest," Dan said.

At lunch with Steve the following week, Marion was too nervous to eat, so she nibbled at her salad until Steve worked his way through a sumptuous bowl of bouillabaisse. Finally, Steve turned to Dan. "So what's my next mega-hit and will it top "Creatures of the Blue Bayou?"

"By a landslide," Dan said and went into pitch-mode. He held up four fingers . . . three, two and pointed to Marion who came in on cue.

"Two preordained lovers grow up on opposite shores of a tropical island, but their families belong to different tribes and refuse to allow the marriage," Marion said. "Battered by insurmountable obstacles, they are ultimately united—but only through divine intervention."

After a long silence, Steve held up his glass and waved to the waiter. Then, he looked at Dan. "That's only thirty-eight words."

"Want to hear the whole story?" Dan asked.

"You're my rabbi," Steve muttered. "Can I say no?" He nodded to Marion.

"Our film is a contemporary love story based on the myth of Orpheus and Eurydice," she said.

"My ass just twitched," Steve said.

"In this case, your criterion doesn't apply," Dan said.

"Why not?"

"Because your ass can't sing and it can't count."

Steve looked at Dan with his familiar smile. "I know I'm about to hear a sermon, but what's the point?"

"Music rights, worldwide. Our movie, *Sunsplash,*" Dan said, "is named after the reggae festival that draws thirty thousand people to Jamaica every year for three days and three nights to groove to the best reggae artists in the world, and that intoxicating rhythm is what drives our film."

"But, Orpheus and Eurydice?" Steve frowned. "You really think millions of horny teenagers will flock to theaters all across America to watch a two thousand-year-old love story?"

"Not just America," Dan said firmly. He took a sheet from his briefcase and handed it to Steve. "In 1960, *Black Orpheus,* a French film built around the same theme, was made for under a million dollars and . . ." he pointed to the list of figures. "As of the last accounting—*with* worldwide music rights, and that's the key—the producers grossed over a hundred and forty-seven million."

Steve carefully studied the lists of itemized revenues. ". . . A hundred and forty-seven million!"

STEVE APPROVED THE FINANCING and nine months later, the movie was screened in Montego Bay for the international press corps.

Word was out and buyers from all over the world descended on the island for a first look at *Sunsplash*. The post-screening party was triumphant. Actors, extras, crew and celebrity guests were all riding high, many literally. Reggae Star, David ben David, TKI, True King of Israel, sat at the piano entertaining the enthusiastic crowd. His reggae score provided the perfect tone for Marion and Dan's film, integrating elements of the Orpheus myth with a contemporary meditation on transcendent love.

When Dan and Marion arrived at the party, David B.D. rose and called for Marion to sit beside him. Amid applause, he kissed her hand and said "Lady Marion, you are de most splendiferous of women. I must write a song dat extols your beauty. What is your favorite word in de whole English language?"

Marion thought for a moment. "My favorite word isn't in the English language," she said. "It's Yiddish."

When she told him the word and what it meant, he laughed, clapped his hands, sat down at the piano and created a song that became one of the biggest reggae hits that year—"Bashert."

"Ja make de woman *basherte* and de mon *bashert* and He place dem bot in de garden of love . . ."

DAN WAS PROUD of the way the film turned out. With *Sunsplash,* he achieved a level of artistry he had always strived for. Marion's reactions were harder to read. She was pleased with the film and she loved the people they worked with, but something else was going on. During the months of writing, pre-production, shooting and editing, Marion felt gracefully guided by her father's loving spirit but when the film was finished, she was struck with a feeling of abandonment, painfully similar to the day of his burial.

Later that night, Dan and Marion watched the sun slowly drop into the horizon from their cottage on the ocean. Their flight was scheduled for the following morning and the magnum of champagne that the producers planted in their room, together with a bouquet of Garden of Eden weed, enhanced the atmosphere of their last night in Jamaica.

Pulsating rhythms emerged from their tape deck, as Marion, cloaked in moonlit melancholy, danced. Her eyes were closed, her motions, subtle and precise. Her body danced but her feet barely moved. High and happy, Dan tried to read her expression, but he couldn't. As if to rein her in, he called out: *"Ha-rey at meku-deshet li* . . . Thou art consecrated unto me!" It was his marriage vow and he didn't know why he felt he had to repeat it at that moment, but he did.

Without missing a beat, Marion said "Does that mean you will never leave me, Dan?"

"Leave you? We are *bashert!* Preordained to be together for all time," Dan said with a flourish.

Still dancing, she opened her eyes and looked into his. "What if I die before you?"

Her tone was chilling. Marion continued to sway in place, expressionless, waiting for an answer. Dan was gripped by a harrowing apprehension. Echoes of the Orpheus myth, the dominant theme of their film suddenly took center stage.

"Will you come and get me?" she asked.

"I will find you and bring you back," Dan said. "This I swear on my eternal soul."

"How will you do that?"

What the hell was happening? Why was she going there? Dan couldn't find anything more to say. His strongest connection to life, his pure love for Marion, was now being challenged.

She studied his face for a long moment. "I believe you will find a way. I'm counting on it."

Dan should have felt relieved. He didn't.

The next song on the tape must have been placed there by a disc jockey from hell. It was in Spanish and although Dan caught some of the lyrics, especially the familiar refrain, he never understood—until Marion explained—that it bore a terrifying message.

When the cello intro began, Marion put her arms around Dan's neck. He followed her lead and they danced into another dimension as Marion translated.

Dicen que por las noches

"They say that every night, he was overcome by uncontrollable weeping."

No mas se le iba en puro llorar

"They swear that even the heavens trembled as he cried out in pain."

Como sufrio por ella

"How he suffered for her"

Ay ay ay ay ay, Paloma triste

Ay ay ay ay ay, no llores.

De passion mortal moria

"She was dying . . . but even his love could not revive her."

Marion closed her eyes and held onto him tightly.

"Dance me, Dan. Dance me . . . to the end of time."

{ Chapter Ten }

"COME, MY BROTHER," Abednego said, rousing Dan out of his reverie. He arranged Dan's luggage amid some trash in the trunk, secured it with a piece of rope and squeezed Dan into the back seat.

"Make yourself comfortable," he smiled and looked across the road. "Don't go 'way, be back in a flash."

Don't go away? Dan said to himself. *Where the hell can I go?*

Abednego returned to the car, carrying two small suitcases. Beside him was a familiar looking woman who smiled politely as Dan made room for her in the back seat while Abednego tied her suitcases to the roof. Abednego settled down behind the wheel, turned the key and to everyone's amazement, the car started.

"We be in Montego Bay in no time flat," he said cheerfully.

"How much is that going to cost?" the woman asked.

"We find out when we get dere, no need to pay in advance," Abednego said.

"But there's no meter in this car."

"What you need a meter for?"

"So we'll know how much the fare is."

"Oh, I already know dat," Abednego laughed.

Dan couldn't hold back a loud chuckle. The woman looked at them both and she started to laugh, too.

Abednego's car rattled on, often moving more slowly than the throngs of celebrants on foot, singing and rejoicing as they paraded towards Montego Bay to participate in the opening festivities of the Jubilee.

Abednego's "vehicle" chugged across the narrow mountain road, surrounded on both sides by dense green foliage, Dan began to relive the first time he and Marion drove across this island. When Abednego's car passed a jerk chicken and pineapple stand, Dan recalled the time they stopped to buy a pineapple from a young boy with a machete as tall as he was. The boy tossed the pineapple into the air and cut off the crown with one slice of his blade, then split it in two with a flourish. Marion hugged the boy and Dan snapped their picture. She wore tall slender boots and a red newsboy cap rakishly draped over her left eye. He still carried it in his wallet.

Travelling this same road without Marion was almost unbearable.

Suddenly, Dan sensed that the woman next to him was staring at him.

"You don't recognize me?" she asked.

"No. Should I?"

"I'm gorgeous."

"Excuse me?"

"I sat next to you on the plane all the way from Los Angeles. As we were landing, you were obviously thinking about someone else, but you looked at me and said, 'Hi, gorgeous.'"

That embarrassing moment on the plane! "Please accept my apologies, Miss . . . I didn't mean . . ."

She smiled. "That's okay. It was sweet even if it wasn't intended for me. My name's Gabrielle. Gabrielle Wallace."

"Dan Sobol," he said quietly.

"Good to meet you, Dan. I must tell you, strange as it was to hear you say 'hi, gorgeous,' I couldn't help but be touched by the joyfulness in your voice. You were obviously thinking of someone special." She gazed at the ring on his finger. "I don't mean to pry but I'm a social worker and I guess it's an occupational hazard. Your wife, right?"

Oh, God! The last thing in the world I need now is to "share"—and with a professional snoop, no less. "Yes," Dan said curtly.

"She's a lucky woman," Gabrielle said, looking at him soulfully.

"My wife passed away over two years ago."

"I'm sorry . . . so very sorry."

Dan thought he would explode. That word, *sorry,* those reflexive condolences always triggered recoil. It was one thing to bare your soul to people who saw you through your descent into hell, but complete strangers? Why does everyone feel the need to mumble greeting-card homilies? *I'm sorry. Very sorry. So very sorry.* Everyone he bumped into whether he knew them or not, every introduction began or ended with someone feeling sorry. What the hell are they sorry about? It would be okay if that eased his pain or made him feel whole, but it never did and when the *sorry* people started to probe, they cut deeper into the remnants of his devastated soul. "Was she sick? Did she suffer?" Jesus Christ! Who dies without suffering? Worst of all was the question occasionally put to him: "When did you know it was the end?"

When? Painful as it was to recall, there was an undeniable moment when he knew the wax under his wings was melting. One morning, about three months before the end, Marion wanted to comb her hair. She couldn't walk by herself so Dan led her to the bathroom and remained at her side to make sure she could stand securely next to the sink. Whole patches of her hair fell out with each stroke of the comb. He winced as he remembered every detail of that horrible moment.

Abednego's car struck a huge pothole and the loud thump abruptly shut down the wheels in Dan's head. Gabrielle had been talking all this time and he hadn't heard a word. When she realized that, her expression turned sad. "Oh, Dan," she said. "I'm sorry. I'm talking too much."

"Not at all," he lied.

"I don't know what it is with me. No matter what I start talking about, it always gets back to medieval divorce laws that cause so much suffering all around."

"Are you going through a divorce," Dan asked, "or are you a lawyer?"

"I'm not a lawyer. As I mentioned, I'm a social worker, but I am involved with someone who's being taken to the cleaners and it's very distressing."

"I'm sorry," Dan said. It's still a meaningless word, but it didn't sound so bad when he said it.

"I'm sorry, too," she said sadly.

She looked so vulnerable, but there was no way he was going to get into her *tzores*. His cupboard was full.

Abednego pulled over to the side of the road. "Is there a problem?" Gabrielle asked.

"No prob-lem, just goin' to help out an old friend." Abednego stopped next to a ragged figure leaning on a tattered guitar case with his thumb in the air. "He is very famous on the I-land. He is called Peacock Man, you must have heard about him."

Without waiting for a response, Abednego got out and embraced the man with long white dreadlocks. He too was a man of indeterminate age, but with the distinguishing feature of a hat bedecked with peacock feathers.

They talked and laughed as Dan and Gabrielle looked on. Abednego picked up the old guitar case and secured it on the roof, next to Gabrielle's small bags. He leaned in through the open window and said, "Honored guests, please meet the world-famous Peacock Man."

The old hitchhiker smiled. "Greetin's, good friends!"

With Abednego's help, Peacock Man squeezed through the front passenger door without removing his feathered hat. Abednego extended the rope to reinforce the door and within minutes, the magical mystery car was on its way.

Peacock Man grinned at Dan and Gabrielle. "Welcome to Jamaica. Are you Rastafarai?"

"No, I'm sorry, I'm not." Gabrielle said.

"Me neither," Dan murmured.

"No prob-lem. Dis is de day of Jubilee for all God's chillen, wheder dey be Rasta or bastad." Peacock Man and Abednego laughed. "De Jubilee come only once in fifty years," Peacock said, "just like it say in de Holy Book: On de day of Jubilee, de enslaved shall be set free, de afflicted will be healed, grief and lamentation will disappear from de land. Paradise lost will be refound and all my chillin will rejoice as in days of old."

"Selasiae!" Abednego shouted.

"Rastafarai!" Peacock Man grinned, they clasped hands and laughed.

Abednego turned to Dan. "Dat's from de Bible. Don you recognize it?"

"I'm afraid not."

Abednego smiled knowingly. "Leviticus 25."

"It doesn't sound familiar," was the best Dan could do.

"When was de last time you checked?" Abednego asked slyly.

"A while ago, I guess."

"I tink de time has come for you to look it up again, brother Daniel." Abednego and Peacock Man slapped hands victoriously and laughed.

"Selasiaie!"

"Rastafarai!"

MOONLIGHT BAY RESORT was a mini-castle, surrounded by an open-air mall and an ocean of colorful flowers and exotic trees. Peacocks swept their blue and green plumage across sculpted lawns where tourists eagerly posed and snapped away on cameras and iPhones.

When Abednego's car arrived at the main entrance, Gabrielle got out first. "It was good to meet you, Dan." Almost imploringly, she asked, "Do you think we could have a drink sometime?"

"Sure."

She shook hands with Peacock Man and handed Abednego some bills as the bellhop carried off her two small bags. Then she whispered something in Abednego's ear.

"No prob-lem," he said. "I keep me eyes on de prize."

Two messages were waiting for Dan when he checked in. The first was a FedEx from Steve. "Damn phones are down!

Have to communicate by Pony Express. Simone's lawyers are trying to drown me with depositions. I'll break away as soon as I can. Dying to hear your take on my new son-in-law."

The other was a handwritten note from Molly. "I couldn't wait any longer. I'll come back this evening. Can't say what time. No clocks in Jamaica on Jubilation Day. I am so happy you've come. You'll love Rocky. I know Marion does. We've got a lot to talk about. I'll pick you up here after sunset. Love, Molly." Her unique signature was how she believed James Joyce's Molly Bloom signed her name.

When Abednego set down the bags in the lobby, Dan extended his hand. "I want to thank you. I don't know what I would have done . . ."

Abednego slowly took Dan's hand, held it tightly and closed his eyes. After a few silent moments, he withdrew his hand and placed it lightly on Dan's chest. "It is all *bashert,*" he said softly. "When de Jubilee come, divine music bursts thru de clouds. De fog lifts and de path is revealed. Journeys converge and separated souls are rejoined."

His tone was as chilling as an Old Testament prophecy.

"From de planets in orbit," Abednego's voice rose and fell ". . . from de spheres below and from infinite multiple universes . . ."

Multiple universes? That was one of Marion's core beliefs. How could Abednego know that? Dan suddenly realized he would have to navigate this terrain without Marion. How could he do that?

Abednego opened his eyes, dropped his hand and left silently. Dan was suddenly struck by the parched emptiness of his lonely life.

DAN'S ROOM was elegant and spacious with a balcony overlooking the beach and an open air mall bustling with gaily dressed locals and a sprinkling of tourists, from aging hippies with gray pony tails to overweight couples in white sneakers and large hats. The bellhop opened the floor-to-ceiling glass doors, accepted the tip and quickly left. The balmy ocean breeze wafted through Dan's nasal passages up into his brain and he fell onto the king size bed. The yielding mattress absorbed him, and soon he was off, floating in space. Gliding on a gentle gust of ocean air, he rose higher and higher in a Chagall-like scene with his arms wrapped around Marion. Blissfully they soared through clouds, flying over rooftops and skipping over chimneys. A rapturous sensation pulsated through Dan's body as he held Marion safely in his arms . . .

KNOCK.

With his eyes still closed, Dan could tell that the sun was dropping out of the sky. A wave of amplified music rolled in through his open window, pushing out all the air that had kept him aloft. He was falling! Panicking . . . his first thought was to save Marion, but she was gone.

KNOCK. KNOCK. KNOCK. "Mr. Sobol?" A voice called from some distant place.

Disoriented, Dan pulled himself out of bed and opened the door. A pretty young girl wearing a hotel blazer handed him a huge bouquet of lilacs in a colorful vase.

"Mr. Sobol? Dese are from my fadder's garden. He say, welcome, brudder Daniel. Jus like dat, he say. Welcome, brudder Daniel."

"Do I know your father?"

"Ya, mon. He drove you here."

"Your father is Abednego?"

"De same."

"Please thank him for me."

She refused a tip.

Dan put the arrangement on a table near the window. One of the last rays of the setting sun hit the glass tabletop, causing it to glow under the vase. He put his face into the flowers and inhaled deeply. "What a fascinating combination of leaves, flowers and buds," Dan thought, "and that lilac scent, so familiar . . . of course! *Garden of Eden herb.* How could he forget? The wrap party for *Sunsplash* all those years ago. That was what they called the special strain of ganja made from an aromatic blend of lilacs, hemp leaves and wild buds. One whiff of the mind-expanding mixture brought it all rushing back. *It exalt de brain, nourish de soul and open de heart."*

The full moon was rising and intermittent flashes of fireworks punctuated sounds of the celebration. Dan went out onto the patio. The unmistakable scent of ganja rose from the happy throngs below. Tourists and locals danced to the music and crowds swirled up and down the street and beachfront. One image captured Dan's attention. A pale, light-skinned woman in a white shawl twirled in and out of the crowd. She was a nymph, weaving and swaying to the music. Dan couldn't take his eyes off her . . . and that shawl. It was exactly like the flamenco manton shawl he bought for Marion in Seville. The woman danced closer and closer and he realized . . . it was MARION!

He ran out of his room, down the stairs, through the lobby and into the street, where he was swallowed up by boisterous revelers. The music was wild and intoxicating. Lilac scented smoke hovered in the air like a gossamer cloud. Dan strained to see the shimmering figure in the white shawl as she wove in and out of the crowd. He felt pressed in from all sides. In the distance, she moved towards two parallel poles where dancers were taking turns slithering under a horizontal limbo stick. Two burly, bare-chested men stood on either side of the support poles. Marion bent back and her white shawl draped across her breasts as her strong dancer's legs carried her through.

By the time Dan got to the poles, she was gone.

{ Chapter Eleven }

A BRIGHT LIGHT flashed to one side of him. A fire-eater spat a huge flame into the air. The fire exploded and was replaced by a balloon of black smoke. Through the vanishing haze, a silhouette appeared. It's her . . . but without the shawl . . . what happened to it? "Marion!" he cried out.

She turned. It wasn't Marion. It was Gabrielle, the woman from Abednego's cab.

"Dan, what a lovely surprise."

"I'm sorry . . . I . . . mistook you for someone else."

She laughed. "You tend to do that."

Dan looked around. *Marion was here . . . I saw her!*

Fenced in by the mob, Dan looked in every direction but Marion was gone.

"Let's get out of here before we're trampled," Gabrielle said loudly in his ear and pulled him through the raucous crowd to a café festooned with lanterns of every shape and hue. Inside, the dark interior reeked of a musty aroma and strands of smoke hovered above the wooden tables that wobbled as they walked by. Three ancient musicians played a washboard, a guitar-cum-harmonica, and a gasoline can that served as a drum.

Gabrielle led Dan through the crammed café to the only table that didn't have a hat or bag hanging on a chair. "I like this place," she said, and sat down. "I was here once . . ."

Dan was trying to process the mind-boggling event he just experienced. *I was standing on my balcony . . . and I SAW her. The walk, the hair . . . and the flamenco manton shawl!*

A waitress set a tray down on their table. "Thank you," Gabrielle said, "but we haven't ordered yet . . ."

"No prob-lem," the young woman said and placed two cups of dark, pungent tea on the table. She smiled sweetly and said, "My fadder aks me to bring you his special brew."

"Your father . . . ?" Gabrielle asked.

The girl pointed to a large window. Outside the café, Abednego, swaying to music, waved. Gabrielle raised her cup. "Many thanks," she mouthed.

Dan was lost.

The waitress waited for them to try the tea. Gabrielle savored the aroma, then, sipped the tea. "Try it, Dan. You won't be sorry."

Dan didn't respond.

"The tea," she tapped his hand as if to awaken him. "I wish you would take a sip. It will lift your spirits."

Dan raised the cup, breathed in the heady aroma and took a sip. His brain immediately perked up. "Wow! Garden of Eden herb, plus!"

"I knew you would like it," Gabrielle smiled.

"We grow dis tea right here on de I-land," the girl said. "Papa say nothin' like it anywhere in de world."

After she left, Dan took another sip. "The girl is right," he said. "I've been there, the rest of the world that is, and this is definitely good tea."

Gabrielle raised her cup as an invitation to toast. Dan didn't notice so they both sat and drank in silence. When their cups were empty, the waitress appeared again and filled them a second time.

Drinking the tea, Gabrielle appeared less stressed than he remembered her in the car. He did recall that she had problems, legal or whatever and he definitely wasn't going there. Still, he had to admit that he felt better being with someone, anyone, instead of sitting alone like a putz.

Sipping his second cup of tea, Dan heard a distant, but familiar voice.

"Dan . . . Dan!"

Through the haze and noise, Dan tried to connect a face to the sound. He studied the crowd and saw Molly! His heart leapt! Dan jumped up, practically knocking over the table. He struggled to follow the face, appearing and disappearing as it plowed through the crowded café.

"Dan! I'm so glad I found you." Molly threw her arms around him and hugged tightly.

Molly . . . when did she start styling her hair like Marion? How did Molly acquire her posture? All the years she lived with us, there wasn't any physical similarity, but look at her now. The resemblance is uncanny.

"Where have you been?" she asked. "When I missed you at the hotel . . ." Molly's face was aglow and she hugged him again.

Dan was about to explain why he had run out into the crowd, but words weren't forming. With her arms around his neck and her high-spirited smile, Dan was so happy to see her, he found himself giggling. Molly's healing smile! He recalled the time Marion was recovering from knee replacement surgery. Dan had been rubbing therapeutic gel all over Marion's scarred leg, but nothing eased the pain until Molly came home from school. She ran straight to Marion's bed with a big grin that was more healing than all the medications. With their noses practically touching, Molly said "I'm here, Mama! Everything's going to be okay now." Marion held onto Molly and the most tranquil smile appeared on her face.

"Molly, I can't tell you how happy I am to see you," Dan said.

Molly picked up Dan's cup, sniffed it and winked. "Welcome to Jamaica." She drank what was left in the cup.

"You want to be careful with that, it's pretty potent," Gabrielle said.

Molly looked at Gabrielle and her smile faded. "You are?"

"My name's Gabrielle. And you?"

"Molly," she replied coldly and looked to Dan for an explanation.

The awkward silence and glances sent a clear message. Gabrielle got up. "It was good to see you again, Dan. Nice to meet you, Molly."

Molly watched her leave. "Who is she?"

"I have no idea. Just somebody I shared a cab with."

"I don't like her."

"Who cares about her? Tell me about you."

Molly grabbed Dan's hand and held it tightly. "We've got so much to talk about."

"Tell me about your husband-to-be. When and how did all this happen? There are a thousand things you have to fill me in on."

"I will, but there is something more important we have to do first."

"What could be more important than your wedding?

"The wedding will happen or it won't, but that's not why I brought you here."

What she said didn't fit anything Dan was prepared to hear. A narrow path opened through the mist in his brain and he wasn't sure he wanted to go down it. "Why *did* you bring me here?" he asked, hesitantly.

"Because of the Jubilee, Dan. It's happening."

"What is?"

"We're going to be rejoined."

"Rejoined?" *Where did Dan hear that word?*

"With your *basherte,* with my true mother."

"Molly, I'm a few frames out of sync, what with the travel and the tea. You do know Marion . . ." Dan couldn't say the word.

"Do I have to teach you Bible, rabbi? Remember my *bat mitzvah?"*

"I'll never forget it."

"What were the most important words spoken that day?"

"I'm not following you," Dan said.

"My bat mitzvah! What was the promise Ruth made to Naomi that I made to Mama?"

"Whither thou goest . . . ?"

"The end of her vow! The essence of the prophecy: 'DEATH CANNOT SEPARATE US."

Confused, he stared at Molly.

"Dan, think about the connection between Marion and your mother."

"My mother? What's that got to do . . . ?"

"Everything. Think!"

After Marion convinced Bertha to move to Los Angeles, the two women became inseparable. Marion made sure Bertha was invited to social events where she could meet new people and expand her life. Bertha in turn became Marion's biggest fan. If someone mentioned a beautiful model or movie star, Bertha's immediate response would be "where does she compare to my Marion?" She told everyone she met about her extraordinary daughter—purposely dropping the *in-law*—whether in the synagogue, at a senior citizens event or even a stranger on the bus, and the photos would come flying out of her purse.

Four months after Bertha arrived, Marion made a birthday party for Dan that was attended by the Hollywood elite, and who was the belle of the ball? Bertha. Most of the guests—producers, writers and directors—were Jewish and many had mothers or grandmothers who sounded exactly like Bertha, so she was warmly received.

"Do you know your mother never had a birthday party?" Marion said to Dan after the guests left.

"Did she say that?"

"She didn't have to. I asked when she had her last birthday party, she didn't understand the question." Not only had Dan never planned a party for his mother or father, it never occurred to him that he should. Marion was determined to change all that, but it wasn't easy. The problem wasn't planning Bertha's party; it was getting her to buy a new dress. "What do I need to spend money on a new dress? I have plenty dresses."

"Bertha," Marion scolded, "this is your first birthday party and I'm not going to let you wear a *shmata*. Period." Before Bertha could mount even a whining defense, Marion dragged her through every boutique on Rodeo Drive. Five hours later, an exhausted Marion triumphantly walked into Dan's study and showed him the most elegant Andre Laug Roma dress. Marion insisted that Bertha put it on to show Dan.

"What am I, a model suddenly? It's a beautiful dress. Who wouldn't look good in it?"

"Bertha! We tried on every damn dress in Beverly Hills. Five hours! I didn't take that long to buy a house. Put it on so Dan can decide whether it was worth it or not."

Bertha reluctantly trudged into the bedroom and when she came out, Dan's jaw dropped. On both sides of the dress were hints of red roses that came together in a fold of black lace at the waist and gave her small body, curves one rarely saw. The hem was just below the knee and revealed tapered legs in two-inch black pumps and there was a slight lift around the shoulders that gave her height, something little Bertha sorely needed. The dress transformed her into someone Dan had never seen. Not the doting mother in an apron who thought only of her obligations to her husband and sons but never herself. This Bertha was an elegant, attractive woman. She looked at herself in the floor to ceiling mirror and even she had to admit she looked good. Dan had never seen her like that, but there she was, standing straight and proud, feeling confident.

"You look fantastic, Mom," he said and saw his mother blush for the first time in his life.

"Turn around, Mom," Marion said. "Show him how you look when you walk in it." Bertha shyly model-walked around the room and Dan applauded. Marion wrapped her arms around Bertha and kissed her.

THE BEAMING IMAGE of his mother nestled in Marion's arms faded as Dan pulled himself back to the café.

Molly looked intensely at Dan. "What does that tell you?"

"Marion gave my mother the will to live."

"More than that! I want you to remember the day your mother died. It is the only way to understand what's about to happen."

"What is about to happen? I'm not following you."

"Please, Dan. I'm asking you to remember every detail of that day. The phone call . . ."

"Phone call?"

"The one you never heard . . . but Marion did."

The call. The secret that had been safely buried in Dan's subconscious all those years.

It was a Sunday morning in January over twenty-five years ago. Dan had been looking forward to watching the Giants and Cowboys in the playoffs. Both were Super Bowl favorites. It was also the morning he thoughtlessly promised his mother they would come for brunch.

"Ready?" Marion called out.

"Do we really have to go today?"

"No. Not if you don't mind breaking your mother's heart."

If Dan could growl, he would have. Instead, he slipped on his leather jacket. When they arrived, Bertha seemed to walk a little slower than usual and tilted to one side. "How's your osteoporosis, Mom?" Marion asked.

"I think I must have slept funny. I don't sleep so good anyhow, but last night I couldn't get comfortable no matter what I did. I started to make the coffee this morning, but I had to sit down awhile until my back stopped hurting, but breakfast, what do you call it, brunch, will be ready in no time." Marion put her arm around Bertha and gently rubbed her shoulder. "Where does it hurt, Mom?"

"When I try to lift up my arm, I get a *shtuch* in the chest."

"I want to go to your doctor with you," Marion said. "Call for an appointment first thing tomorrow." Bertha shrugged and hobbled towards the kitchen.

"We can't let this go," Marion whispered to Dan. "Her bones are so brittle, one fall could do her in."

"What can they do for her? She's had severe osteo for a long time now. There aren't any cures so far as I know. All they can do is put her on heavier pain medication."

"Then let's do it if that's the problem, but osteoporosis affects the spine, not the chest." Marion proceeded to set the table while Dan flopped onto his mother's Barcolounger to watch the game. Brunch passed uneventfully. By the time Dan and Marion got home, the second half was just beginning. It was an exciting game, evenly matched, with both quarterbacks at the top of their form. "Turn down that damn TV! I can't hear a thing," Marion said angrily at the doorway to the den.

Dan didn't think the TV was too loud at all, but he didn't want to get into a discussion about his hearing problems just then. But the way she said it bothered him. They never talked to one another that way. If the TV was too loud, particularly if one of them was working or on the phone or reading or just thinking, they merely asked the other if they would mind turning it down a little. Never, "turn down that damn TV!" But he let it go.

Fourth quarter. Marion came into the den, wearing her jacket.

"Where are you going?"

"I need to buy some fruit."

"Call Chalet Gourmet. They deliver on Sunday."

"No, I have to pick out some stuff we might want later."

"Where will you go?"

"To the Persian market."

"We never shop there. That's all the way back near mom's house. Why go that far?"

"Gotta go," she said and left.

That was strange. Dan knew he would be thinking about it later, but for now, his mind was on the game. A half hour later, the phone rang. "Dan, meet me at the emergency room of West Pico Hospital."

When he arrived, Marion was at the admittance entry standing next to Bertha, who lay on a gurney with an IV in her arm. Dan rushed to his mother's side and touched her hand. She was awake, but her eyes seemed to wander. "Isn't Marion wonderful? I don't even remember calling but she heard me and came," Bertha said groggily. The doctor, who was barking out orders waved them away quickly and motioned his aides to follow the gurney.

Dan was stunned. "What's going on? When did she call you?"

"She didn't. Not by phone, anyway,"Marion said. "I just had this urge to go to the Persian market. I wasn't sure why, so when I got there, I went up one aisle and down the next and that's when I saw her. Bertha was sitting on a chair, half-dazed, next to the manager's office with a package of strawberry blintzes on her lap. She stared at me. It took a minute for her to focus. Then she thanked me for coming."

Dan felt such love . . . and guilt.

Marion continued. "I could see she might black out any minute, so I told the manager to call 911. She said West Pico Hospital was right across the street, so I figured it would be quicker to bring her over myself. That was when I called you."

Dan paced around the small waiting room. "What do they think? Did they tell you anything at all?"

Marion shook her head. Dan stopped asking, but couldn't stop pacing. What seemed like hours later, the doctor came down to the waiting room carefully filling out a form on his clipboard. Dan ran to him. "How is she?"

Dan expected him to say the usual, that they were performing tests and would know more within hours. The doctor didn't say that. He stopped writing and said, "She didn't make it."

Dan didn't hear him at first and he asked the doctor to repeat what he said. He did, with professional detachment. "I'm sorry."

Dan was stunned. He tried hard to keep those words from sinking in but they finally did. "She's dead?"

The doctor nodded discreetly. Dan couldn't hold back the wail that shook his body. Marion put her arms around him and the Doctor explained. "She had a massive stroke and there was nothing we could do. She probably had the first of several embolic strokes yesterday, which accounts for the chest pain you told me about, and another stroke just before you found her. The final shock waves came as we were trying to intubate her."

"Can we see her, please?" Marion asked. She locked her arm in Dan's and followed the doctor to the operating room, which was abandoned except for the gurney bearing Dan's dead mother. As the doctor pulled back the sheet, his beeper erupted. He excused himself and walked quickly down the long corridor.

Bertha was so still. On her chest was the intubation tube.

"She never looked so serene," Dan said softly.

Molly leaned across the table until her face was inches away from Dan. "What Marion told me about Bertha and how she responded to the call no one else heard is what I'm trying to get you to understand. They were on a frequency only they could access. That's what Marion and I have. Trust me when I tell you. I hear Marion. I speak to her. She speaks to me . . . clearly and unmistakably."

"What does she say?"

"She says she's waiting, Dan. Marion is here, waiting for you."

"Waiting?"

"To be rejoined."

{ Chapter Twelve }

A BURST OF MORNING SUN filled Dan's room. The bouquet of Eden weed on the table next to the bed still exuded its captivating aroma.

When did I fall asleep? I don't even remember taking off my clothes. What a dream!

Sitting up he saw a handwritten note on his night table. The Molly Bloom signature was unmistakable.

> You passed out. I brought you to your hotel and put you to bed. Still wearing Jockey briefs, eh? Sexy. I hope you feel better when you wake up. It's essential that we get together tomorrow. We have important things to do. Phones still aren't working. Not even cells. Jubilation Day, remember? A friend will be waiting for you whenever you wake up. He'll take you to he Israeli consulate in Kingston. When you get there, ask for Colonel ben-Solomon. Rocky will know where to find me. It was wonderful seeing you last night. Love, Molly.

Everything started to swirl. Molly *was* with me last night and she *did* say . . . *Marion was here . . . waiting?* The word she used was *rejoined!* Is that some kind of cruel joke? Molly has gone through weird stages, but she was never cruel. Is it conceivable that the woman I saw in the crowd . . . ? Dan quickly dressed and ran downstairs. In the lobby, he saw a man with a tall hat decorated with peacock feathers. The man walked towards Dan, waved and shook his hand.

"Good to see my brother again. Beautiful day for a drive to Kingston."

"You're the driver?"

"As a favor to Molly, Peacock Man happily takes his new friend where he needs to go."

"A favor to Molly?" That was a connection Dan would never have made. How does Molly know Peacock Man?

At the main road, Peacock stopped and looked, apparently for his car. Dan looked and didn't see anything. "Is your car nearby?" Dan asked.

"Be here in a flash." Soon a car came by and Peacock Man raised his hand and waved. The driver waved back and kept driving. Then, another car approached. Peacock stuck his thumb up, but the driver ignored him and drove on. He smiled to Dan then turned at the sound of another car. As it approached, Peacock stuck up his thumb again and the car drove by without slowing down.

"You do have a car?" Dan asked, trying to appear patient.

"Not to worry," Peacock smiled, "we got everyt'ing what we need. No prob-lem. I get you dere."

Another car came by and up went the thumb. Again the car drove by without even slowing down. "Excuse me. Are we hitchhiking?"

Peacock Man ignored Dan's question but there was no

point pursuing the matter. Obviously there was no car and Dan's only hope was that someone would stop. After a raft of drive-byes, Dan gave up. There was nothing for him to do except stand around like a *putz*. No point talking to Peacock Man. All he'd get would be more smiles and assurances that everything was according to plan.

Finally a truck filled with boxes of mangos chugged down the road and up went Peacock's thumb. This time the driver stopped. Dan's escort ran to the rear of the truck where a group of gaily dressed hitchhikers sat on boxes. One of the larger women helped Peacock Man up, then reached for Dan who chose to pull himself up, but thanked the woman, who smiled brightly and said, "Happy Jubilation Day."

The truck moved bumpity-bump down the road as the new arrivals took their seats atop two available mango crates, surrounded by several other cheerful passengers. Peacock Man was warmly greeted. A woman wearing a bright red turban that must have been a foot high asked if he was going to perform at the Jubilation Day Carnival. "I be dere dis year and every fifty years, dead or alive." They laughed in unison.

"You gonna sing de same Greetin's what you did fifty years ago?" An old man wearing a tattered straw hat called out.

"Got to. I know you be disappointed if I don't," he said and they all laughed. A handsome woman next to Peacock passed him a *spliff*. He took a long hit, then exhaled a cloud of lilac scented smoke and passed it to Dan who refused, but there were many other enthusiastic takers.

"Give us some of dem greetins, mon!" the old fellow traveler shouted. Several of the riders created a slow, pulsating beat by banging on mango crates. Peacock stood up, miraculously maintaining his balance, while the driver cautiously navigated around pilgrims on foot lining the road. Peacock shuffled around several crates, hugging the ladies, then declaimed.

"Greetin's on dis great festival of Jubilee. I greet you all in de name of our holy prophet Ja who has revealed himself dis day in de personality of his imp'eral majesty, Emperor Haile Selassie, de first. Selasiai! Rastafari!"

Peacock's eyes closed and his voice rang out.

On dis day of great jubilee

De trut is revealed for all to see

Circumcised hearts rise to de sun

De livin' and dead rejoined' as one

On de Jubilee

Great Jubilee

Every passenger on the truck joined in and sang . . . and sang and sang. *On dis day of great jubilee* . . . repeating . . . *circumcised hearts* . . . r e p e a t . . . *de livin and dead* . . . r e p e . . . a . . . t . . . *rejoined as one* . . . passing lilac scented spliffs as they chanted trancelike with Peacock Man.

Who are these people? Dan thought. They live in a different dimension of time from everybody else on the planet. They speak English but their combination of words is unlike anything he ever heard. Every conversation is on at least two levels, like the one he had with Peacock while they were waiting for a car, a vehicle, anything to take them to Kingston. Dan asked him how he knew Molly.

"Everybody on de I-land know everybody else on de I-land," Peacock said.

"Did Molly tell Abednego to meet me at the airport yesterday?"

"What you tink?"

"I don't know. I'm asking you."

"Why you no ask Abednego?"

"He's not here, that's why I'm asking you."

"And I ask *you* what you tink?"

"It doesn't matter what I think"

"Oh, it matter more dan you tink."

If Marion were here, Dan thought, she could make sense of all this. She had access to what Professor Abrams called, the ineffable. Dan first recognized that shortly after they met. Standing in front of Van Gogh's "Starry Night" at the Museum of Modern Art, Marion explained the essence of the painting. "It was a premonition of his death and transmigration through a shower of asteroids. Surrounded by whirling clouds, shining stars and the curvy cypress tree, typically associated with burial grounds, Van Gogh saw the end of his life as the beginning of a bright hereafter filled with glittering stars that made everything that was millions of light years away, not only familiar, but accessible." *How did Marion know that?!*

The next time the spliff was offered, Dan didn't refuse. Inhaling deeply, he recalled how David ben David, True King of Israel, described Garden of Eden ganja. "It exalt de mind, nourish de soul and open de heart."

Mellow: *Marion is here* . . . mellower . . . *she's here waiting* . . . mellowest . . . *she is here waiting for me!* The repetitious chant fueled his ascent and he was flying with Marion through clusters of dazzling galaxies, each composed of three stars. "Each is a triad," she explained as they sailed through the starry, starry night. "A trinity, a triumvirate: Abraham, Isaac and Jacob . . . Jesus, Mary and Joseph." After a couple more hits, Dan *got* it and he sang along with the celestial choir in his head, stretching each word into three syllables. *Abraham . . . Peacock man . . . multiple . . . universe . . . circumcised . . . jubilee . . . Marion . . . even death . . . CANNOT SEPARATE US !*

The screech of grinding gears and gush of worn brake pads jostled Dan from his deep sleep. His escort, still wearing the peacock bedecked hat, smiled and pointed to the imposing building where the mango truck had stopped. A blue and white Star of David flag rose above the inscription: Consulate General of Israel, in English and Hebrew.

"You be in good hands now, my brother," Peacock said. "Happy Jubilation Day. Selassiai! Rastafarai!"

Dan jumped out and waved to his fellow travelers as the mango truck chugged away.

THE SQUAT QUADRANGULAR BUILDING, topped by cameras, radar and massive electronic surveillance equipment, looked menacing. Getting through the gates was a daunting process. Security checks were even more intrusive and burdensome than American airports after 9/11. There were pat downs, passing through X-ray machines and an enclosed booth that made sounds like a CT scan and surrounded Dan's body with intermittent flashing streaks of light.

After passing through the final metal detector, showing his passport and responding to the same two formal pages of questions twice, the first time to Jamaican guards outside the main entrance and the second time, Israeli guards two feet away, but inside the front door. Dan hoped there was no residual *ganja* fogging his brain. Apparently there wasn't because his answers must have been acceptable—every time—and he was instructed to proceed to the welcome desk.

A young Israeli woman with a long, braid down her back and three stripes on her rolled-up shirtsleeve, sat behind a small desk. The nameplate read Sergeant Dorit Jacobovich in Hebrew and English. She was pretty in a challenging sort of way. A cigarette dangled from the edge of her mouth and her face showed not a trace of emotion.

"Your business here?"

"I'd like to see Colonel ben-Solomon."

"Is he expecting you?"

"Yes."

"And you are?"

"Dan Sobol."

"May I see your passport?"

Dan handed her his passport, which she placed under a screen connected to a computer on her desk. She pointed to a chair and he sat down.

She studied the computer screen as she smoked. "I see you speak Hebrew. Where did you learn?"

He answered in Hebrew with a quote from the Book of Jonah. "I am a Hebrew and I worship the One God who created the sea and the dry land."

"Very flowery. We don't speak Hebrew that way in Israel today."

"To my great distress," he responded using a classical Hebrew phrase.

"You are distressed because . . . ?"

"Because biblical Hebrew sounds elegant to my ear and what I hear on the streets of Tel Aviv sounds coarse and vulgar."

"I wouldn't want to offend your sensibilities," she said with a smile that looked like a cobra toying with its prey, "so let us continue in English. My question was where did you learn Hebrew?"

"At the Jewish Theological Seminary. I'm an ex-rabbi."

"Ex as in excommunicated?"

"No. Ex as in former."

"I see. You were a rabbi but now you are not. What do you do now?"

"I'm a retired film director."

She read something on her computer. After a few moments, she smiled. "I see you directed *Tomboy.*"

"You saw it?"

"I did," she said, without looking away from her computer screen.

"How did you like it?"

"It was crap." No longer smiling, she inhaled and puffed smoke.

"It was number three in box office receipts, worldwide," Dan pointed out. "Millions of people disagreed with you."

She shrugged and continued to read her computer screen, scrolling down. *"Summer Father* . . . never heard of it . . . *Haunts* . . . never heard of it. *Greater Love,* I saw that. Made in Israel." She looked up and smiled. "That was crap, too . . ." then, seemingly impressed, she said, "You also made *Child2Man?"*

"So you liked that one?"

She pondered the question. "It was flawed."

"What are you, a critic?"

"I just like movies."

"I never would have guessed."

"Well, good ones."

Dan smoldered as she continued to scroll.

"Beyond Evil . . . *Graduation Day* . . . *Commando Squad* 1 *and* 2 . . ." She looked at Dan with a grimace. "No wonder they retired you."

"They, whoever they are, didn't retire me. I retired for personal reasons."

"What reasons?" She casually flicked her ashes into a porcelain dish, overflowing with butts on her neat desk.

"Personal means none of your goddam business. Would you please call Colonel ben-Solomon and tell him I'm here?"

The sergeant handed back his passport.

"He's expecting you.

"You knew that all along?"

"I knew the Colonel was expecting someone named Dan Sobol, but how could I know that was you?"

"You and all the other guards saw my passport which reads Daniel Sobol."

"Passports, shmasports."

Dan got up. "Sergeant Jacobovich, I assume that's your name, or would you rather I called you Che Guevara?"

"Whatever the passion of your soul dictates," she said in flowery classical Hebrew with an edge of sarcasm.

Dan was furious. "Do you ever wonder why some people don't like Israelis?"

"No. I never wonder about that."

"Maybe you should."

"Maybe you should make better movies. Two flights up. First door on the right."

Dan steamed as he climbed the second flight of stairs. Out of breath, he stopped at the door marked Colonel Ben-Solomon. Before he could knock, the door swung open and a tall, handsome young man wearing a form fitting khaki shirt, smiled broadly. Rocky looked like a model out of GQ, except for the combat ribbons on his chest and the smile that was vintage Israeli, warm, but not unguarded.

"Dan," Rocky said as he grabbed his hand. "Come in," he pulled him inside. "I've heard so much about you."

"You have?"

"Well, Molly talks mostly about Marion, but your name runs a close second." He pointed to a chair alongside his well-organized desk. "Make yourself at home."

"I hope I'm not late," Dan said, "but my ride here was . . . different from what I expected."

"Everything in Jamaica is different, especially on holidays. As it turns out, the one road that spans the island is totally clogged. We're going to have to sit it out for a while. Like some coffee, meantime?"

"Sure."

Rocky went to his electric percolator next to a wall that was entirely covered with snapshots of Molly and Rocky, including the one Dan remembered from Steve's iPhone. Rocky poured two cups and handed one to Dan, then, rather than sit behind his desk, he pulled up a chair next to him.

What a *mensch*, Dan thought. He savored the aroma and took a sip. "I forgot about Jamaican coffee. This is great brew."

Silence settled on the room. *What do I say?* Dan wondered. He was eager to talk about Molly and the inscrutable things she said last night, but he had no idea how to broach it.

Rocky appeared equally uneasy, so they both sat in silence, sipping coffee and waiting for the other to say something.

"So . . ." Rocky smiled.

"Yeah . . ." Dan said.

"How was the trip from L.A.?"

"Fine."

"I'm really glad you came."

"Me, too."

More silence.

"You're a fascinating man," Rocky ventured. "I googled you."

"So, all my secrets are exposed."

"Not all. Obviously, the *yarmulke* is gone, but I don't see you carrying a riding crop and megaphone, either."

"When I retired, I had to turn those in."

"Why would a director retire? Didn't you love the life?"

"Retirement in the movie business is unlike most other professions. There's no gold watch and no drunken office party. The only way a director knows he's retired is when nobody returns his phone calls."

Rocky laughed. "Molly said I'd like you. She's right."

"She said the same thing about you."

"I didn't mean to sound flippant about the career trajectory, but Molly says I'm her Dan, so I'd like to know how you think I fit that mold."

"She said that?" Dan felt the lump in his brain drop into his throat.

"She told me she knew I was her *bashert* the very first time she heard my voice. She said she didn't care if I looked like Yasser Arafat—she's glad I don't—but the voice is what captivated her and apparently the only other person who sounds like me, is you. Molly is convinced that she, Marion, you and I are connected in mystical ways."

"Do you share that belief?"

"I'd like to." Rocky's smile was irresistible.

The intercom on Rocky's desk beeped five or six times before he clicked the on-button. Dan heard someone screaming on the other end. Rocky listened calmly, but frowned and gesticulated to Dan that there was some unnecessary fuss going on. Obviously the screamer—probably Sergeant Mary

Sunshine from the welcome desk—was upset about something that Rocky kept insisting was no big deal. He clicked off the intercom and breathed deeply, then got up and walked to the reinforced bulletproof window.

"Something important?" Dan asked.

"Singularly insignificant," Rocky sighed. "A *nudnik* arrived from Tel Aviv last night who was supposed to be here an hour ago. He's a TV commercial producer and I have to provide waivers for him to get his equipment through customs. Apparently, he's stuck in traffic so he'll be here when he gets here. That's the catastrophe *du jour,*" Rocky said sarcastically, then threw up his hands and rolled his eyes.

Dan looked out the window. The road below, lined with cars, buses and trucks, looked more like a vast parking lot than a highway.

"Do we have a battle plan for getting through all that, Colonel?"

"Yes, we wait until it eases. "More coffee?"

"No thanks,"

Silence settled on the room again. "I'm sorry," Dan said, "but I seem to have forgotten what we were talking about."

"Yarmulkes and director's paraphernalia," Rocky said. "You've got to admit, you travelled one hell of a career arc. How does one go from being a rabbi to directing films?"

"My advice to anyone who wants to make movies is first to enroll in rabbinical school."

"That's what my professor at M.I.T. would call sleight of mouth," Rocky winked. "Somehow I think there must be more to it than that."

"Not really. Not in my case, anyway. A member of my congregation happened to be head of a studio and he got it into his head that I would be better suited to making films, so he nagged and pestered me until I finally agreed to leave the rabbinate and became a director."

Beep. Beep. Beep. Rocky clicked on the intercom." I'm busy! Don't bother me," he said and clicked off.

"A member of your congregation pestered you to leave the rabbinate to become a film director? That's the weirdest thing I ever heard."

"I don't doubt that, but it is true."

"Who is this guy?"

"Steve Weisman."

"Molly's father? You were his rabbi?"

"And his closest friend. Have you met Steve?"

"Not yet. I've spoken to him on the phone, but from our conversations, I can't imagine that the two of you had much in common."

"I hear Molly talking now. To everyone except his daughter, Steve is the perfect Renaissance man, absolutely brilliant and the kind of unstoppable energy I had never seen before. We met when he joined my congregation in the Pacific Palisades. He said he was fascinated by my sermons and became an avid fan—and sometimes harsh critic. 'Each one,' Steve said 'was like a story conference at the studio, only without the crazy writers.'"

Deep in his reverie, Dan smiled as he walked to the percolator. While refilling his cup, Dan recalled those first meetings with Steve and silence settled on the room again.

"I hope there's more to this story," Rocky said.

"The story? Oh, yes, my story. I left the rabbinate, became a director and the rest, as they say, is the rest."

"Whoa! You skipped the most important part. With all due respect, what made Steve Weisman think a rabbi with no training or background in film could become a director?"

"Great question. You should ask him."

"Come on," Rocky said. "You must have done something to plant that seed in his head."

Dan sipped his coffee. "I guess a seed was planted, but not by me."

"If not you, then who? Molly?"

"That was long before Molly was born."

"Do I have to ask twenty questions? Come on, Dan. This is a great story."

Dan slid into his chair and took another sip, "As I remember it, Steve called late one night."

PART FIVE

Come Together

{ Chapter Thirteen }

"I HOPE I DIDN'T WAKE YOU," Steve said.

"I wasn't sleeping. What's up?"

"You'll never guess who I met tonight. The famous Professor Abrams, the guy you like to quote in your sermons."

"The most inspiring man I ever met," Dan said. "I'm sure you two found a lot of common ground."

"More than I expected. Why didn't you tell me about your sordid past?"

"Which part?" Dan asked.

"That my rabbi—and I thought, my best friend—is a closet director."

"Well, not much of an exposé there. I directed one play, off-Broadway."

"Way off-Broadway as your Professor Abrams tells it. Brooklyn, I think, but that's not the point. You and I have to talk."

"What about?" Dan asked.

"An offer you can't refuse."

THE NEXT AFTERNOON on his patio, Steve opened a bottle of vintage Pommery and handed Dan a glass. "I've been thinking all week about your sermon last Friday night, Dan." He raised his glass. "To the hero of my rabbi's sermon," he said. "Sir Lawrence of Arabia."

Dan was curious to find out what the offer was that he couldn't refuse, but Steve didn't give him an opening. Instead, he took a long sip and settled into his chaise lounge.

"The story as you told it was mesmerizing. You started when T.E. Lawrence came to New York at the end of World War One with the tribal leaders of the forces that drove the Turks out of Arabia. Suddenly, floods broke out on the top floors of the Waldorf Astoria, where they were housed in preparation for their presentation to the League of Nations. After the maintenance people found the source of the problem, Lawrence confronted his comrades. When he asked the sheiks and sharifs if they had anything to do with the flooding, they responded by proudly opening their luggage where every spigot and pipe from their hotel rooms was on display. The Arabs had hacked off all the plumbing and could barely contain their glee, telling Lawrence that when they returned to the desert they would no longer have to dig wells. They could just turn on those faucets and have all the water they would ever need."

"So, look what you did," Steve continued. "In the first minute, you set up the entire premise of the movie. I know, I know, the sermon. You grabbed the audience immediately and they were with you, ready to go anywhere you wanted to take them. The message was simple and powerful. Pipes and faucets only work when they are connected to a water source, otherwise it's useless junk. That's great story telling and believe me, as someone who works with writers every day, it is a rare gift, my friend, and has applications far beyond preaching from the pulpit, if you get my meaning."

"I'm not sure I do," Dan said.

"I spoke to someone this morning I think you should meet. He spent his life doing what you did last Friday night, only he doesn't preach sermons. His name is Dore Schary. Does that name mean anything to you?"

"A movie producer, isn't he?"

"A Hollywood legend! Head of production at RKO, then MGM where he kicked out Louis B. Mayer! He retired a few years back and, among other things, he's on my Board of Directors. Brilliant, shrewd, incredibly talented, Dore Schary is the most elegant man I ever met but he can also be the crassest son of a bitch on the planet. He lives in New York but he's in town for the E.S.I. board meeting day after tomorrow. I told him about you. I said you were the best preacher I ever heard and he said he would be happy to meet you. Interested?"

"Of course, but why would he want to meet me?"

"Because I told him to and he owes me big time. Besides, he already knows about the rabbi who directed a play in Brooklyn. Tell me about that."

"Not much to tell. I once adapted a Gogol story for the stage. It was called *The Overcoat* and it only played eight performances. Some good reviews, but there was no money for promotion, so it closed."

"You never talked to me about your interest in the theater. Where did that come from?"

"Mainly from my wife, Anne, who you unfortunately never met. Anne was a successful Broadway actress and she was the spark. She took me to see every play in New York.

I took acting classes, writing courses and even joined an improv group. It was a magical time for me and with her encouragement I seriously considered a career in the theater. But Anne died in the third year of our marriage and the fire went out. I haven't thought about it since. How did Dore Schary hear about my play at the Brooklyn Academy?"

"It seems that your Professor Abrams went to see it and made a point of talking to Schary about you. He said you were one of his promising students but he believed your talents might find better expression in the arts, specifically the dramatic arts."

"Now you've lost me."

"I don't think so, Dan. What I'm getting at scares the hell out of you, as I expected it would. If it doesn't, you should be hospitalized. Very simply, it's time for you to leave the rabbinate and move on to the next stage of your life."

"What is the next stage?" Dan asked. "You think I can become a movie producer? Director? Screen writer? I don't know the first thing about film."

"Don't worry about the nuts and bolts. A man with your intelligence can easily acquire the skills, so that's not an issue. The real question is what role do you want to play in this human tragi-comedy? Think of the truly successful priests, ministers and rabbis you've known. Their greatest satisfaction in life is comforting the afflicted. It's a lofty calling, but in your heart of hearts, you know you are not one of those people. Sure, you can play that role and we both know you can fake it, but it will never light your fire."

"And what do you think will?" Dan asked.

"I can't say for sure, but what I do know is that you have a twelve-cylinder brain and you will be cruising on only two for the rest of your life because your real talents will never find expression. Nothing makes life more disappointing."

Steve refilled his glass and leaned back on his chaise. "In one of your early sermons, you told the story of Rabbi Zusha, remember that?"

"I do."

"As I recall, he was on his death bed, surrounded by his students, weeping hysterically. Am I right so far?"

"You are, and I'm flattered that you remember." Dan said.

"I remember every sermon you ever gave, Dan. So what was Rabbi Zusha crying about? Was he afraid of dying?"

"No. Reb Zusha made it clear that he had no fear of death. Everyone born of woman is destined to pass on. What terrified him was that when he approached the gates of heaven, God would ask him to give an accounting of his life. Zusha wasn't worried that he might be asked why he never became a great leader like Moses or a fearless warrior like David or a scholar like Maimonides because he could say in his defense, if that's what You—God—wanted, You should have made me a Moses or a David or Maimonides. What terrified him was that God would ask him why he didn't become the best Zusha he could have been."

"I rest my case, Dan."

"Steve," Dan said, trying to clear his head of all the fireworks he set off. "Either the champagne or what you're saying is making me tipsy. If you had asked anyone in my acting classes, creative writing courses, anyone who ever mounted a school play, what they would most like to do in life, they would say direct a movie. Why do none of them ever make it?"

"First and most important of all," Steve said, "Because they don't have me. Secondly, dreamers always go about it the wrong way. They focus all their energy on where they want to end up. They visualize success. They can taste it, but they will never achieve it. Why? Because they don't know where to *begin*. Whenever I set my mind on someplace I want to be, I look for one thing: a point of access, where to start. Without that, there is nothing."

"I hear what you're saying." Dan said, "But even if I were to consider the upheaval in my life that you're talking about, I have absolutely no idea where I would begin."

"The place for you to begin is the Bel-Air Hotel. I arranged for you to meet Dore Schary tomorrow morning at ten o'clock on the patio. He's expecting you."

AFTER WAITING NERVOUSLY for nearly twenty minutes at the outer gate of the Bel-Air hotel, Dan was instructed to go to the visitors parking area where a bellhop would accompany him to the place where he would meet his "host." Names were conspicuously avoided.

Dan was led to an elegantly tiled patio bordered by a huge lawn. Schary was easy to spot since he was the only one there. Dressed in a fashionable but conservative three-piece suit and a tie that had just the slightest hint of flair, he sat at a round antique glass table under a sun umbrella, talking on the phone and sipping what looked like a serious drink at ten in the morning.

As Dan approached, he waved. "You must be the rabbi," he said aloud and pointed to the chair opposite him. He extended his left hand—while talking on the phone—shook Dan's right, and motioned for him to sit.

"Sorry, Orson, I have no time for your bullshit. My rabbi needs me," and he hung up.

Schary smiled as he sized up his guest, then took the last swig of his drink and called for the waiter, who came over immediately.

"So, Rabbi Sobol, is it?" he asked.

"Yes sir, Dan Sobol, and I want to tell you what an honor it is to meet you, Mr. Schary."

Ignoring the compliment, Schary said to the waiter, "Two more Sapphire martinis, Carlos, straight up, very dry." Turning to Dan, he said, "That okay with you, rabbi?" Dan nodded, *sure*. The waiter carefully picked up his empty glass and walked back across the lawn to an outdoor bar.

Still smiling, Schary said "Steve Weisman tells me you are planning to forsake the rabbinate to pursue a career in motion pictures."

"I am exploring that possibility," Dan said, trying not to sound intimidated.

"Were you defrocked or are you merely unsuited?"

That sounded like a prepared pun and without waiting for Dan to reply, Schary laughed out loud, enjoying his own *bon mot*.

"Neither," Dan said, but smiled to let him know that his humor wasn't lost.

Schary's smile faded. "I have one question for you, Rabbi Sobol. Are you out of your fucking mind? You clergymen are the most revered people in our society, pun intended. Nobody criticizes you publicly, nobody demeans you personally. When you appeal to your flock to donate money for some bullshit charity, they don't tell you to go fuck yourself. When you give a speech or Bible lesson that bores the shit out of everybody, they listen respectfully and respond with applause or at least, some polite *A-mens*. In your current profession, old ladies open doors for you, rabbi. Become a film maker and they will slam them in your face. Can you tell me why you want to make that glorious transition?"

Dan refused to be intimidated. "I have never let an old lady open a door for me, nor would I." He wanted to let Schary know he had suffered a lot of disappointments too, but was interrupted by the waiter, who carefully set down the drinks, then quietly slipped away. Schary took out the olive, placed it on the side of his drink and took a long sip. Dan looked at his glass, not knowing whether to eat the olive or put it aside. Dan took a small sip of the martini and felt it in his eyeballs. While Dan was dealing with his drink, Schary glanced at a copy of *Daily Variety* that was next to his phone and grimaced.

Not knowing what to do, Dan reminded him that he was there. "You were saying . . ."

"I was saying that life in the business we call show is not all glamour and you had better be prepared, emotionally and spiritually, to absorb the mendacity, hyperbole and outright lies you read in the trades every day," he angrily tossed his *Variety* onto the freshly trimmed lawn.

Dan had heard about the backstabbing that went on in Hollywood and he wanted Schary to know that he wasn't entirely unprepared for the challenges.

"Wrong," Schary said. "Nobody stabs you in the back. In Hollywood, they stab you in the chest so they can watch you die."

Dan couldn't let that go. "But you have done well in the system, however you characterize it," he said. "You not only survived, you made important films that affected the lives of millions of people all over the world. Why do you do it, year after year if it's so ugly?"

To Dan's surprise, he actually stumped him. Softly, Schary said, "Because . . . I'm addicted to talent and spending my days with the most gifted artists on the planet is the best way I know to live my life. Working on a soundstage is like living in Montmartre at the turn of the century, surrounded by artists. I see it when I walk onto a set that looks exactly like Oliver Twist's bedroom, down to the bedbugs and urine stains on the one mattress all the boys sleep on, or when I watch a director of photography light a scene with haunting echoes of terror that sends chills down my back. For me, there's no greater high and that's where I choose to live, but it exacts a heavy toll and I don't recommend it for the faint of heart."

Dan was determined to make the point that his heart wasn't all that faint when the phone rang. Schary picked up the receiver. He listened briefly, bristled then shouted. "Yes, I just read it. Kiss my ass!" He slammed down the phone, took a moment to collect himself then turned to Dan. "Steve Weisman said he talked to you about access."

"He did, but frankly I didn't know what that meant."

"Access, my boy, where to begin, learning to do the breast stroke so that someday you will be able to do double flips from the high board. How does a smart rabbi with no background in film break in? Where's the point of entry? I'll give you a clue. Do you know how many feet of film was shot by the top three studios last year?"

If everything depended on Dan knowing the answer to that question, he was sunk. He didn't know how much film was shot last year, he said, but he could find out.

"Don't bother. The reason I bring it up is because I'm on the board of directors at McCann-Erickson and what I discovered is that this one advertising agency shot more film last year than the top three movie studios combined. So, if you do the math you will discover that the film business in America today is supported not by feature films, but by advertising.

The sound stages, crews, equipment are all working at full capacity—making TV commercials."

What the hell was he talking about? Dan asked himself. *TV commercials?!* He was horrified. *If Schary or Steve thought he was the least bit interested in advertising, they were way off track.*

"So, why am I talking to you about TV commercials?" Schary asked. "You want to make movies, not sell depilatories, right?"

"Absolutely right, sir!" Dan wanted to make that clear before they got too far afield.

"I know where you want to go and what I'm talking about is how to get there, a point of entry. Even if you're as good at creating a story as Steve Weisman says you are, you must first master the craft or you will never have the opportunity to tell it. Of course, you don't want to die with a bottle of Pepsi Cola shoved up your ass. I know that, but TV is the best place to acquire the skills to move on to feature films. What's more, it's a field that's wide open. Why? Because movie directors think television is beneath them so there is a vacuum. The process is the same. The crews and equipment are the same, only the stories are different and in the end, a film succeeds or fails depending on how well the story is told, whether it's *All Quiet on the Western Front* or Schaffer is the one beer to have when you're having more than one. From TV, the leap to feature films is still at best only a possibility. That may or may not happen, but if it does . . ."

He told Dan what classes and lectures to attend and gave him a list of books to study on staging, camera, lighting, editing and everything else a film director needs to know. Not surprisingly, the list of essential reading included Schary's tell-all best seller, *Actors I Have Known and Loved . . . And Then Some.*

He recommended only one book on advertising. "The

entire industry is total bullshit," he said. "There are no guidelines, only what sells, but David Ogilvy's book *My Life in Advertising* lays all that out. It won't tell you anything about advertising you didn't know, but it clearly drives home the point that nothing matters except story, not just the story of the commercial, but the stories you sneak into casual conversations to sell yourself and your product, the smoke you blow up the asses of everyone you want to impress from clients to actors to the ad agency hierarchy."

Schary summed it up. "If you can create intriguing stories about ex-Rabbi Dan Sobol who brings that *ex-tra something* to his films, you just might have a shot."

At that moment, Dan knew he had found the direction his life had to take, but what about all the years of study and preparation for the rabbinate?

THE DECISION to sever the umbilical cord came one night in Laurel Canyon a few days after his meeting at the Bel-Air Hotel. A friend of Dan's in the music biz invited him to a party at the home of Mama Cass. Sitting on the Persian rug next to a very tall girl with long, straight red hair, Dan was passed a joint. He had never smoked anything, let alone marijuana, but he decided to go with the flow and took a puff. Nothing happened. He tried again and again and waited to experience *something*. Still nothing. Having demonstrated that he could smoke as much as he wanted without getting stoned, Dan took several more hits, held it in and slowly released the fragrant smoke. After a few minutes, the redhead started to laugh.

"Why are you pulling at your hair?" she asked.

"I'm trying to take off my yarmulke."

"But you're not wearing a yarmulke."

She was right. The yarmulke was gone.

As the evening wore on, Dan remembered laughing and dancing, until his friend came over and said, "I think we should go now."

"Why? I'm having more fun than I have in years."

"Put your clothes back on. I'll explain later."

The following day, Dan called the president of the temple and announced his decision to resign.

He took courses and read the books. Schary had arranged for Dan to visit sound stages where commercials were being shot, and it was fascinating. The intricate choreography of staging a scene that requires precise interaction of actors, director, technicians manning cameras, cranes and sound booms to make magical moments happen, made Dan feel energized and he knew he was smitten.

Shortly after he moved into an apartment in West Hollywood, Dan got an important phone call. Steve had pulled a few strings and Dan was being considered to direct a commercial for U.S. Steel, of which Steve was a major shareholder and board member. Within days, Dan was on a plane to the Big Apple for a meeting with U.S. Steel's ad agency, BBD&O.

THE AGENCY had convinced U.S. Steel that with their worldwide sales sinking and Japanese exports cornering the market, they had better remind the public that they were still in business. The visuals featured happy steel workers in Pittsburgh pulling molten steel out of a Bessemer furnace with the message that their star—cut to the U.S. Steel logo superimposed on the fiery furnace—still shines bright.

It was obvious why Dan was in the running. As written, the commercial was so anemic it was impossible to get it wrong, so the agency would be taking very little risk assigning a novice director. Dan was appalled. This was his big chance and he wasn't going to waste it. He needed to design a 60-second film that would make Madison Avenue sit up and take notice. What they needed was a powerful *story* and without knowing it, they came to the right place.

When Dan was ushered into the posh suite on the top floor of 777 Madison Avenue to make his pitch, he went balls out and told the agency execs, as gently as he could, that they had no story. That sent the creative team into a frenzy, but Dan was Jimmy Stewart in *Mr. Smith Goes to Washington,* pleading the cause of justice and the common man and nothing could stop him.

"This is the age of the Beatles, for God's sake, and revolutions in music, the arts, fashion and business. It's essential that we portray U.S. Steel as the world-class leader of a revolution in manufacturing, light years ahead of the Japanese and all other competitors, ushering in a whole new era of prosperity and abundance for all Americans."

He was silent for as long as he thought he could sustain it then picked up the pace. Speaking softly at first so that they would really have to listen, Dan continued, "Visualize the Imperial Valley, the heart of the California breadbasket, bordering on the Mojave Desert. Camera moves in tight on an iguana, basking on a blisteringly hot sandy rock. The camera then slowly moves past the iguana and crawls up a barren sand dune, emphasizing the bleak nothingness of the desert, accompanied by the theme from *Lawrence of Arabia*. But when the camera reaches the summit, the screen is suddenly filled with a panoramic view of the valley below. The music swells to an arousing crescendo. Thousands of acres of juicy melons, ripe tomatoes, peaches and tall corn are sprouting out of what was once a parched desert, as far as the eye can see. A farmer in a vast field of lettuce stands next to an irrigation ditch. Beside him is a culvert made of U.S. Steel, four feet in diameter emerging from the ground. The farmer lifts the metal shield and torrents of fresh water gush forth, soaking up the dry land as it surges through canals, between rows and rows of sumptuous fruits and vegetables. Then we follow several quick cuts of culverts opening and water filling trenches all over the farm. A resonant announcer's voice fills the track. 'U.S. Steel culverts carrying fresh water from inland lakes turn barren wastes into fertile farmland to feed millions of people here in the U.S. and around the world. Join us. We're U.S. Steel, pioneers of the new, greater America, leading the world to a better tomorrow.'

Dan was hired to direct the commercial. It ended up winning a Clio and U.S. Steel shares got a significant uptick. Dan's new calling was exciting *and* lucrative. He couldn't believe what they paid him, for something he loved as much as directing film . . . well, commercials, and there's the rub. His crew told fascinating stories about what it was like to work on *African Queen, To Kill a Mockingbird, Paths of Glory.* All Dan could talk about was how skillfully he sprayed Freon on a bottle of Budweiser to get just the right flow of sweat dripping across the label.

It wasn't long before he found himself back in LA sitting on a small fortune but feeling nothing but emptiness. His goal was to make meaningful films but all he saw in his mirror was a rich huckster. Dan couldn't sleep; he lost weight. When he did doze off, he had recurring nightmares that he was running through a supermarket wearing a tallit pursued by a giant can of Ajax. Who could he talk to? He was reluctant to dump his problems on Steve after all he had done, but who else was there?

Over lunch, he told Steve in general terms how he felt. After two martinis—Dan never really developed a taste for those things but the habit came from a year of hanging out with Madison Avenue lunatics—he couldn't control himself and it poured out of him. "The work is great but life is horrible," he ranted, while Steve sat silently. He shared his thoughts about wanting so badly to make films that told real stories, but he was stuck with that bottle of Pepsi Cola shoved up his ass. Dan finally realized he had taken up all the ether. "So . . . how are things with you?"

"Good," Steve said. "Same old, same old. I did read a screenplay I liked a lot but I'm not sure what to do with it. A coming-of-age story, but it's missing something. I'd like you to read it if you have the time."

Dan said he'd be happy to.

"It's called *Grace*. The characters are well drawn, but the story wobbles. I'll send it over."

"It will be my pleasure, Steve."

"Be sure to let me know what you think."

"Of course."

"It's important that I know what you think."

"What I think?"

"Let me know if you think you're up to directing it."

Dan was so excited he could hardly see straight for the first dozen readings. He wrote two full pages of notes for every page in the script.

The film wasn't a huge hit, but it got some good reviews and made a decent profit. Critics made a big deal about Dan's *nouvelle vague* style, long lenses, hand-held chase sequences, back-lit sun flares and well placed voice-overs instead of direct dialogue. Those techniques had often been used in commercials but at the time, were rarely seen in movies.

Steve's favorite review was the one that said, "*Grace* soared with the passion of a Sunday morning prayer meeting." Dan was featured in a *Newsweek* article on "The New Directors" with Joe Dante, Brian de Palma and Billy Friedkin.

After that, Steve brought Dan into his company and produced all his early films.

{ Chapter Fourteen }

ROCKY LISTENED INTENTLY to Dan through the entire twisting tale of his life. He smiled, applauded, and proclaimed, "It's the American dream!"

The intercom beeped again. "Nu?" While Rocky listened impatiently, Dan walked to the wall of snapshots. Studying the photos, he *kvelled*. Molly and Rocky were so wholesome, so youthful, so much in love.

Rocky clicked off the intercom and joined Dan.

"A threesome?" Dan pointed to a close shot of three faces. Molly on one side, Rocky on the other and a camel between them

"That's how we met," Rocky said. "Didn't Molly tell you?"

"No. Where was that?"

"On Mount Sinai. You should appreciate that, rabbi".

"Were you looking for the lost ark of the covenant?"

"Not exactly. I was part of a joint Israeli-Egyptian patrol trying to stop Bedouins from harassing tourists in the Sinai desert between El Arish and El Tur. I was taking a coffee break with Hassan Ali, my Egyptian counterpart, when we heard bloodcurdling screams. *'Rahim Allah yahmini!'* In my meager Arabic, I asked Ali what was going on. He motioned with his finger across his throat. I picked up my Tar 2 assault rifle and ran to the top of the hill.

"Below, I saw a female tourist wearing only a shirt and underwear swinging a club at a screaming Bedouin who was pulling on a camel's bridle, apparently trying to steal it and possibly worse. I fired one shot in the air and the sound was enough that everybody stopped and stood in place. When we approached, the Bedouin looked terrified but the girl stood tall with her cane poised."

Rocky's expression softened. "She was . . . stunning! Like a mirage you would see if you were dying of thirst. I couldn't take my eyes off her. I tried to think like a professional but the situation was surreal. There stood the most beautiful girl I had ever seen, in her shirt and panties, holding a club in striking position and a cranky Bedouin tugging on a camel's rope halter. I was speechless, but Ali talked to the Bedouin to find out what the screaming was about. Unable to look at her for fear I would start stuttering, I translated Ali's meager Hebrew. The Bedouin was not trying to steal anything. The camel is his and he was protecting himself from the crazy girl swinging the cane. 'Bullshit,' the girl said, 'and if he comes one step closer, I'll clobber him.' Ali translated and the Bedouin pulled his camel away to put as much distance between himself and the crazy girl as he could.

"Dan, I couldn't stop staring at her! I asked what she was doing in the middle of the Sinai desert. 'I am with the tour group from Beersheba just over that hill,' she said. 'I finally found a solitary spot to take a much needed pee when this idiot and his camel attacked me.' The Bedouin had a slightly different story. He was also doing something personal on another hill when his camel drifted away and innocently nudged the girl from behind in the middle of her business. It was bizarre and hilarious and I was seriously smitten by the appearance of this magnificent girl in the middle of nowhere. I asked her to please stand down while my Egyptian friend salved the ego of the Bedouin with ten Israeli shekels and sent him off. I wanted so much to talk to her."

Dan was smiling. "This is very romantic. Go on."

"I wanted to tell her how incredibly lovely she was, but what came out sounded like a traffic cop. I said to her, 'I don't know how familiar you are with the rules of the desert, but here, camels are the highest form of life and one shouldn't hit them with a cane, not even when they poke their nose into your business. Speaking of your business, you might want to put your pants on.' She was totally unfazed. She picked up her hiking shorts, shook out the sand, and said, 'Turn around.' I motioned to Ali, who didn't understand English and we both turned around. I'm sorry we caught you in your underwear, I said over my shoulder, as she put on her shorts and adjusted her belt, but please don't be embarrassed. Her answer was priceless, Dan. She said, 'Why should I be embarrassed? I kicked that Bedouin's ass, didn't I?'"

Dan laughed. "If I were thinking of a way to describe Molly, that story would tell anyone all they need to know." He liked hearing stories like that about Marion's daughter, who had acquired all the moxie and spunk of his *basherte*.

Rocky continued as if retelling a dream. "As I walked her back to her tour group, she was silent. I felt like my heart would burst. She turned to me and said, 'Did you like what you saw?' I don't know what made me say it, but I did. 'Yes. Yes and yes. I liked everything I saw and there's something I'd like to say, but I don't know how.' She said, 'Say it.' So I blurted out, 'you have the most beautiful eyes.'"

Rocky turned to look at Dan. "Later, when she mentioned that voice thing again, I asked her what I said that she found so appealing. She said, 'It wasn't anything you said. It was the sound. It's as though I heard a familiar melody and I wanted to sing along."

The mystical drama was unfolding. The words Rocky said to Molly were exactly the same as Dan's when he met Marion at that play reading so many years before and to see the connection Molly made between the sound of his voice and Rocky's was too compelling to dismiss. Dan was beginning to sense that he actually was part of a matrix connecting the four of them.

"The truth is," Rocky said, "everything in my life fell into place when I saw her face. She was like an incandescent flame in the desert. I'm not religious, but that was as close to seeing a burning bush as I'll ever come. I was fascinated by this vulnerable creature in a harsh landscape without language or protection who wasn't afraid of anything . . . and so beautiful!"

"And on the holy mountain, yet," Dan said. "That's what I call an auspicious beginning."

"And I wasn't going to let it end there. The group she came with was leaving for Beersheba the next morning. I had a three-day pass before returning to my base so I asked if she would like to come with me to see the world's largest collection of fifteen hundred-year-old human bones."

"Interesting pickup line," Dan said.

"It worked." Rocky smiled. "I thought I had pictures of the place," he said as he looked through the wall of photos. "I don't remember where they are but you can google it."

"I have heard of the Monastery of Santa Caterina, if that's what you're referring to," Dan said, "and I'm trying to understand why you decided to entertain this fascinating young woman you just met by taking her to a mortuary."

"I beat myself up about that at first, but we were in the middle of the Sinai desert. I had to find something that would be more enticing than going back to her tour bus and that was the first thing that popped into my head."

"How did she react when you finally got there?"

"She was fine but I was afraid I had made a terrible mistake. I just met the girl of my dreams and what do I do to impress her? Bring her to a mausoleum, reeking of death, bodies and bones! What kind of weirdo must she think I am?"

"What was it like?"

"Eerie. Bones. Everywhere, bones! Huge piles of gruesome, ghoulish bones. Aside from us, there were twenty or thirty evangelical tourists from the U.S., sitting on the dirt floor while their pastor walked back and forth, Bible in hand, preaching. I whispered to Molly. 'I think we've seen enough, don't you?' 'Sshhhhh!' she said, then grabbed my arm and led me to where the faithful were sitting. She sat on the dirt floor in the last row. What could I do? I sat next to her."

"Good introduction to Molly," Dan said. "Never anticipate, never underestimate. Did she get you to convert?"

"No," Rocky said, "but she did open my eyes. I never thought much about TV evangelists other than they are probably charlatans, milking the poor, so when this guy raised his hand and stared at the ceiling, I whispered to Molly 'you know we don't *have* to stay . . .' But she shushed me again, only louder. 'This is what I've been looking for!' she said."

Rocky looked at Dan. "What was I supposed to think?"

Dan smiled. "I'm sure she let you know."

"She did. In a way I never could have imagined. Once the preacher began to spout fire and brimstone, Molly locked onto his every word. 'And He set me down in the midst of these hills-ah. And it was full of bones!' Molly held my hand in a tight grip. 'Ezekiel 37!' she said. 'This is important. Listen.' At first I thought the preacher was just a showman, but slowly . . . something came over me. I can't explain it, but sitting in that place, next to Molly, with her hand tightly holding mine, I was feeling something I never had before. Surrounded by stacks of bones, the Pastor looked up at the ceiling." Rocky waved his arms in the air as the charismatic preacher did when he looked heavenward. "'And God said unto me: Son of man, can-these-bones-live?' The pastor suddenly stopped and turned to the congregation. 'What? Is GOD asking ME if these bones can live?' That's when the hall started to rattle and shake. 'Yes He is, Pastor!' 'Go on, tell 'im,' the whole congregation joined in. 'Speak truth to the Lord, Pastor!' 'Don't be afraid.'"

Rocky stopped waving his arms. "Then a voice rose above the crowd. It was Molly. She was steadfast and spoke with the timbre of a prophet. 'We say unto Him, YES, LORD!' she cried out. 'From the earth below and the heavens above, from the spheres, galaxies and all the multiple universes, YES, LORD, as my soul liveth this day, the spirit *will* reenter these bones and they *will* live again.'"

Rocky paced around his office. Dan was rapt.

"Weeping, cheering and endless *a-mens* filled the chamber like a well-rehearsed gospel chorus. Everyone felt they not only heard the words of Ezekiel the prophet, they heard the *voice* that Moses heard right there on Mt. Sinai all those years ago and the strangest thing happened to me," Rocky said. "For the first time in my life, I felt that I truly believed!

"Outside the catacomb, Molly's face was radiant. I had just experienced the most inspirational event of my life. I can't say I understood what she said, but I knew it was true. I put my arms around her. I said *'ah-men'* and in that embrace, we both felt something neither of us ever had before. It was a transcendent moment."

Still deeply inside himself, Rocky said: "We walked along the hills outside the monastery in silence. Molly put her tiny hand in mine. Tall and statuesque as she is, Molly has the smallest hands I have ever seen. I suddenly realized that I did not have a single thought in my head, but my heart was pounding. I stopped and looked at her. She was an ethereal angel and her aura engulfed me. I held her close and felt her heart beating in rhythm with mine. She looked up at me, with tears in her eyes and said, 'We *can* return life to the ones we love, if we truly believe. That's what I heard on this holy mountain today and in my heart of hearts and I know it's true.'

"I don't know what made me say it but the words rolled out of my mouth. 'I believe it, too,' I said. To this day, I can't say that I do believe or I don't. All I know is that my role in life from that moment on was to support and protect and love Molly."

As joyful as it was to hear Rocky speak of Molly with love and admiration, the talk about *returning life to the ones we love* had a disquieting resonance for Dan, echoing the words of Abednego: *separated souls are rejoined.* It took a moment for Dan to get his voice back. "And then?"

"It all happened quickly. I was ordered back to Tel Aviv for intelligence training. Molly came with me. It was the most exciting time of my life. We were together every minute I could get away. Every night was perfect bliss. We called that time 'here's looking at you, kid,' because our love affair was straight out of the movie, *Casablanca.* We laughed and danced. Life was glorious. We soared through those days and nights, falling more deeply in love."

"That film and especially the montage sequence in Paris was one of our favorites, too," Dan said, "but as I recall, that particular episode didn't turn out so well."

"I was getting to that. I couldn't imagine life without Molly. But how do I go about this? What do I do? I thought of so many scenarios. Should I do the bent knee? Let her accidentally find a ring in a plate of hummus? While I was considering all the options, we were in bed one night, drinking champagne and watching our favorite movie. When Bogie said, 'of all the gin joints in all the world . . . ' I heard myself say, 'Don't you think we should get married?'

"I don't know what I expected. A hug? Tears? Whatever I was hoping would happen, didn't. She put down her glass, turned off the TV and sat quietly on the bed. I was going nuts. Did I do it wrong? What could she say? No, she doesn't think we should get married? Impossible! We love each other. There's no question about that. It seemed like forever before she said 'Of course I want to marry you . . .' I wanted to breathe easier, but the pause ruled that out . . . 'but before I can, there's something important I have to do.'

"Important! What could be that important? I walked around the room asking a hundred questions, but nothing Molly said made any sense. I was confused and upset. She hugged me, pressing her head to my chest. 'Do you trust me?' 'Of course! I'm asking you to be my wife, to share my life . . . but you'll have to share yours with me.' 'I am and I will,' she said, 'but there is something I have to do myself. I love you with all my heart, Rocky. If I could explain this to you I would, but it relates to . . . a spiritual realm, one that you simply can't access yet.'

"I told her she did awaken something spiritual in me outside the monastery, but she said there was more to it.

"I couldn't hold back any longer. This is about Marion, isn't it?"

"'What are you saying?'

"'I'm saying that I love you and I want to marry you. I know you love me too, but you're bound by this idea that you can't do anything unless and until Marion gives the go-ahead. I understand your love for Marion and your allegiance to her, but she passed on. She's dead. You have to accept that. She lived her life. It's time for us to live ours.'

"'Do you know why I came to Israel?' She asked. 'Do you have any understanding of how you and I met?'

"'It was the most important event of my life! I gladly acknowledge that. You can call it whatever you like but the fact is that you and I were in the same place at the same time. Our eyes met and we fell in love. It's not mystical or magical, it's nature.'

"Molly looked at me with the saddest expression. 'What you see is real but it's only one layer of who we are and what we are destined to be.'

"'Is that all I am to you? One layer out of many in your mystical world?'

"'No, that's not what I'm saying. I do think we are *bashert,* but . . .'

"'You're not sure?'

"She looked at me with tears in her eyes. There were no more words. I embraced her. She kissed me and we made the most beautiful love. She fell asleep in my arms and all the weird stuff drifted away. But when I awoke, she was gone. Her note read,

> I love you more than words can describe. Do I want to marry you? Of course! I beg you to trust me. I am leaving now. I hope with all my heart that when I return, I will be ready to become your wife and that you will still want me. I understand the terrible risk I am

> taking, but I must do this. I know how much pain it is causing you and I am so sorry. I feel it as deeply as you, but there is no other way. You have my love, dearest man, and I need your trust. I carry your heart . . . I carry it in my heart. Please, please be here when I return.
> —Molly

"'I am leaving now?!' Rocky fumed. "That's all her note said. I felt like I was hit by a thunderbolt. Leaving? And going where? You'd think she would at least tell me. A friend of mine who works in customs pulled a few strings and found out. She was on her way to Nepal. NEPAL?!" Rocky howled. "How do I contact her? Is she in Kathmandu . . . maybe one of several hundred other cities or maybe a thousand ashrams . . . maybe . . . who the hell knows? And for how long? Forever? Molly was suddenly gone, swallowed up in some inscrutable quest. I wept like a child, screaming and crying, She had become the epicenter of my life and suddenly she was gone. What do I do? Recite *Kaddish?* Kill myself? I spent the next two months in unspeakable agony."

Dan put a hand on Rocky's arm. "Rocky, I . . ."

Still in a frenzied state, Rocky said "A few weeks before I was assigned this post in Jamaica, she called. 'Rocky, I love you so much . . .' 'Where are you?' I asked. I couldn't think straight. I was relieved that she was alive, but angry as hell. 'I'm in Bangkok waiting for a connecting flight to Tel Aviv. I'm so happy! Everything is in place. I had the most exhilarating time with Marion . . . and we can get married!'"

"What did she say about Marion?" Dan couldn't control what came out of his mouth.

"Nothing else and I didn't ask. I was livid. She talked to a dead person and now she's ready to marry me? What do

I say? Yes, I'll take you back as though nothing happened? You didn't disappear? You didn't break my heart? You didn't turn my life into a nightmare? I felt like breaking something. I was enraged. Yes, and vengeful. What did she expect? I wanted to tell her to go to hell for all the crap she put me through, but the words that came out of my mouth were, 'Please, please, please come home. I am so miserable without you.'"

Rocky closed his eyes then exhaled. "So, Molly and I are here in Jamaica. Happy, I guess, but with so many things unresolved."

The intercom beeped. Rocky looked as though he was ready to smash the damn thing. He clicked on, caught his breath and shouted, "All right already!"

"Dan, I have to step out for a few minutes." He held his hands out apologetically, palms up. "The TV producer I told you about finally arrived. He's here to shoot a tourism commercial for El Al. I didn't think he'd get through the traffic but he did. I have to sign a bunch of forms so he can get his equipment through customs. You're welcome to come along. I'm sure he'd be thrilled to meet you."

"No thanks. Anything having to do with TV commercials gives me hives."

"Didn't you start that way?"

"Yes, but that was a long time ago. It was like a fraternity initiation. Once you're past it, you want to forget it ever happened."

"It may not be great art, but what's wrong with travelling to all those dazzling locations for a few weeks at a time photographing sexy models?"

"Pure fantasy. Scantily dressed models are there to work. Every commercial shoot is miserable in its own way, trust me. The only thing that stays with you after it's all over is the exotic disease in your intestines. Once you've broken through to features, there is only one reason to go back to commercials, and that is if you're totally broke . . . and even then . . ." Dan was suddenly distracted by what he was saying.

"Even then?" Rocky asked.

"Even then, it's not worth the nightmares."

"Nightmares? Are you talking about the encounter with the shaman?"

"What do you know about that?"

"Just what Molly told me."

"What did she say?"

"I don't remember all the details but she said it was the most terrifying event of Marion's life."

The intercom began to beep again. "I'll be back in five, tops." Rocky left but the machine continued to beep until it stopped abruptly.

The most terrifying event of her life? I never heard Marion use those words. *Strange? Hurtful?* Yes, and when we got home she did have nightmares, but eventually they disappeared. We even joked about it. I assumed Marion had finally driven out whatever demons were unleashed during that grotesque encounter in Chechuacan. Clearly I was wrong.

What were we doing in the bowels of a Guatemalan jungle, anyway?

". . . there is only one reason to go back to commercials and that is if you're totally broke."

It all came rushing back with the fury of a tidal wave from hell.

PART SIX

Risky Business

{ Chapter Fifteen }

"WHAT DO YOU MEAN, you're not going to the opening?"

"It's not about you, Dan," Marion said. "I just can't spend an evening posing for paparazzi with Steve Weisman."

"After all he did for us . . . ?"

"For us?" Marion was seething. "We brought Steve the only Golden Globe nomination he ever received and, to this day, he laments ever making *Sunsplash*. In all his extravagant self-promotion, he never even mentions our film."

"I hear what you're saying, but tonight isn't about Steve. I directed the film and if it does as well as we hope, it could open all kinds of doors for us."

"Doors to where?" Marion held up a copy of *Daily Variety*. "'*Graduation Day*,'" Marion read aloud, '*E.S.I.'s biggest-budget release ever, is expected to yield bango-big bucks. The critics are unanimous. Dan Sobol's socko-boffo direction takes no prisoners. Ninety-seven minutes of pure carnage spells huge profits.*'" Marion threw the paper into the garbage basket. "Pure carnage?

Bango-big bucks? Is that the door you want us to go through? Is that what you want engraved on your tombstone? Steve Weisman is not your friend."

"That's not fair. Steve gave me a shot when no one else would, and a whole lot more. He was always straight with me. E.S.I. makes films for the great unwashed. Those were his conditions and I agreed because it gave me a chance to prove myself. I know what you're upset about but that's not entirely Steve's fault. We convinced him to try it our way once and we made a good film, but even with the Golden Globe nomination, *Sunsplash* lost money, so I've got to help him recoup. That's all this is."

"We will make our own films again, Dan. Won't we?"

"We will, but tonight I have to go to the opening of *Graduation Day* and I need you to be with me."

I SURVIVED GRADUATION DAY was on all the banners and badges worn by screaming young fans, dancing to boisterous rock music outside the Pantages Theater on Hollywood Boulevard. When Dan and Marion's limo arrived at the star-packed, klieg light gala, they were met by Steve and all three were swallowed up in the crowd.

When the film began to roll, the young audience cheered. They laughed, hooted and screamed at the graphic action, accompanied by an ear-splitting soundtrack.

Dan noticed that Marion seemed distracted. There were some hilarious scenes, but she didn't laugh once.

"I'm sorry," she whispered halfway through the film. "I have to step out for a few minutes."

"Are you okay?"

"Fine," she said and quietly left. After what seemed like a

long time, Dan went out to look for her. She was in the lobby, sitting on a large red upholstered chair, alone.

"Go back in, Dan," she said. "You have to. I don't."

"What's going on?"

"I'll see you at home," she said and walked out of the theater.

When Dan entered the house, he was steaming. "What the hell was that about?"

"I'm sorry, Dan, but it was just too humiliating."

"Was the film that bad?"

"No. It wasn't a bad film at all. By every measure, it was a hit. Kids were cheering, hooting and laughing, especially during the decapitation scene."

"So what's the problem?"

"If anyone else had made that film, it wouldn't bother me in the least. But you, Dan, are possessed of a soul, a brain and talent! You should be making *Nights of Cabiria, Doctor Strangelove, Four Hundred Blows*. Instead, you squander your gifts on mindless exploitation crap. For what? Is this why you left the rabbinate? Is pandering to the masses with B films any better than making commercials for vaginal sprays?"

Dan was stunned. He didn't know what to say. He was angry and wanted to strike back or at least defend himself, but how could he? She spoke the words that were in his gut since he screened his first commercial. He fell into his chair and couldn't speak. Marion knelt beside him and held his hand.

"You know more about the art of film than most directors working today and you're a captivating storyteller. You should be making great films. You are capable of it, Dan. You have the gifts. Don't squander them on *drek*."

That night, while Dan was asleep, Marion went to their study and printed a copy of the three-page treatment she had been working on. The next morning she prepared a breakfast of fresh papaya and mango, with French roast coffee and a whole-wheat baguette, his favorite. After pouring the coffee, she placed the pages next to Dan's plate. The title was *Child2Man*. The story was loosely based on the horrific riots that devastated whole neighborhoods of Los Angeles just a few years prior. The style called for a blend of realism and surrealism to confront the audience with scenes of hopeless desperation against an explosive backdrop of neglect.

Dan had his coffee, a bite of baguette, and started reading. The silence was deafening. Finally, Dan spoke. "Brilliant. It's real . . . it's all heart . . . and it's powerful. What stars do you have in mind?"

"None," Marion said. "This story demands real people, whose style and manner of speaking can draw the audience into the world of poverty and violence that spawned them."

"No stars? Who would finance a film without stars?"

"You convinced Steve once," she said.

"*Sunsplash?* He swore he'd never go down that road again."

"Never?"

Dan read the three pagers again . . . and again. "This is the best treatment I ever read."

"Isn't it worth a try?"

"How long before you have a screenplay?

TWO MONTHS LATER, they sent Steve a script and within days, he invited them to the Paladin Club for lunch. When he arrived, Steve was in a particularly good mood. After the hugs and smiles, Steve raised his glass.

"To *Graduation Day!* Congratulations, Dan. We're already

shit-deep in profit and we haven't begun to sell foreign, let alone, ancillaries."

"That's great news," Marion said unenthusiastically.

Dan downed his glass and waved to the waiter. "Another bottle, please."

Their lack of enthusiasm wasn't lost on Steve. "Obviously we're not here to celebrate Dan's latest triumph," he said.

"Did you read *Child2Man?*" Marion asked.

"I did."

Dan couldn't hold back. "What do you think?"

"Beautifully written. Clearly, you want to make a relevant film that will impact people's lives and I mean it when I say my heart is with you."

There was a long silence as Dan and Marion waited for the shoe to drop.

"Unfortunately, despite the quality of the writing, I have to pass. E.S.I. isn't a little indie anymore, you know that, Dan. We're part of a conglomerate now. Despite the brilliance of your screenplay, Marion, and I mean that sincerely, there is no way I could convince my partners that *Child2Man* will attract *Graduation Day* audiences and without stars, they won't even read it. The only way to finance a film like this is with private investment and in my current situation that would be major conflict."

Private investment? That was one part of filmmaking Dan never learned and he didn't have the slightest idea how to go about it.

Private investment . . . private investment . . . Marion was possessed. She called relatives in New York and some entrepreneurs she met through her work at the studios. She got a lot of encouragement and invitations to visit Baja or Cannes, but precious few offers to invest money in an independent film without stars.

Marion was intent on finding a way. "Aren't there ways to cut corners?"

"Corners?"

"You said when you first started out you were a master at stealing locations and shooting on the cheap. Why can't we do that?"

"First of all, that was a long time ago. I was just breaking in, desperate to get a credit."

"How did you raise the money?"

"I didn't. I was making sample reels, using short ends I *schnorred* from labs when I met a guy who worked for Honda. He told me they wanted to make a low budget movie featuring their new minivan like Volkswagen did a few years back with *Herbie, the Love Bug.* It was a funny script. The title was, 'From those wonderful folks who brought you Pearl Harbor.' Every bid came in over a million and Honda wouldn't go for it. My friend said if I could bring it in for six hundred thousand, I would get the job and I grabbed it."

"How did you know you could do it?"

"I didn't. I just knew I had to find a way."

"How did it turn out?"

"Great. Honda loved the film, but making it was a nightmare. Six weeks of shooting from Louisiana swamps to the Grand Canyon with a fifteen-man crew in two Winnebagos, two equipment trucks, and a fleet of Hondas."

"So?" Marion was excited.

"So what?

"Why can't we make our film like that?"

"First of all, because we're not Honda. Remember, they put up the six hundred thousand."

WEEKS WENT BY and the prospect of getting their film produced seemed like a fading dream. At a tax-planning session with his lawyer, Nate Schlosser, Dan found his mind wandering. Those yearly meetings were so boring Dan usually brought a magazine to read while Nate rattled off a lot of tax jargon, but he forgot this time and had only his *Hollywood Reporter* to skim while his lawyer rambled on.

"You've got a huge tax hit coming this year, kid." Nate was only five years older than Dan, but he called everybody kid. "I haven't bothered you with it in the past, but Congress just castrated FATCA."

Dan looked up, uninterested. "FATCA? Is that good for the Jews or bad for the Jews?"

Nate tried to appear patient. "Bad. Very bad for everybody but the friggin' government. Foreign Account Tax Compliance Act is what kept your savings from being eaten by the IRS. I really wish you'd take more of an interest. The point is, with offshore havens shutting down, we have to find you some new shelters and that's not easy. We did good these last few years, kid, but like all good things . . ." Nate picked up an attractively designed brochure. "None of the domestic shelters pay dividends like we're used to, but this one isn't bad," he said as he moved it across his large round table. "Check it out."

Dan put down his *Hollywood Reporter* and browsed the pamphlet unenthusiastically. Nice looking modern style buildings surrounded by lush gardens. "What's this got to do with me?"

"Nursing homes in Arizona," Nate said. "Good tax benefits, not great, but guaranteed four percent interest. In ten years, your six hundred thousand dollar-plus nest egg could be worth over . . ."

Dan stopped listening. *"My . . . six hundred thousand dollar-plus nest egg!"*

He knew he had saved some money during his commercial days but he never thought about how much, and the checks from E.S.I. went straight to his lawyer who paid his and Marion's bills, so it never occurred to him to ask how much money he actually had. They lived well and had everything they wanted so it was a surprise to hear that he had amassed that kind of nest egg, a thrilling, wonderful surprise!

"I FOUND AN INVESTOR," Dan bellowed when he burst through the door.

What followed was the best creative honeymoon they could have imagined. Living inside each other's heads for the next weeks and months brought Marion and Dan closer than ever. If Marion would say, "Why don't we stage the scene this or that way?" Dan's inevitable response was, "I can't believe it. I was just going to say that!"

Child2Man wasn't written as a low-budget film, so Dan had to find ways to save a nickel here and a dime there. Working for E.S.I., he never had to manage costs. That was left to the bean counters, so how could he bring in a major film for a fraction of the original estimate?

He calculated that by deferring all of his and Marion's fees, hiring non-SAG actors and calling in every favor he was owed, he could just about cover the budget. He saved on everything but skimped on nothing. Expensive caravans for wardrobe and makeup? No way. Actors can dress and do their own makeup in port-o-potties, but film, special equipment, computer graphics? That's where the money will be spent. Shooting will be a major challenge . . . but *Child2Man* will be a cinematic masterpiece.

Even though Dan controlled the budget with a tight fist, he was generous when giving out profit points to both crew and cast. "If they're willing to work for less than they deserve, they're de facto investors and if the film does half the business we expect, they should be rewarded."

"I'm glad to see that the rabbi in you is still alive and well," Marion said proudly.

With a little luck, Dan and Marion actually stood to see a significant profit, but they weren't making this film to become rich. Even a small return on their investment would enable them to continue to make their kind of films, and that's all they hoped for.

MARION'S SHOOTING SCRIPT was electric and rehearsals brought tears to cast, crew and everyone on the set. *Child2Man* was a gritty story of a lost generation of kids growing up in the human detritus of the hood, struggling to stay alive. Despite the long hours and difficult locations, when Marion and Dan heard their words emerging from the mouths of these young actors who actually lived the story, they knew they were precisely where they should be at this magical time of their lives.

The film was a hit. Enthusiastic receptions at film festivals—they won first prize in both Houston and Toronto—confirmed their belief that they had *made it*. Marion couldn't have been happier and more fulfilled—until they returned home and Dan confronted her with the bad news, the very bad news.

Despite the overwhelming success of the film in festivals, no major studio was prepared to invest a significant amount of money on prints and advertising to distribute what they considered an *art film* with no marquee value. The only offers came from specialty houses or art theaters, which by definition meant small venues in only a handful of cities and negligible, if any, returns on their investment. The bottom line was that while reviews continued to glow, the impact on their personal finances was disastrous.

Marion was perplexed. "I don't get it. Everyone who saw our film loved it, so what's the problem?" There was no way she could understand Dan's dilemma. She was raised to appreciate the art, not how much it was sold for. They set out to make a significant film and they succeeded. What more could they have done? Marion knew that some films earned a lot of money and some didn't, but who cares?

"I care," Dan said, totally defeated. He cared because they had deferred their fees and spent every cent of their own money, well over the six hundred thousand dollar budget. Normally, the distributor assumes the biggest postproduction expenses—prints, advertising and promotion—but they made this film without a firm distribution deal. Dan just assumed that every studio would be competing for the picture, especially after all the glowing praise it garnered. That didn't happen and the result was that the unpaid bills remained with Dan.

After tallying the costs of travel to Houston and Toronto with their press agents and cast members, they were barely left with enough for basics. Dan had never been in this situation before. He was always bored by the number crunchers, the bankers, and sales reps who never made a creative contribution, but knew how to make cash presales so that producers never had to face the abyss he was staring into now.

"Hubris! Stupid, totally my fault!" Dan castigated himself mercilessly. He had made a colossal miscalculation and the humiliating result was that they lost everything. They weren't just low on cash; they were broke. To make things worse, the losses from *Child2Man* continued to pursue them. After reviewing bills due for legal, accounting, and a whole stack of invoices he thought were paid but were not, Dan was so depressed and angry with himself, he hardly spoke a word for days.

To get another film going would take months. *How would they survive?*

{ Chapter Sixteen }

On one of the many gloomy days that followed, Dan got a phone call from his lawyer, Nate Schlosser. "I'm sorry about the way things turned out, kid."

"Yeah, well . . ."

"I really am sorry, but this isn't a condolence call. How would you like some good news?"

"I'm listening."

"You're booked on a flight to New York day after tomorrow. I got you a gig. You start shooting in three weeks. Good money, all up front."

"What kind of film?"

"Not a film, exactly. It's a package of very well paying commercials for BBD&O. You apparently have some clout there."

"That's the most depressing news yet, Nate. I can't go back to making commercials. Those were the worst days of my life. I don't have the stomach for it anymore."

"I got them to offer you a hundred thousand dollars for

eighteen days of shooting plus some prep here and in New York. Okay, that's less than you lost on *Child2Man,* but it's enough to put you back on your feet. Didn't you hear what I said? You are not going to starve! I'm waiting for you to tell me how badly you want to kiss my ass."

"Commercials?! Please, Nate. I can't do it. I just can't."

"Dan, let me put it another way. You're not the only one who got screwed on *Child2Man*. I hate to bring this up kid, but you haven't paid me in nearly a year. I know what that film meant to you, so I carried you—out of pocket. The bottom line is, you're into me for nearly twenty grand and I won't even take a commission for getting you this gig. Eighteen days, Dan. I put in a hell of a lot more time than that on your film. I've got a big nut to crack and I think it's fair to say, you owe me."

Later, when Dan told Marion the news, she was aghast. "TV commercials! What's this one for, rat poison?"

"It's an innovative brand of cigarettes for women," Dan said.

"Cigarettes?! What's the innovation? Breast cancer in addition to lung cancer? Rat poison is definitely more benign, unless you're a rat," she fumed. "Dan, advertising is the asshole of American culture. Legalized deception, lies piled on lies and presented by actors pretending to be doctors or hot-looking models who promise every manner of sexual delight if you buy their shaving cream. Don't you see how cynical that is? It kills me to think you'd go back to it."

"Eighteen days," Dan said. "I've got obligations and I can't dodge them. The way I look at it, it's a light sentence. I deserve a lot worse."

The new brand, sponsored by National Tobacco, was called I.M.W.O.M.A.N. The agency considered every possible location to shoot the commercials. The one they selected was perfectly suited for their message: Chechuacan in central Guatemala, once capital of the great Mayan empire.

Dan had spent enough time on Madison Avenue that he wasn't surprised at some of the far-fetched claims advertisers used to sell their products, but how could the smoking habits of a culture that disappeared a thousand years ago have any relevance for contemporary women?

The creative director had that covered. "Everyone knows about the Mayan calendar. At least they think they do, but they are wrong. Some think it predicts the end of the world but that was not the intention of the Mayan astrologers. What it predicts is that male domination of the world will end this year and women will finally be empowered to make their own choices."

"How do we prove that?" Dan asked.

"We can't prove it exactly, but who's going to contest it? Montezuma?"

"Montezuma was Aztec, not Mayan and he's dead," Dan said

"Excellent points," the creative director conceded, "Our legal department studied the plan and those two facts are precisely what makes our position unassailable."

"How?"

"The only way to refute our claim is to find a Mayan witness from the tenth century and that's not likely. As for Truth in Advertising, all the FTC requires is that we bring an expert on Mayan history to the location so we have a name on a document. We've already arranged that, so we're covered."

While Dan slogged through endless meetings with the agency's creative team, Marion decided to make the best of a bad situation. She devoured every book she could find on

Mayan culture. Impressed as she was by their advances in astronomy and science, Marion was captivated by the superior quality of their art. The grand pyramids were adorned with extravagant representations of heroic warriors, fearsome animals, regally attired princes and queens, all magnificently rendered . . . but there was also a troubling aspect to those sculptures. Central to every carving was a graphic depiction of some hideous form of torture inflicted not only upon enemies, but their own nobility, who graciously accepted punishment as proof of their power and position in the hierarchy.

For the Maya, violence—no matter how or where it was directed—was honorable and perpetrators and victims were held in high esteem.

Human sacrifice was practiced as a regular form of communal worship. This act, an inseparable part of their culture, was graphically portrayed in well preserved monuments. In one superbly crafted stele at the base of the great pyramid at Tikal, a Jaguar Priest feasts on the hearts of his victims. Often, those sacrificial offerings were daughters of the very priests who wielded the obsidian knives.

AFTER AN UNEASY FLIGHT from Guatemala City, the key crew and agency reps drove four exhausting hours in a caravan of off-road vehicles through dense tropical forest before they finally arrived in the village.

A deep sense of mystery hovered over the place. Ruins of Chechuacan, once jewel of the Mayan Kingdom, lay half-buried in the feral undergrowth like a camouflaged army. Only the twin pyramids in the center of a vast clearing stretched high above the neighboring terrain, arrogantly proclaiming the power of their endurance.

Unlike the Roman Forum or even the Parthenon, Chechuacan was not smothered by fume-spewing traffic and noisy pedestrians reducing their glorious achievements to relics of the past. The heart of Maya still beat loudly in their jungle kingdom. The grandeur that radiated through the remnants of this exalted civilization—eerily enhanced by the absence of life—was awesome.

Most of the shooting was to take place around the Twin Pyramids. One was known as Shrine of the Jaguar and the other, Plumed Serpent. The imposing structures faced one another and between them lay a deep pit that received the hearts of thousands of maidens sacrificed to the god *Ah Puch*.

Dan spent long hours mapping out shooting schedules, placement of set pieces, cameras, lights, and rehearsing actors to read stilted advertising copy, but the hardest thing he had to deal with was being separated from Marion all day. When they worked on *Child2Man,* they were together all the time, working in perfect synch and feasting daily on a rich exchange of ideas. Those were happy times and he was confident they would return, but for now Dan was resigned to do penance: eighteen days of purgatory in the service of I.M.W.O.M.A.N.

Concerned about distracting Dan from his mission, the agency made it clear that Marion's presence wasn't required on the set. Given her contempt for admen and their convoluted sense of "truth in advertising," Marion was happy to spend her days exploring the wonders of that amazing civilization whose presence in the surrounding jungle was palpable.

Early one morning, while Dan was riding atop a crane following the sun as it rose between the pyramids, Marion set out to explore the treasures she had read about. A short walk from her hut, she found a clearing and followed it. There was an aura of wonderment in the diverse array of tropical plants:

red and yellow lobster claws that grew waist high and swayed in the breeze, metallic silver Bromeliads wound around huge Sapodilla trees and a dazzling array of huge orchids, violet, orange, blood-red and yellow. A symphony of birdcalls welcomed Marion as she entered their domain.

Navigating the narrow path was easy enough and soon she was greeted by a stream of humid mist that led to a vast garden of megalithic tombs. Sculptures and monuments of all sizes were strewn amid giant Mahogany and stately Ceiba trees.

The first tombstone that caught her attention was a warrior, wearing a black stone helmet, poised to attack with a sword in one hand and a spear in the other. At first, Marion was intrigued by the subtle contours of the sculpture, but her curiosity turned to revulsion when she realized that the reddish-gold curved half-moons growing out of his face was fire. The same rendering of flames covered the bottom of his tunic and all around his feet. Clearly the warrior was being burned alive.

Another superbly rendered gravestone featured a group of women, each holding hands with a child. They all wore feathered black ceremonial bonnets. It was clear that every character, women *and* children, had gaping holes in the left side of their chests. Droplets of red blood flowed down their bodies and filled the entire base of the stone.

The monuments differed in size and shape, but the central theme was always some form of unspeakable horror. The pictures in her guidebooks were often unsettling, but standing on the very ground where the victims were buried, she was stung with a sense of dread. This wasn't a gallery or museum. It was a vast slaughterhouse where pain and death were memorialized in monstrous images.

The incessant calls of jungle birds became increasingly dissonant and Marion found herself reliving that terrible day in the cemetery on Long Island. She recalled the deafening screech of crows circling overhead as shovels of dirt piled onto that box, pushing her dead father farther away from her.

Walking unsteadily, Marion continued down the narrow path, practically bumping into a huge stone sculpture. It was the image of a queen or princess in regal garb and crown, with large knives peeling flesh from her neck, arms and chest.

Suddenly feeling faint, Marion leaned against a tree. The first rumblings of an earthquake shook the ground beneath her. Looking down, she saw a pool of blood. Before she could scream, she looked again and the blood was actually a huge florescent red orchid that rose past her knees.

Marion stumbled as she ran back up the narrow path.

When she arrived at the twin pyramids, Dan, his A.D. and D.P. looked on as department heads from the agency argued fiercely while costumed actors stood by, waiting for instructions.

"Why in hell are the actresses barefoot?" The head copywriter was furious. "Some kind of slipper or moccasin would be sexy. Barefoot, all we see are a lot of ugly bunions."

"Authenticity, jackass. Mayan women always walked barefoot," the art director stood his ground.

"Who knows that?"

"I do."

"You don't know shit."

When Marion approached, the quarreling ad agency execs suddenly became silent. "Can we do something for you, Marion?" The account executive said, obviously offended by the intrusion.

"Can we talk for a few minutes?" Marion whispered in Dan's ear.

The hostile looks of the ad execs sent a clear message.

"Can it wait?" Dan asked gently.

Marion nodded and as soon as she left, the arguments flared anew.

DAN WAS UP BEFORE SUNRISE every morning to get a variety of predawn angles and was unavailable for the rest of the day. Dinner was served to the entire ensemble after sunset, at which time Marion hoped she and Dan could find a few peaceful moments to examine the impact of her discoveries, but there was always some nervous agency nudnik badgering him.

"Remember, we need to get real passion out of those actors," the head copywriter insisted. "When the sacrificial virgin blows smoke in the face of the priest holding a sharp blade at her chest and she says defiantly: '*I* smoke 'em because *I* like 'em,' I want to hear Lady Macbeth!"

Just when Marion thought she wouldn't survive the full eighteen days, relief came with the arrival of the "qualified professional" required by the FTC. Her name was Dr. Linda Ramirez, a world-renowned expert on Mayan culture from the Universidad de San Carlos de Guatemala. When they met, she took Marion's hand and said "I saw *Child2Man* and loved it."

Marion felt her heart jump. A lifeline in the form of a kindred spirit! "I have no idea why I'm here," Professor Ramirez said. "It is well documented that the Mayans smoked tobacco and a variety of hallucinogens, but that's in my books. They didn't have to bring me to the location to substantiate it."

"It's called Truth in Advertising," Marion said.

'What's that?"

"It's an oxymoron, but one that will save them millions of dollars if anyone tries to sue."

They both laughed. "I can't tell you how happy I am to meet you, Dr. Ramirez. I have a thousand questions to ask you."

"Call me Linda, please. I'm here for the remainder of the shoot, so fire away."

SINCE THERE WERE FEW demands on her time, Linda offered to be Marion's personal guide. Together, they explored awe-inspiring terrain, pristine lakes and water falls, dizzying varieties of plants and whole cities now underwater, but clearly visible.

When Marion expressed her revulsion over the many scenes of death and mutilation she had witnessed, Linda explained a key tenet of Mayan theology. "In their culture, death was not the end, but a transition to a loftier reification and was received with joy as a gift from the gods. When one spouse left their body and journeyed to the spirit world, the survivor, eager to rejoin their beloved, rarely stayed alive long after the burial."

On the last day of shooting, Linda brought Marion to a small Indian enclave in the heart of the rain forest. The village was fairly empty. Chickens scampered about, avoiding the pigs, dogs and goats. A few women were doing laundry at a communal pond and old men dragged carts along a dirt path. The loudest sounds came from children, running around and around and around for no apparent reason. Marion took photographs of the huts and some of the locals. One of the larger shacks caught her attention. On the door was a poster of a radiant young woman in regal attire, complete with a crown and knives, peeling her flesh. The connection was immediate. It was the woman in the sculpture Marion saw on her way out of the burial grounds.

"This is the home of a Shaman," Linda said. "Her name is Ixchel and people come from distant villages for *advice,"* she snickered.

"Is that her . . . the Shaman?" Marion asked, pointing to the poster.

"No," she laughed. "Ixchel, the Shaman is much older. That is a picture of the actress who played the goddess on stage in Guatemala City. The Shaman put that picture on her door so visitors who want to find out what their ancestors are doing in the afterlife know where to go."

"So, Ixchel is a goddess?"

"The Mayan goddess of love and fortune. The natives believe she knows who is true and who is false, who will bring happiness and who will cause trouble."

"By she, you mean Ixchel the goddess or Ixchel the Shaman?"

"According to the Shaman," Linda said with a cynical smile, "she is an incarnation of the goddess and therefore possesses her powers. The natives believe she can predict the future."

"I have to meet her," Marion said. "Would she do a reading for me?"

Linda was taken aback. "I didn't think Americans believed in sorcerers."

"I'm not what you'd call devout, but this exotic place with

its underwater cities and fascinating artifacts is so full of mysteries, I feel I would be missing something if I didn't meet the shaman."

"I'm glad you were able to explore our ancient treasures," Linda was unusually defensive, "but I would not equate the genius of the Maya with crystal gazing utterances of a self-proclaimed shaman."

"I can't explain it, but I feel I must do this. How long can it take? I already found my true love so there's not much she can tell me about that. I know he's not false and I'm sure he won't bring trouble. Let's just take a peek at my future. If it's half as good as my present, that goddess is in for a big tip."

{ Chapter Seventeen }

A BURLAP CURTAIN HUNG over the opening to the tiny hut, making it hard to discern anything other than a gnarled old woman, presumably shaman Ixchel, incarnation of the Goddess of Love and Fortune, sitting cross-legged on an embroidered yellow and brown quilt. A large wooden cross hung on the wall. The only furnishings were a small wooden cabinet with a Bible resting on it and a tree trunk covered with a swatch of red carpet. On the dirt floor, next to the Shaman, in a clay ashtray, was something that looked like a freshly lit cigar, but the aroma gave it away. The shack was so full of peyote, Marion was afraid she was going to pass out.

With her eyes closed, the ageless crone said something in a dialect that sounded close to Spanish, but the fact that she had no teeth distorted any words Marion might have recognized.

"She asks you to sit," Linda said, pointing to the tree trunk. Marion made herself as comfortable as she could while Linda squatted on the dirt floor, between them.

Silence.

Marion looked at the shaman and smiled. The shaman's eyes remained closed.

More silence.

Marion was aware that time means something very different in these remote villages, but she didn't want to sit there all day. "Should I pay her now?" Marion asked Linda, who translated into dialect.

The shaman opened her eyes. Her blank gaze made it clear that she was blind. After a long pause, she responded. "No pay," Linda said. "You are an honored guest," she laughed nervously. It was clear from her tone that Linda, an archeologist and historian, was uncomfortable in this milieu.

Marion was getting impatient.

The shaman reached for her "cigar" and took several rapid, deep puffs holding her breath for an incredibly long time before exhaling. Some minutes later, obviously long enough for the peyote to grease her brain, she rested her hands on her lap, palms up and with her eyes closed, chanted something unintelligible.

Marion was beginning to feel a little woozy, definitely getting a buzz from the smoke. Slowly, the shaman raised her hands high above her head and waved them back and forth, then stopped abruptly. Her eyes still closed, she listened, apparently receiving a detailed communiqué.

Finally, she dropped her hands back in her lap and opened her sightless eyes. A luminous, toothless smile emerged. She spoke rapidly in Marion's direction for quite a long time, modulating all the way between falsetto and unintelligible murmur. She seemed to be delivering the most cheerful message. Marion couldn't wait to find out what she was saying.

She picked up a few words, but the dialect was nothing like the Spanish she knew.

"You are in love with a man," Linda translated. "He is your husband and he loves you. You have a very, very happy marriage."

"Tell her she's right on," Marion said, smiling. "The woman obviously has psychic powers."

The Shaman closed her eyes and nodded, apparently receiving more insights. Then, she spoke again in Marion's direction. Linda translated. "You will have a beautiful child."

"Whoa," Marion said. "I'm sorry to interrupt but I feel I have to interject a medical reality here. My ovaries burst when I was very young and I can never have a child."

Linda translated. The Shaman listened and shook her head. "You will have a child. She will be just like you, tall and fair with long wavy hair."

Marion whispered to Linda, "How did she know I was tall and fair with long wavy hair?"

Linda shrugged. The Shaman took another long hit on her cigar. She inhaled deeply and closed her eyes again. After a long, hazy silence, she burst forth with an incantation full of weird modulations that sounded as though the peyote got stuck in her throat and squeezed her vocal chords. When she finished, Linda was conspicuously quiet.

"What's going on?" Marion asked.

"Nothing. Foolishness. It is time for us to leave," Linda said.

"What is it?" Marion asked again.

Linda, clearly embarrassed, tried to evade the question with a frown. "Meaningless chatter. We should go now."

"Come on,' Marion pleaded. "I have to know what the woman said."

The shaman's sightless eyes opened and she was still smiling her toothless smile in Marion's direction. "Please," Marion said. "I have to know."

Reluctantly, Linda translated. "The Shaman says . . . your child . . . she will be tall and fair and beautiful, with long, wavy hair, just like you . . . and . . . she will care for you . . . when the love of your life dies."

Marion felt her heart stop. "When the love of my life dies?!" She screamed at the old crone, "It's a curse! Linda, please. Tell her to take it all back."

Linda said something rapidly in the dialect. Ixchel sat motionless and continued to smile. Marion waited for the shaman to say something, but she didn't. "NO! NO! NO," Marion cried. She was trapped. The curse was engulfing her and she had to undo it. She stood up and screamed at the old witch. "I can't live without my husband. Dan is my *bashert*. That means he is my soulmate forever. Do you understand that? Please, lady! I don't know if I believe any of this crap, but you are scaring the hell out of me." She turned to Linda. "Please tell her to take another hit of that peyote and invoke her Mayan ancestors or whoever the hell she talks to and get rid of that horrible, disgusting curse."

Linda translated and the woman nodded, but said nothing.

Marion was shaking like a leaf.

The shaman spoke again. Linda, who by now was very upset, translated. "Ixchel says one dies and one lives but no *llores,* no crying, because the one who dies, lives, and both die and both live. No *llores,* no tears because the child remains."

Marion started to bawl. She was confused, frightened. She didn't know what to do.

The old witch then said something in an uncharacteristically appeasing tone.

"What?!" Marion wailed barely able to speak.

"Ixchel says . . . be happy. Death means happy forever."

When Linda and Marion returned to the village, the crew was barbequing a whole goat for the wrap party. Marion ran to Dan, who was standing at the base of the twin pyramids. She threw her arms around his neck and held on for dear life.

"All of it is crazy. You know that," he said after she had told him what the shaman predicted. He gently guided her back to their hut.

"Of course I know," Marion said, but she didn't stop crying until they had a couple of shots of tequila straight from the bottle. "But the thought, however remote, that you would abandon me pulled the heart right out of my chest," Marion said.

"I will not abandon you and I am not dying anytime soon."

"But you will someday. What will I do then? Dan, let's make a pact. We die together."

"I'll call Nate Schlosser and ask him to draw it up."

"I mean it, Dan. I can't live without you."

"You won't have to. We have many beautiful years to celebrate our love together. We're *bashert,* remember? That's the deal and it doesn't change because some illiterate witch high on peyote says so."

"So you're not dying?"

"I am not dying and I will never leave you."

"You promise?"

"I promise. Cross my heart and hope to . . . no, forget that. Just the promise part, okay?"

"Okay," she was laughing even though the tears continued

to stream down her face. Dan embraced her and held on, but she pulled away suddenly.

"But she's Mayan. Those people knew things nobody else did."

"Her great-great-great ancestors knew some things, but they made a lot of mistakes too, remember?"

"Like what?"

"Like disappearing a thousand years ago."

Marion had nothing more to say, but she held onto him as tightly as she could.

"Instead of rushing back to L.A.," Dan said, "why don't we go to Cancun for a few days and depressurize? You love to snorkel."

"The old witch also said to tell my husband to stay away from the water. She said you're not a very good swimmer."

"Okay, now that's a challenge I accept," Dan said. "I'm a great swimmer. Not as good as you, but nobody is. This will give me a chance to prove that the Goddess of Love and Fortune doesn't know which end of her peyote is up."

He had barely fallen asleep that night when she suddenly screamed. "Dan! Dan!"

"I'm here, Marion. I'll always be here. Always."

She was adrift in a vague, demi-world, her eyes closed. Dan searched for a way to ease her anxieties but he was too tired to think straight. Having worked eighteen straight fourteen-hour days, he couldn't keep his eyes open and passed out.

Sometime later, he woke up and heard music coming from their tape deck. Apparently, unable to sleep, Marion got out of bed and put in the cassette, then crawled back into his arms and passed out while Jacques Brel and Rod McKuen sang the song that Dan and Marion had danced to so often.

Ne me quitte pas

Ne me quitte pas

If you go away, and I know you must

There is nothing left in this world to trust

Just an empty room full of empty space

Like the empty look I see on your face

I can tell you now as you turn to go

I'll be dying slowly till the next hello

Ne me quitte pas

Ne me quitte pas

Ne me quitte pas

Dan leaned back so that his tears wouldn't awaken the one he loved more than life.

SNORKELING IN CANCUN was pure delight. Gliding through the warm waves, Marion was in her element. She flirted with short blue tang fish that turned yellow and puckered as if waiting to be kissed and frolicked with schools of luminous four-eyed butterfish.

At home in the shallow reefs, Marion's energy returned. When she popped up to breathe, her bright smile erased Dan's anxieties and the stress of the past days drifted out to sea. "One of the things I don't believe in," she said, "is the Zodiac, but even as an astrological atheist, I cannot deny that I am a Pisces. I was born a creature of water, only to spend my days on land, but water I am and to water I shall return."

It was a welcome relief to see her enjoying herself with such abandon. Marion slid into the waves and within minutes her snorkel with the blue and white ping pong ball emerged twenty yards away. She popped up and laughed.

Unlike Marion, who was fearless, Dan never let down his guard. Determined to be the responsible protector, he kept a wary eye out for sharks, barracuda, eels, jellyfish, sea urchins and any other lurking danger.

"Where are you, intrepid lover?" she taunted. "I thought you were going to prove what a great a swimmer you are. If I have to depend on you to swim across the River Styx to bring me back, you are not engendering confidence." She bit her snorkel and dived deep.

Back on the sand, sitting on a colorful beach blanket, sipping Margaritas, Dan said, "If you are planning to swim all the way to Guam, please let me know."

"Wrong Ocean, Cap'n Ahab. I'm headed for Portugal."

Dan grabbed Marion's hand and dragged her back into the water. "Last one to reach Portugal is a rotten egg." They leapt through the waves and swam into each other's arms.

Marion wrapped her legs around Dan's waist and rolled with the surf. "I have not been to heaven, but it couldn't be better than this." Marion's face shone in the sun and her perfect smile soothed Dan's soul. Her worries about him dying seemed to be gone, no more hassles from the Madison Avenue crazies, no distractions from beach combers, just the two of them alone in an ocean of bliss.

"No *llores?*" Dan asked.

"No tears and no fears," Marion said, scrubbing off any vestige of that curse. Dan's wet lips met hers. With her eyes still closed she said, "If I were a girl, I'd be ringing."

THAT NIGHT AT DINNER, a four-piece band featured a vocalist with a pleasant enough voice who sang the familiar Mexican songs tourists expect to hear.

"I'm so glad we're alone, Dan. Whenever we expose ourselves to other people, the best we can hope for is that they're only wasting our time. The worst is that they leave a stain in the form of a curse. And a special finger to you, Shaman Ixchel! Talk to me about Adam and Eve, Rabbi. They were living in paradise before the snake offered to take them on a tour of the special trees. Why didn't they just tell him/her/or whatever gender the snake was, to bugger off and leave them alone to enjoy their sublime togetherness for all eternity? What I'm saying is we must never allow anyone or anything to contaminate our lives."

"I absolutely agree." Dan said. "It always heats up the grate."

"What grate is that?"

"The point of a classic Yiddish film, *Gan Eden Farloren,* starring a young Emmanuel Goldenberg and an even younger Hedwig Keisler."

"Sorry, never heard of any of them."

"Of course you have. They're among your favorite screen actors, only you know them by their *goyishe* names, Edward G. Robinson and Hedy Lamarr. The title *Gan Eden Farloren* would be *Paradise Lost* if it was ever translated, which it wasn't."

"I've seen a couple versions of *Paradise Lost,* but none in Yiddish. What's it about?"

"Briefly, *Gan Eden Farloren* is a love story about mice."

"How could I have missed it?" Marion loved the way Dan

revised films in the telling to enhance whatever point he wanted to make. Clearly, a literary device he acquired preaching from the pulpit, a lifetime ago. "So, nu? I'm all ears, Rabbi."

"Two mice lived happily in a cage that was part of a medical research project. One could even say lovingly, if mice are so inclined."

"Considering their accelerated increase in population over the millennia," Marion said, "I would have to agree that there is sufficient attraction between the sexes."

"It's been a long time since I saw the film, but it made a powerful impression on me. As I recall, the mice are doing what comes naturally, when the lab technician—played by the great Meshilim Weisenfruend, as he was known then, or Paul Muni, to you—tries to gauge the amount of external pressure mice can tolerate. He heats the grate inside their cage and the mice become stressed. As the temperature rises, they begin to fidget, then, they chase each other around the cage. As the tiny enclosure gets hotter and hotter, they become aggressive, bare their teeth and soon, the loving couple viciously attack one another. Before the mice can kill each other, the technician turns down the heat and the grate returns to normal. Slowly, the mice stop assaulting one another. Some observable skepticism remains for a while, but unlike humans, a mouse's memory isn't good enough to hang on to grievances for very long. With the passage of time, they return to their benevolent behavior patterns. For the mice, there was a happy ending.

"Not so for the humans in a parallel story. A loving couple played by the young Hedy and Edward G. are blessed with an ideal marriage. Totally devoted to one another, they build an enchanted cottage in the woods. They read, talk, go for walks, laugh, make love. In every way, their life is pure paradise.

"One day a boyhood friend of the husband arrives and asks if he can stay for a while. Who can say no to an old buddy? But when the husband isn't around, the friend mocks the wife and treats her contemptuously. Soon, the friend's reason for his visit emerges. He is jealous of the wife. She angrily confronts her husband for allowing this person to enter their perfect world and demands that he leave. From there, the movie cuts back and forth between two parallel stories: mice in a cage and young lovers in their personal paradise."

"Ah, my rabbi turned director. Tell me which is which, so I'll know who to root for." Marion beamed at Dan.

"The film opens on a tight shot of the cage. The technician turns up the thermostat. Immediately, the mice become agitated and hostile. Intercut with the couple: The husband's boyhood friend becomes abusive towards the wife. Cut to the lab. The technician raises the heat again. The mice bare their teeth and chase one another around their cage. Intercut with the couple: The wife demands that the husband tell his friend to leave, but the husband can't do that. They spent so much of their youth together, first as classmates, then roommates sharing all the experiences of adolescence. When the husband sees his friend treating his wife disdainfully and the wife fighting back, making equally stinging accusations about the friend's sexuality, he tries to placate them both. The guest is appalled that his best friend—and possibly more—has turned against him and leaves. Close-up of mice. The grate gets hotter and they viciously claw one another. Back to the couple: She feels betrayed by her husband's lack of loyalty to her and angrily belittles him, suggesting that his confused sexuality is the core of the problem. He feels his manhood is threatened and they find themselves verbally assaulting one another. Back to the mice. The lab technician turns down the grate. The heat that once inflamed them is gone and over time, the mice resume their peaceful behavior. Intercut with the couple. Their grate does not cool down. To the contrary, it grows hotter over time and even though the friend is long gone, the couple cannot forgive the insults they heaped on one another.

Dan paused for effect.

Marion almost jumped out of her chair. "So how does it end?"

"Final shot of the cottage. A blazing fire fills the frame, obliterating everything. The paradise they once cherished is lost forever."

"We must never allow anyone or anything to heat up our grate," Marion said, a serious look on her face.

THE NEXT MORNING they were snorkeling again, but the water felt strange. Dan looked around for Marion. The blue ping-pong ball in her snorkel bobbed up and down, but she didn't stay in very long. When she returned to shore, she silently wrapped the large beach towel tightly around herself. Marion was shivering, despite the intense heat.

"Are you okay?"

She nodded but her teeth chattered.

"Did you catch a chill?"

She didn't answer.

"The water did feel different today," he said.

Marion nodded.

"There were warm spots that turned frigid. Then, a few feet away, the water heated up again." Dan said. "Did you notice that?"

She nodded. "I'm tired," she said. "Let's take a nap before dinner."

OUT OF A DEEP SLEEP, Marion let out a horrifying shriek.

"What's wrong?!"

"I just got a burst of pain that started in my hip and radiated all the way down my leg, like a sharp knife slicing through my flesh."

"Does it still hurt?"

"No. For a moment, it was terrible . . . but now it's gone."

Dan said he told the concierge that the water felt strange. "He said this time of year, currents from the Gulf Stream bring in diverse tides and fresh water mingles with brine from the ocean. Do you think that's what caused it?"

She shrugged, clearly troubled.

"Want me to call a doctor?"

"No."

"How about a massage?"

"That won't help."

She wasn't up to going out for dinner, so they ordered food in the room. When she didn't eat anything, Dan began to wonder . . . and worry.

"Maybe you overdid it with all the snorkeling yesterday. Would you like a Tylenol?"

She shook her head. A deep gloom settled over her.

"Talk to me. What do you think it is?"

She waited until she could speak the word that haunted her throughout her childhood. "I know what it is . . . lupus."

"What's lupus?"

"It's a curse. That's what my grandmother called it. Lupus is a malicious auto-immune disease that attacks every joint in the body. The ankles and wrists swell and the pain is unbearable. It feels like you're being skinned alive. My grandmother lived a horrible life and died a worse death . . ."

"But your joints aren't swollen."

"No . . . not yet."

PART SEVEN

Pangs of The Messiah

{ Chapter Eighteen }

NOT YET . . . *lupus . . . a horrible life and a worse death . . .*

Sitting alone in Rocky's empty office, those words scraped the walls of Dan's brain like fingernails on a blackboard. He recalled the hints and intimations Marion picked up over the years. She saw it all coming. He never did.

Rocky flung the door open and rushed in fuming. Less than a step behind was Sergeant Jacobovich, who made a point of ignoring Dan. "I'm sorry to keep you waiting," Rocky said. "I didn't think it would take this long." He went straight to his desk and searched through a pile of neatly stacked folders. The sergeant with the personality of a vampire stood opposite him, hands on her hips, cigarette dangling from her mouth.

"It's a holiday. Nobody is checking permits today!" Rocky was obviously angry.

"No permits, no release," she said without emotion.

Rocky continued to look through his desk drawers, one at

a time. Finally, he came up with a document and handed it triumphantly to the sergeant. She read it carefully and turned to the door without a word. On her way out, she looked at Dan. "Think about what I told you. *Commando Squad* . . . ? *One* and *Two*? That's your legacy?" She sneered and left, not bothering to shut the door.

"What?!"

Rocky stood at the window sizing up the traffic below. "Don't take it personally," he said. "Busting balls is what she's paid to do. It's a lousy job but she's good at it. The road is still pretty congested but it's as good as it's going to get," Rocky said. He removed his khaki shirt and took a bright festive one from the coat rack.

When they approached the exit, the guard asked them to show their passports, which were carefully read and recorded. When that was approved, they were subjected to a complete body check, emptying of pockets, pat downs and a slow walk through the X-ray machine.

"They don't know me," Dan said on the way to the parking lot, "but you? Do you have to go through this every day?"

"In the twenty-first century, security is the new oxygen. Without it, we don't survive," Rocky said.

Traffic was heavy on the narrow highway, but there was movement. The greatest hazards on the road were throngs of happy revelers on foot, bicycles, skateboards and a variety of improvised carts that snaked between tightly packed cars, trucks and buses. At the first intersection, Rocky turned onto the road bearing a sign that read: Ochos Rios, 67.3 km.

"I thought you guys lived in Port Antonio."

"We do, but Molly thought it best if you and I join her at mid-point rather than chase each other around the island. It's always a madhouse during holidays."

"What's she doing in Ochos Rios?

"She's spending the morning with her Obeahman."

"Her what?"

"Obeahman. That's an honorary title for what is essentially a tribal psychic."

"So, that's where Molly is? With a psychic? Oy," he sighed, unable to withhold his disappointment.

"Not a psychic, exactly. More like a Hasidic rabbi slash yogi on an acid trip."

"So what does she do with this guy? Pray, stand on her head or hallucinate?"

"None of the above. He's teaching her how to access miracles."

Dan looked at Rocky and couldn't decide whether he was joking or serious. Finally, he asked as gently as he could, "Do you have any idea how weird that sounds?"

"I think you should know," Rocky said, "that Molly's life is totally about finding ways to invoke the miraculous."

Dan said nothing but his silence could be read several ways, none of them positive.

"What . . . ?" Rocky said. "You don't believe in miracles or you don't think it's possible to access them?"

"I am not a believer," Dan said, not sure if Rocky was serious.

"Have you never experienced something you couldn't explain rationally?"

"Who hasn't? Like everyone else, I've witnessed many baffling phenomena in my life, but I can't honestly say I attribute them to miracles."

Rocky let that sink in.

"What do you believe, Rocky?"

"I pretty much agree with Moshe Dayan. As a military

strategist—and secularist—he said that he could not *believe* in miracles, but he *depended* on them."

"So you're not a believer, either," Dan said. "You just assume the cosmos will deliver whenever necessary, but if it doesn't, it's cool because you didn't really think it would in the first place."

"That's about as far as I go with miracles."

"Obviously Molly goes farther?"

"A whole lot farther, pretty much halfway around the world."

"Did she tell you why she went to Nepal?"

"She said it was the shock of suddenly being abandoned. When Marion was no longer 'on this plane' as Molly describes it, she was confused and needed direction, but didn't know where to find it."

"And she thought it would be waiting for her on a mountain in the Himalayas?"

"Not in the beginning. For reasons she'll have to explain, her journey began on Mount Sinai and as we all now acknowledge, that was an important stop, but the more she found herself falling in love with me, the more complicated it became. How should she proceed with her life? She needed guidance, which had always come from one source, Marion. Not being able to consult her was maddening, so she set out to find the Shrine in Kathmandu that Marion once visited, but when she arrived she discovered it had been destroyed in an earth quake years before. Not knowing where else to go, she entered the nearest Ashram."

"How did that work out?"

"It didn't," Rocky said. "That particular sect believed that in order to achieve enlightenment, the body must be disciplined to embrace suffering. Molly was in so much pain at the end of her first day, she knew she was in the wrong place. Marion definitely did not believe there is anything virtuous about suffering, especially invoking it voluntarily, like walking barefoot on hot coals, even if you think you don't feel the pain. Her advice, according to Molly, would be, 'why in hell are you walking on hot coals? What are you, stupid?'"

Dan laughed out loud. "That was Marion talking. No doubt about it. I could actually hear her saying that. So, why did Molly stay in Nepal?"

"She needed to get her bearings. There was no point running around the world. She wouldn't find Marion that way. The only place to go was inward. She recalled the *mind-travel* exercises she and Marion shared when she was a child. Meditating deeply, Molly was able, not only to visualize, but to experience the exhilaration of being together with Marion at specific moments in time. Those images formed virtual bridges in Molly's mind and she traveled across them every night, hoping to connect with Marion. Finally, one night during a final phase of the moon, lights appeared in the sky resembling an aurora borealis and through it, Marion emerged amid a shower of meteors."

"How did she look? What did she say?" Dan couldn't help but ask.

"Molly said she looked ethereal. Passing through countless sources of flashing lights, Marion told her that she must access the realm of parallel universes. That was all she said and her image faded. Molly tried hard to understand what that meant. '*Parallel* universes?' She had long accepted Marion's idea of *multiple* universes, but she understood that to mean sequential, so that when we pass from this plane, that is, when we die, our soul becomes an incorporeal form of energy and continues to evolve to the next level. But the idea of parallel universes suggests that all forms of life—in every incarnation—exist simultaneously. That sounded totally different and she struggled to understand what that meant.

"After more weeks of meditation, Marion appeared again. The lights were just as bright, but more stable and she stayed longer. Marion told her, 'Once you enter the realm of parallel universes, you will find true enlightenment and you will be linked to your soulmates for all eternity.' Molly had only one question: 'How do I get there?' Marion told her to return immediately to Israel. From there, she and I would both proceed to Jamaica, a place of miracles, during the Jubilee, a *time* of miracles. Then, everything would be revealed."

Dan tried to clear the fog in his head. His bedeviling recollection of what Molly said last night: *"Marion is here, waiting for you!"* was maddening. But to hear Rocky casually repeat that this was the precise time and place where fantasies were to materialize, was totally disorienting. After all, Rocky was a rational, secular man. But he talked about Molly's search for the miraculous as though she were shopping for a pair of patent leather pumps. *Everything will be revealed*? What will? When and how? And why Jamaica? Didn't he ask Molly how Marion knew he would be assigned to Jamaica before he did? Dan had no doubt that it all came from Molly but how could Rocky simply repeat it as though it was acceptable fact? He said he doesn't believe in miracles! So, what *is* he saying . . . and why?

Dan's insides were roiling. To say that he and Marion will be *rejoined* was too painfully cynical to be anything but wishful thinking and he didn't dare get too close to the edge of that cliff. He had awakened too many nights soaked in sweat and bathed in tears with a heart broken in a thousand pieces lamenting a life that was and will never be again. *Rejoined?*

That's the word she used. What kind of heartless delusion is that and how can Molly taunt him with false hope? Doesn't she understand how that exacerbates his suffering? All he thought about since the night he met Marion twenty-nine years ago was being together. If he could have kept her body in his home, breathing or not, he would have—or so he thought on those weird, drunken nights when he did think about that. The brutal fact is that she's gone and his life during the past two years had turned into instantaneous crying fests. He watched an old movie of Al Jolson singing *Kol Nidre* to his dying father in *The Jazz Singer* and he wept uncontrollably. He saw snatches of *Love, Actually*. Every scene was about love and lovers and his heart broke again and again. He had become the weepy old man he always feared he might turn into if he lived long enough—and God damn it, he had. But . . . recalling how intensely Molly spoke to him—her face inches from his—with complete conviction: *"Marion is here, Dan . . . she's waiting for you,"* and she really believes it!

Dan knew all about believing and what it was like to possess perfect faith. In his youth when he prayed he spoke directly to God. His heart surged when he inhaled the first flowers of spring. The message was gloriously clear. All's well with the world! But that was when Dan was young. The problem is life. It strikes a mortal blow to the very soul of the believer and shows him—indisputably—that his faith is naïve. Bad things happen to everybody. It doesn't matter if you believe or not. Aside the momentary good feeling that things will turn out for the best, the reality is that they rarely do, so every decision must be based not on faith or even her weak sister, hope, but on figuring out how to survive the worst possible outcome of every situation.

On the other hand, look what happened since last night.

His comfortable cynicism was being seriously challenged. His new dilemma was not that he didn't believe anymore. At this point in his agonized life, he couldn't trust himself not to! For the past two and a half years he felt like Prometheus bound to a rock, only instead of the eagle coming to eat his liver every day, the most formidable challenge he had to confront was getting out of bed in the morning. His life was a witch's brew of tears that boiled over at every inopportune moment. He had no more control over his weeping than he had over any other part of his miserable life. She's gone and everything he lived for was taken from him, so what's left, other than to sit on death row and wait his turn? But all of a sudden, when he was next in line and prepared to die, he is being told—and despite himself, really considering the possibility—that he is about to be . . . rejoined? He should be ecstatic, not filled with dread, right? So, why wasn't he? Is it because he is afraid to trust the words, mere words . . . but actual words—spoken by Molly, who swears that the message she bore came directly from Marion?

The clash in his soul became so intense, he felt his head was about to explode. Turning to Rocky, he said. "I need you to clear up something for me right now."

"If I can."

"Why am I here? Is there going to be a wedding or was I brought here to be part of some phantasmagoric Mardi Gras pageant?"

The usually amiable Rocky suddenly became visibly upset. He forced the car to the side of the road, turned off the engine and stared at Dan. "You're asking me if there's going to be a wedding? How the hell do I know? I was counting on you to tell me!"

"Me?"

"I thought for sure Molly confided in you."

"Why would you think that?"

"When she came home last night, she was elated. She said, 'It's all set. Now that Dan's here, everything is in place. It could only happen through him.'"

"What does that mean?"

"I assumed she was talking about the wedding. What did she say to you?"

"All she said was that there will be a wedding or there won't, but that wasn't the reason she brought me here."

Gentle Rocky went ballistic. "Is that a yes or no or maybe we should wait until our souls transmigrate to some version of Disneyland?" Rocky was in pain and his eyes pleaded with Dan. "What do I do?"

Dan said nothing. The traffic in his own head was far too congested to hear Rocky's cries for help.

"So," Rocky said, "am I supposed to pretend that I don't know if the sun will rise after it sets? It always has and it always will despite—forgive me for saying this—some inscrutable message Molly received from Marion. That's when she accuses me of obstructing the process by trying to manipulate what I call the future. What I call the future? What does the rest of the world call it? The whenever?" Rocky steamed. "So, in answer to your question, why are you here? As far as I know it is to conduct a wedding, which according to Molly, will happen or it won't. 'First things first,' she keeps saying. What I would like to know is where our marriage ranks in her order of priorities."

After a long silence, Rocky spoke hesitatingly. "In one of her recent *encounters,* she says Marion told her that what appears to be miraculous in our sphere is commonplace in others. According to what Marion *transmitted* to Molly, when one successfully accesses parallel universes, it is entirely possible to transit from one incarnation to another. Dan's brain was suddenly pinched. "You mean a person who can access the *program* can travel back and forth between life and death?"

"According to what Molly says, yes."

"Did she say how one accesses that program? I mean, are only certain people endowed . . ." Dan stopped because he realized that what he was saying was as incomprehensible as anything he had ever heard or uttered, drunk or sober, but how could he not ask?

"Whatever Molly was searching for, she is convinced that this is where she's going to find it," Rocky said. "Here in Jamaica, on the Day of Jubilation when journeys converge."

"Where did you hear that expression?" Dan asked, wondering if Rocky had also fallen under the spell of the Island.

"Everywhere I go, people are singing about journeys converging. Damned if I know what it means."

That tingling sensation was challenging the walls of Dan's cynicism again but this time it might have found a breach. *A program that can be accessed . . . ?* That possibility tip-toed furtively around his brain.

"Molly says she has been communicating regularly with Marion . . . but more frequently now that you're here."

Dan didn't respond.

"According to Marion, via Molly, I understand . . . you had a personal experience involving miracles," Rocky said. "Didn't Molly talk to you about that?"

"No."

"It is true that Marion went to Nepal, isn't it?"

"Yes."

"You went with her?"

"Rocky, if we're going to be as close as I hope we will, say what you mean."

"I have to know if I'm about to marry an elevated soul or a crackpot, assuming there will actually be a wedding. You can help by telling me about Nepal. Did Marion experience a miracle? And if you were there, did you witness it? I know what Molly believes. What I have to know from you—is any of it true?"

"What happened in Nepal . . . is it true?" Dan repeated the question and tried to find words to describe the indescribable.

"J'ai vu. c'est vrai. C'est passé."

"C'est vrai?" Rocky repeated. "Then, it *is* all true?"

C'est vrai. C'est passé. Those words, first uttered by the French rheumatologist in Jerusalem in answer to Marion's frantic plea are what set the pilgrimage in motion. When the doctor told them what his patient experienced in a Nepalese village, it was as though a whole new dimension of light entered the room. But even then, the doctor insisted that he did not—could not—believe what he saw with his own eyes. As a physician, he could not accept what actually transpired because it defied every scientific principle he lived by, but *"c'est passé,"* it did happen. When he described—in detail—the miracle he witnessed, Marion believed every word. Dan did not.

Marion was right.

Dan wasn't wrong because what the doctor told them was incredible . . . even though it was entirely true.

{ Chapter Nineteen }

THE FIRST SYMPTOMS of Marion's disease appeared while they were snorkeling in Cancun and by the time they returned to Los Angeles the pain was unbearable. Lying on an antiseptic examination table, Marion stared angrily into the cold florescent lights overhead as her rheumatologist Dr. Alan Marcus moved her legs and feet in circular patterns to determine the range of motion. Dan sat in a plastic chair opposite her, feeling every twitch of Marion's aching body. When she experienced a sharp pain, Dan's face showed it and Dr. Marcus stopped.

"I'm cursed," Marion seethed.

"You could say that," Alan said sympathetically. "Unfortunately, you are suffering from the onset of lupus."

"I knew it! The same fucking curse that made my grandmother's life a misery,"

"Fortunately, we have a variety of palliatives today that weren't available to your grandmother and we can relieve many of your symptoms, but what we know for a certainty is that stress defeats every medication we have, which is why I'm urging you to find a less frenzied way to earn a living."

"And do what, Alan? I make films. That's all I've ever wanted to do. It's who I am . . . who we are. Dan and I are a team. I can't just quit."

"Your body sent you a warning. If you refuse to acknowledge it, you run the risk of serious lupus flairs."

"As bad as Cancun?"

"I can't say for certain, but there's always the possibility that they can get worse, maybe much worse."

MARION SPENT HER TIME READING and occasionally writing, but after six months of trying to decide how to spend the next day, she began to feel her life slipping away. Marion was a workaholic and a gifted film editor. She loved her work and was nourished by it. Marion tried hard not to nag, but with each week that passed, she became more and more frustrated.

"If God wanted me to loaf around all day, He would have fashioned my back in the shape of a hammock. I need to work, Dan."

"I know, honey. I would love nothing more than for us to do another film, but remember how cruel this disease can be. Alan knows how eager you are to get back to work. He'll be the first to tell you when he thinks your body can handle it."

"I'm taking all the pills and they work wonders. I'm in better physical shape than I've been in years. I think I'm ready, Dan. I really do."

At their next visit to the rheumatologist, Marion was determined to show how supple her body was. She dropped to the floor and did five perfect pushups.

"You are doing a great job and your symptoms have

decreased substantially," Dr. Marcus said, "but your microscopic tests show that the synovial fluid in your joints is still at a low level of viscosity. Not the best news, I'm afraid. I'm glad you're feeling better, but you're a long way from resuming your former lifestyle."

After another six months of restless "resting," Marion was climbing the walls when she discovered that E.S.I. was sending *Valor* into turnaround. *Valor* was an original screenplay based on a true story that she and Dan wrote several years before. Steve had agreed to finance it and it was the perfect vehicle for them to start working together again. The thought that it was going into turnaround, the cemetery for great screenplays that never get produced, made her furious.

"Why is Steve doing this? I thought he loved *Valor.*"

"He does. He said it's the best war story he's ever read but when I told him we didn't know when you'd be ready to go back to work . . ."

"Are you crazy? I'm ready now! I have never been this ready. I want to make that film, Dan. I can do it, dammit."

"Marion . . . there are a dozen hazardous stunt scenes, synchronized sea chases with boats blowing up, parachute jumps, multiple weapon underwater battles and close combat in caves. You should know that. You wrote the script! An action film like that is like stepping into a giant pressure cooker."

"Talk about pressure," Marion said, "I've spent over a year reading every damn book since Guttenberg and I'll burst if I don't start working again. When I'm working, I feel alive. Loafing just squeezes every ounce of energy out of me and that's making me really sick. I mean it, Dan. I can't live like this."

"But Dr. Marcus said . . ."

"I love Alan but it's my life, Dan. *Valor* is the perfect vehicle for us now. Look where we'll be. Rome. I love that city almost as much as Paris . . . and Israel! You've always wanted to take me there. We're lucky to be alive and together. This is our time. Let's not squander it!"

Dan's dilemma: He was aching to do another film with Marion but . . .

"Please, Dan." The look on her face left him no choice. He felt his head throbbing as he tried to think of ways to create a protective environment. He could make sure Marion had the best assistants and working conditions, but beyond that . . . he prayed her decision was the right one.

Dan called Steve and said Marion felt great. They were ready to go back to work. He asked Steve to put the production elements together. Steve agreed, and wished his friends luck . . . and good health.

Marion was right about Rome. The first few weeks of shooting were like an extended holiday. Marion was back in her old cutting rooms at Cinecitta. Since the more complicated scenes hadn't been shot yet, the light editing schedule allowed for long lunches with old friends and dinners with Dan in Trastevere.

Israel was another story. Problems with traffic, terrorism and daily labor strikes were minor compared to the bad news Dan got at the end of their sixth week of shooting.

"They're pulling our C-147s?" Dan couldn't believe what Mookie, the Israeli co-producer, just said. "Half the shots we need are either in or around those damn troop carriers," Dan fumed. "I thought that was all arranged."

"It was," Mookie said, stopping to light a new cigarette from the stub he had been holding. There's an incursion on the norther border. Joint Syrian and Lebanese forces launched a surprise attack and we've got to send troops to block their advance."

Dan was fuming. "How long will that take? A day, a week, a month?"

Mookie was too depressed to try to answer, which he couldn't in any event.

"So, what do we do?"

The conference call to Steve was brief and to the point. "I hate news like this. I don't want to say I warned you about shooting in a war zone, but I did. Pull the damn plug and cut our losses."

Mookie, who had put up half the budget, was visibly shaking.

"Pull the plug?" Marion was angry. "What about trying to figure out how to save the film?"

"Any ideas?" Dan looked around the room.

No words but lots of sighs.

In the silence that followed, Dan noticed that all eyes were on Marion. She studied the shooting script and made notes on a dozen pages.

"Nu?" Mookie finally asked the question that was on everybody's mind: "Is there any way to edit the scenes that were scheduled for the C-147s without actually being in the planes?"

Dan frowned. He had been in these situations before. Shutting down a production is painful for everyone but it's a fact of life and he accepted it.

Marion did not and she wasn't about to give up without a fight. Finally, she closed the manuscript. "I don't know, she said. "I'll need at least a week to go through all the footage . . . maybe two. We'll talk then."

Marion worked long hours every day, piecing together

scenes, frame by frame, ordering stock shots, recording musical stings and reprinting weeks of dailies. Dan insisted on sitting with her in the editing room.

"I've got three assistants working two shifts," Marion said. "Why don't you go back to the hotel and get some rest?"

"I'm fine," Dan yawned. "I want to be here in case you need anything."

"We all know what I need," Marion said, "a couple of C-147s . . . ."

Dan was fast asleep on his chair. Marion couldn't help smiling. She loved the way he looked when he slept. Her love flowed and she felt energized by his presence.

Ten days later, department heads sat nervously in the screening room as Marion narrated the new version. The editing worked wonders. By pacing and inserting quick cuts, focusing more on tight shots of actors and less on the plane, relying more on creative sound and stock visual effects, it was possible to believe they were actually in flight!

"These aren't the best stock shots," she said, "but we can get the ones we need. It will cost a few bucks but nothing compared to what you'd lose if we had to pull the plug. We'll need at least a week to build mockups on a soundstage and a few days to shoot inserts. We'll have to call back a few actors but that shouldn't be a problem either . . ."

Marion saved the film and the producers were ecstatic. At the screening, a few people commented that Marion appeared to have lost a lot of weight. Dan didn't notice. To him, she was always perfect, but in Israel, everybody noticed. Among Jews, an adult who is cadaverously thin is more upsetting than a twelve-year-old who brings home a B- in Algebra.

"Why are you so skinny?" The taxi driver, who picked her up that morning, was alarmed. "What did you eat for breakfast? You call that a meal? Let's stop at my house. My wife will feed you. It's not good a grown person should look like you look." Marion had never seen the man before and shook it off. In Israel everybody is *mishpocha!*

At the wrap party, the producers gave Marion a silver-covered Bible. They were grateful to her for preserving the integrity of the film while saving them a bundle of money.

THE NEXT MORNING, they drove to Jerusalem and settled into a charming room in the King David Hotel with spectacular views of the Mosque of Omar and the Judean Hills. That night they went to an Arab restaurant in the Old City. Dan ordered *marouch* with dates and a fine French Bourgogne, which he and Marion devoured. For the first time in many weeks, she was in great spirits. On the way home, they walked hand in hand through subdued cobblestone streets, harmonizing. ". . . like a bird on a wire . . ."

Back in the room, they fired up a doobie and topped off the evening with delicious, holy sex. The next morning, they slept in, read the paper and had lunch plans with a former teacher of Dan's, now living in Jerusalem, to look forward to.

YEHOSHUA KLEIN was a charismatic young professor when Dan was a student at the Seminary. Teaching a class in medieval Hebrew poetry, Yehoshua invited students to his home. There he laid out tables filled with dates, figs and vats of wine as was the custom in twelfth century Malaga. The price of entry for each student was an original poem in classical Hebrew extolling the pleasures of wine, women and song. Yehoshua inspired his students and they loved him.

Marion and Dan waited patiently in the elegant hotel dining room. Dan heard that Yehoshua had been afflicted with a severe form of multiple sclerosis and was not surprised when he arrived in a wheelchair. Ziva, his wife, was a charming woman who said she remembered Dan as a student. A young man they introduced as their nurse also accompanied them. Dan embraced Yehoshua in his chair and noticed that he leaned heavily to one side, but his broad smile heralded the robust, energetic scholar Dan remembered so well. The minute Yehoshua met Marion, they engaged each other with such zeal, Dan could hardly get a drink order out of them.

During that conversation, Yehoshua introduced her to Gilgamesh, the legendary Mesopotamian epic. That story was particularly poignant for Marion in that it praised youth and vigor as the foremost blessings of the gods.

"But every one of their benefactions carries with it an equally menacing curse," Yehoshua expounded. "Those who receive the gifts of beauty and health are condemned one day to bear the torment and burdens of age and decrepitude. *'If only we could live forever,'* was Gilgamesh's dream and pursuing immortal youth was his enduring goal, which of course, he never achieved."

Marion was intrigued and wrote voluminous notes. Delighted to have found such an eager student, Yehoshua declaimed his favorite passages from Gilgamesh, first in Sumerian, then Acadian and finally, English. *"Youth is as beautiful as it is transitory and the dynamism that propels it cruelly passes away with age."*

Marion was so taken with the allegory of Gilgamesh and his meditation on the inevitable decomposition of the body that she had to express her opposition to the Hebrew God's seriously flawed plan.

"It's hard for me accept a God capable of creating heaven and earth, omniscient and all powerful, who could have been so stupid as to place a serpent in the garden. Life could be perfect if we didn't have to face death. Is that the best an infallible deity could come up with?"

"Unfortunately, or fortunately, we are the way God fashioned us," Yehoshua said. "In His plan, life is terminal."

"That is because God is an underachiever," Marion proclaimed.

"God is an underachiever?" Yehoshua howled with laughter. "That is the funniest thing I ever heard."

Later, when Dan recalled what occurred next, he understood why Marion associated it with her worst fears.

While Yehoshua was laughing so hysterically at Marion's joke, his body began to shake uncontrollably. He was obviously having a seizure of some kind. The nurse immediately took restraining belts from the pocket in back of the wheelchair and secured Yehoshua firmly in his seat. He took a syringe from his black bag and injected it into his forearm.

Marion was white as a ghost.

"This happens sometime when he gets excited," Ziva said. "He'll be okay once I get him home."

They said goodbyes as best they could and promised to stay in touch. In the elevator on the way back to their room, Marion was in shock. "That's going to happen to me, Dan," Marion whispered.

THE NEXT MORNING Marion woke up with a shriek. Lupus in all its fury assaulted every joint. Her wrists and ankles were swollen and every time she turned over in bed or tried to sit up, she let out a bloodcurdling scream. Dan was dumbstruck.

Marion had experienced Lupus flairs before, but nothing like this. Her eyes bulged and her face twisted in agony. It was as though the life was being squeezed out of her. Where to turn? What to do? Dan's mind froze. This was worse than terrible. It was . . .

Her scream shook Dan to his core.

"Where do you keep your pain killers?" He panicked.

"Over the sink!"

Dan rummaged through the glass shelf, past the comb, brush, makeup, glasses, tooth paste . . . floss . . ."I don't see them."

"In my bag . . . God! I can't stand this!"

"Which bag?"

"The green one next to my hair dryer . . . never mind, I'll . . ." she tried to get up and fell back with another chilling scream.

Dan found the green bag and nervously ruffled through it. What was he looking for? How would he know? He ran back to the bedroom with the bag, but Marion didn't have the strength to take it. The pain was excruciating. She rolled from side to side, unable to find even the slightest relief. Dan found a large bottle with a label that sounded familiar. It was Ultram E.R. He grabbed a glass of water from her night table, gently picked up her head and tried to get her to swallow two pills.

"That's worthless, you idiot!" Marion screamed. Dan froze. "I'm sorry, Dan . . . I just . . . E.R. means extended relief! I need help now! God . . . this is so awful. I can't stand it!"

Dan was totally immobilized by Marion's helplessness—and his own! She groaned in waves of pain. Obviously the Ultram E.R. wasn't a good idea. What is? He fumbled through the other bottles in the green bag but none of them looked familiar. He ran to the phone and called the hotel desk. "Help me. I need a doctor, immediately, a rheumatologist if you can find one, but you've got to get him up here right away. My wife is in excruciating pain . . . *Dachuf, dachuf,* urgent, urgent!"

The sympathetic concierge said he would do his best but there was a hospital strike and every available doctor was manning emergency wards.

'This *is* an emergency, damn it." Dan shouted, then pleaded, then cajoled. "Please! My wife is suffering terribly. You must help me," he said in Hebrew, then in English, but neither seemed to get anything more than sympathetic sighs. The concierge assured Dan that he understood and promised to do everything possible to find a doctor. Meanwhile, Marion's pain became increasingly worse.

"I can't take this!" she mumbled. "Please God, let me die."

Dan was horror-stricken. He had to do something.

"Where does it hurt?" How stupid of him to ask, he thought. What could he do if he knew, but he had to say something. He never felt so helpless or in so much sorrow as he watched his beloved tremble in agony.

"Every part of my horrible body is exploding!" She said. "I want to die. I have to get away from this!"

Dan realized he was still holding the phone. Something. He had to think of something! "Send up compresses . . . how the hell do you say compresses in Hebrew? Lots of small towels and plenty of ice, and . . . and quickly, *dachuf! dachuf!!*"

He hung up and wondered if ice was the right thing. Maybe he should have ordered heating pads. What to do? He finally found a Percocet and gave it to Marion with a glass of water. That would take some time to kick in too, but at least he was doing *something*. He had to let Marion know that he was totally there for her. There would be compresses and a doctor was called and there will be an end to this nightmare. At least he hoped that was the message she was getting by his running around the room, opening the door and yelling at the maids in the hall. He needed help badly and didn't know where to find it.

The towels and ice finally arrived and Dan did his best to apply compresses, but Marion was still writhing from side to side. She couldn't find a position that didn't feel like she was being burned alive. He derived some comfort for having ordered ice rather than heat because the swelling seemed to respond to the cold. He tried to keep her legs from flailing off the bed, so that the ice, wrapped in towels would stay on. Hopefully that would reduce the swelling.

After what seemed like an eternity, the Percocet kicked in and despite the anguish, her voice began to exhibit modest signs of relief. "This is intolerable. Why am I living? Is this what my life is going to be like from now on?" Her wrists were still red and tender. Dan tried to help her . . . but how? He didn't know exactly . . . just warm her hands, calm them, maybe.

She pulled away and screamed. "You can't touch my wrists! I don't mean to shout at you, but . . . why is God hurling these plagues at me? Lupus is the eleventh plague and our dim-witted God is smiting me with it. Why? Am I worse than frigging pharaoh? He only got ten! Mine just keep coming. They're endless! Our God is so unfair! We picked the worst God ever. He's not only cruel and stupid, He's worthless. I'm going to pray now, God, even though I know You don't give a damn.

"Heavenly Father, please drown me in the Red Sea! Don't part the waters. Just mind your own business and let me sink. Can you do that much, you slacker?!"

Through all the anguish, watching Marion's humor emerge, however dark, Dan felt a hint of relief. Her strongest survival weapon had always been her droll wit, if only she could draw on that.

The ice did help. The swelling diminished. The tremors passed and slowly, her breathing became more or less normal, although she was totally exhausted.

She lay for several minutes, quiet, miserable. Finally she said, "At least there's one crumb of comfort. That old witch in Chechuacan was a fraud. I don't have to worry about you dying before me."

"Don't be too sure. Lupus hurts like hell, but Dr. Marcus said it's rarely terminal."

"Oh, my God! What if I'm cursed with a long life? That's the worst nightmare of all. Honey, believe me, I know how horrible it would be for you without me and I would do anything to prevent that . . . but I can't take this. It's too much . . ." She sat up in bed. ". . . and I have to pee. Bad."

"Do you think you can make it to the bathroom?"

She tried to get out of bed, but couldn't. Desolate, she shook her head. "What am I going to do? Pee all over the bed? This is so humiliating."

Dan bent over and tried to lift her. Marion never weighed more than a hundred pounds and now even less but the king size bed was unusually low and she was in the center of it. He had no leverage. She squealed when he tried to raise her.

"Let me lift you by your armpits." Moving very slowly, Dan put one hand under her arm and the other, behind her back to nudge her to the edge of the large bed. He put his hands under both armpits and slowly lifted her. She stood up apprehensively, holding onto Dan as he walked backward, guiding her uneasily to the bathroom. When she got to the toilet, Dan positioned her so that she could sit, but when she tried and couldn't, she let out a scream.

"I can't bend my left knee! I can't sit . . ." and urine began to trickle down her legs into a puddle in front of the toilet.

It was painful to look at her face. Such utter misery. Dan grabbed a large piece of toilet paper and began to soak up the yellow liquid as quickly as he could.

"Stop!" She cried. "I will not live to see you clean my diapers!"

Dan stopped, stood up and tried to embrace her. He hoped that the urine would fall on him and she could see that it doesn't mean anything. It's an accident, certainly nothing to be embarrassed about. But she resisted, defiantly keeping him at arm's length. Dan waited until the driblets down her leg ceased. She stood silently, ashen, holding onto a metal bar on the wall. Dan took a towel from the hanging rack and started to wipe her legs. Marion wept. Embarrassed, sad, mournful tears.

Back in bed, Dan placed clean towels under her legs and back. Marion was not crying anymore but she was in total despair. He found her robaxin, a muscle relaxant, and valium. She swallowed the pills, but said nothing.

The maid came in with a pile of fresh towels and was cleaning the bathroom when the phone rang. It was the concierge.

"Honey, they found a doctor who can come over. He'll be here as soon as he can find a taxi, which is also on strike."

Marion was in such despair there was no way she could respond.

"Hopefully, the meds will kick in soon," Dan said trying to sound upbeat. He tipped the maid and she left.

The room was deathly silent.

"Are you feeling any better?"

She said nothing, but covered her face with her hands.

Dan thought maybe he shouldn't have said anything, but

he didn't know how to control himself. He wanted so badly to do the right thing. If only he knew what that was. "Marion, accidents like this happen. It's nothing to be ashamed of. If this is the worst, I'll be grateful."

"You will? You don't think this is the worst? Please tell me what is so I'll know what to expect. Come on Dan, say it. We both know what's coming."

Dan knelt down beside her on the bed and put his arms around her as gently as he could. "I know how hard it is now. It's painful and wretched and unfair, but we've been through rough times before, honey. Nothing this bad, but eventually it will pass, it always does."

"This will pass?" That was a *cri de coeur,* not a question.

He didn't know what to say.

"Dan, let's be real. Okay, so this grossly humiliating episode where I piss all over my husband, my lover, will pass. But then what? I can't afford to turn a blind eye to it anymore and neither should you. Don't you see? Everything is telling me to get out of this diseased body. Even your love, which I cherish with every cell of my being, will sour over time and that is a punishment I could never bear."

"Marion, you are the bravest, dearest, most beautiful girl on God's earth and the only thing I could never bear is losing you. What happened, after all? Your knee went into spasm at a particular moment when you had to pee. What's so awful about that? It's not the end of the world."

Marion started to cry.

"Talk to me, sweetheart. Please tell me why losing momentary control of your bladder is so terrible."

She looked at him with the most sorrowful expression and said "it's not *just* that, it's what will happen next."

"Maybe nothing will happen. Maybe something. Whatever it is, we'll deal with it."

"I will deal with it. *My way."*

Marion's attention was suddenly drawn to the large bedroom window. On the sill facing her was a perfect small yellow canary with a collar around its neck. When Dan approached the window, the canary turned and flew away.

"An omen?" Dan asked semi-seriously.

"Isn't it obvious?" Marion said and Dan saw how bloodshot her eyes had become.

"Not to me."

"When was the last time you saw a canary flying in the open air?"

"Probably never. It is unusual but I'm not sure I got the message, if there is one."

"It's perfectly clear to me," Marion said, with a solemnity Dan had rarely heard. "Gilgamesh predates Christianity by over two thousand years but the Mesopotamians understood original sin far better than Augustine. We suffer in this life not for the sins of anyone, but as ransom for the blessings we enjoy. As we advance towards the exit, for every pleasure, an equivalent punishment is exacted."

"You got all that from the canary?"

"What I got is that free will isn't free. Not for that bird, not for Yehoshua, not for me."

"Do you believe Yehoshua's life was so excessively privileged that he deserved to be stricken with that terrible disease?"

"What I believe . . . what I know, is that once payment comes due, the suffering gets worse . . . unbearably worse. What happened to Yehoshua *will* happen . . ."

Dan had to cut her off and change course immediately. "I know how upsetting that was," he said, "but wellness and sickness are random. Not everyone is similarly blessed and we are not equally cursed . . ."

While he talked, Marion lay back and covered her eyes with a compress.

Platitudes! Dan was embarrassed by his empty clichés but her reaction to Yehoshua was so frightening, he couldn't stop himself. He blurted out whatever flew into his head, desperately hoping to deflect her anxieties. Judging from her silence, it seemed to have the opposite effect.

Finally, Marion said, "I will not live my life in a wheelchair and I refuse to be an object of pity. When that happens to me you must promise that you will kill me."

Dan was stunned. At first he didn't want to believe he heard what she said, but he did and it demanded a response. He walked back to the bed and stood over her. "There is no correlation between what you have and Yehoshua's . . ."

"All I want to hear is that you will do what I am asking," she said calmly, her eyes still covered by the compress.

Dan's brain petrified. He sat down on the bed next to her. His thoughts couldn't get traction. "I know you're upset, honey . . ."

"I need you to answer me," Marion said without emotion.

"I can't put a bullet through your head."

"Okay, will you provide the morphine I need to do it myself?"

Dan was speechless.

"Don't be afraid," Marion said calmly as she removed the compress and leaned on her elbow. Her red eyes, inflamed by lachrymal dehydration, stared into his. "I would do it for you if you asked. Please, Dan. I'm waiting . . . everything depends on your answer . . . our marriage depends on it."

Dan's mouth dropped. "Our marriage . . . ? That is sacrosanct! We are *bashert* . . ."

Her suffering eyes pleaded with him. She had said all she was going to say. The rest was up to Dan. She had exposed the full extent of her desolation and Dan was struck with horror. The pain she deals with every day is bad enough but what's worse is the haunting fear that her torment and degradation will only increase. How bravely she has endured it but how much can a person take? She was pleading for mercy. How could he withhold it? How could he not? Participate in the murder of his *basherte*? He would gladly take the morphine himself if it would eradicate her pain but who would care for her when she needed it most? Is that how the curse of the shaman is to be revealed? Dan's brain shut down. Marion lay back down on the bed and covered her eyes with the compress. Tears burst out of his eyes and he reached for her hand.

"Yes, my perfect love," he could barely stop crying as he said "I will do whatever you ask, but you must promise never to do anything without me."

With the compress covering her eyes, she raised his hand to her face and kissed it as he wept.

{ Chapter Twenty }

JERUSALEM was as silent as it must have been in 70 A.D., hours before sixty thousand Roman legionnaires sacked the city, destroyed the Holy Temple and eventually massacred one million, one hundred thousand Jewish men, women and children by sword, fire and crucifix.

The phone rang as Marion and Dan watched the sun set over the Judean hills.

"The doctor is on his way up."

A pale, thin man in his sixties entered the room and introduced himself: Doctor Marcel Ephrat, a recent immigrant from France. His card, in Hebrew, English and French designated that he was a rheumatologist and listed his addresses, both in France and Israel. He spoke very little English and his scant Hebrew was strongly influenced by his mother tongue. Marion picked up the accent immediately and decided to make his life easier.

"Je crois que ce serait plus facile si nous avions parlé français," she said.

"Tres aimable de votre part," he smiled, bowed slightly and they continued in French. He put his stethoscope to her back and listened intently, then checked her heart and lungs. He examined her knees, calves and ankles, revolving each leg slowly to gauge range of motion, then moved her forward, backward and to the sides to determine flexibility.

"Pas beaucoup?" Marion asked nervously.

He didn't answer. Instead, he pulled a chair close to the bed and asked a number of questions, making notes on a small pad. He asked if she had been diagnosed for rheumatoid arthritis or lupus.

"Lupus."

He grimaced like one who hears what he hopes he didn't hear. He put the stethoscope into his small black case and asked what medications she was on. She didn't know the French names, so she told him the English. He translated in his head and wrote on his notepad.

"What you have been experiencing," he explained, "is a classic lupus flare, *in extemis*. Terrible, terrible affliction, lupus." He asked if she had been under a lot of stress lately. She translated that for Dan and they both laughed bitterly.

"Either you've got a great sense of humor, doc," Dan said, "or you've never been on a movie set."

Marion translated.

The doctor did the familiar shrug and extended lip gesture Frenchmen do when there is no answer.

Dan wondered if he should mention Yehoshua's seizure yesterday. Might Marion's severe reaction have triggered the flare? He decided not to butt in.

Doctor Ephrat closed his notepad and asked if her physician in Los Angeles informed her that although there was no available cure at this time, important advances were being made in the treatment of lupus.

"Are you talking about the silver bullet?" Marion's tone was cynical.

Not comprehending, he shook his head and inhaled simultaneously as only the French can.

Reverting to French, Marion said "My rheumatologist in Los Angeles told me that a Swedish consortium had discovered a magical cure for lupus but the sons of bitches in the medical establishment wouldn't allow them to put it on the market."

"Cure isn't a word I would use," the doctor said, continuing in French. "But the research clearly demonstrates that their discovery can prevent painful flairs, like the one you experienced today."

"So, why does the goddamn medical profession refuse to alleviate my suffering?"

"In all fairness, that particular medication is based on a revolutionary theory that frightens many doctors. The treatment essentially *weakens* the immune system, the body's only protection against microbes and viruses. Victims of lupus have an overactive immune system. When your body mistakenly perceives a viral attack, it releases excessive amounts of synovial fluid into the body to protect you. The attack never comes but the viscous liquid is discharged into your system. That is what produces painful swelling of the joints.

"By weakening the immune system, the synovial fluid is not released. There is no swelling and no pain, but the downside is that you would be more susceptible to a variety of viral infections."

"A little sneezing and a stuffy nose verses excruciating pain?

Hmmm. What a tough choice. Trust me, Doctor Ephrat, anyone who's gone through what I did today, would happily opt for the *médecine* to relieve the misery, no matter what the side effects."

"There are apparently legal problems as well," the doctor said. "Pharmaceutical companies fear there would be an avalanche of lawsuits challenging a drug that diminishes the patient's natural ability to resist disease."

"Catch-22!" Marion steamed in English.

Once again, Dr. Ephrat didn't recognize the allusion, but he got the gist.

"Je suis désolée," he said and looked genuinely sorry. The doctor's face was the soul of compassion but he had nothing more to offer.

Gloom settled on the dark room. After an awkward silence, the doctor prepared to leave but before he could close his black leather bag, Marion asked him something that stopped him cold. He appeared reluctant to answer, but Marion would not let up. She asked one pointed question after another and he responded warily. Her probing seemed to embarrass the doctor, but she persisted. Finally, after a long, protracted answer by Dr. Ephrat, Marion said *"alors c'est vrai!"*

Almost apologetically, the doctor said *"J'ai vu . . . Je dois dire que je ne crois pas, mais . . . c'est vrai. C'est passé."*

After the doctor left, they ordered dinner in the room. Dan took it as a good sign that Marion picked around her salad and actually ate a small roll with jam and tea. The pills were holding and he prayed that she wouldn't have another attack. He was eager to find out what was so compelling in her conversation with the doctor that he didn't understand, but he didn't want to sap her energy. He waited, hinted, but Marion was uncharacteristically subdued.

"So . . . how do you feel now?"

"Better than before," she murmured.

"How did you like the doctor? Nice guy, I thought."

Marion nodded, but said nothing.

That was troubling. Marion was never at a loss for words.

That night, Marion tried to sleep but couldn't get comfortable, even with all the pills. Dan lay next to her and read her favorite T.S. Elliot aloud. *"Ah, my friend, you do not know, you do not know what life is, you who hold it in your hands . . ."* By the time he finished *". . . what can you receive from one about to reach her journey's end?"* She was asleep, peacefully, cooing softly, like an infant.

Sleep did not come easily for Dan that night.

The next morning, she was up, resting comfortably and actually ate a slice of melon, part of a blueberry muffin and drank a cup of tea. That was an encouraging sign and Dan felt as if a boulder had been magically, if temporarily, lifted from his shoulders. He sat down to compose a letter.

"A love note?" Marion asked.

"Yes, but not for you. This one is for God. I'm going down to the Wailing Wall to have a little chat with you-know-who," he said, pointing upward. He folded the paper so it could be stuffed into a crevice between the coarse stones.

"Send my regards," she said blowing a kiss.

STANDING BEFORE THE WALL, Dan's head throbbed as he recalled the sounds of Marion's agonized groans. He took the note out of his pocket and squeezed it into a crevice. It was a highly charged moment. He felt that he was actually in *The Presence.* Apprehensive and more than a little fearful, Dan pleaded with God to heal Marion. He leaned against the wall with both hands and closed his eyes. Trying to visualize her, pain-free and healthy, he spoke softly but passionately.

Suddenly, someone bumped into him, hard. Annoyed, he turned and saw that it was a young Hasid, with an overly wide-brim felt hat, long twirled *payos* and a black frock coat. The *kacker* couldn't have been more than nine or ten years old. He walked a few feet away and stared at Dan contemptuously.

Dan tried to overcome his irritation so he could get back to his prayer. Seconds later, another bump. It was the same kid.

"What is your problem?" Dan asked the kid in Hebrew.

"You don't talk Yiddish?" The young Hasid said in Yiddish.

"This is Israel," Dan responded in Hebrew. "I speak the language of the people who live here in the twentieth century."

"You American, no?" he said in English with a strong Polish inflection. "Whata you doin' here at de wall?"

"I'm praying to the God of Israel, my God, if it's any of your business."

"Of course it's my business. Det's why I'm here. So, what a'you, some kinda Jew?"

"Very much some kind of Jew."

The kid stroked his chin, as if expecting to find a beard on his smooth baby face. He then opened the slender volume he was his holding and stuck it in Dan's face. "If you a Jew, you can read dis."

Dan looked at the book. "It's the introduction to *Berachot,* the first tractate of the Talmud, and who the hell are you to be testing me? Talk to me after your bar mitzvah."

The Hasid suddenly got angry. "You tink I'm not bar mitzvah yet? Ignoronamus! How could I be wearing dis hat if I wasn't bar mitzvah already?"

"Anyone living in seventeenth century Poland could wear

that hat and not look foolish, but in case you haven't noticed, you're four centuries out of style."

The kid waved his hand disparagingly. "Let's get down to business. So, who are you talkin' to wit your eyes closed?"

"I was praying until you bumped me—twice! What is it with you? Do you just happen to be the rudest person in Jerusalem today or are you on some kind of mission?"

The young Hasid grimaced and waved his hand at Dan again, only more disparagingly this time. "Praying? You call det praying? You talkin' wit your eyes closed. Det's nuttin wit nuttin. You wanna say prayers? I'll give you prayers to say. You tink you can just come here and schmooze wit de Holy One? Det's stupidness. You stand dere talking like you talk to de chemist in de drug store. You tink you're so smart you can write prescriptions and send dem to Him tru de wall and He'll fill dem for you? *You* telling *Him* what to do? Who de hell are you? Talk about rude. Det's de rudest ting anybody can do. Where do you come off telling *der Aebishter* what's right and what's wrong and what He should do about it?"

Why was Dan angry, he asked himself? Because he couldn't win an argument with this little automaton? Or, was it that he made Dan feel suddenly embarrassed about petitioning God for a special favor? True, he wasn't asking for wealth or fame. He was pleading for Marion's life, but can he deny that his prayer for Marion to find remission from pain was not inherently different from someone else's wish for success or fortune? In the final analysis then, is prayer nothing more than a shopping list? Dan stood silently watching this miserable little *kacker* disdainfully wave his hand at him again.

"Don't interrupt me again," was the best Dan could come up with.

"You're not woit de trouble," the young Hasid said, then turned away, looking for new victims for his unique brand of aggressive, ultra-orthodox fanaticism.

When Dan got back, Marion saw how distressed he was. As he recounted the story, Dan became even more infuriated at that rude, vulgar little *vance*. "I should have picked him up by the *payos* and thrown the bastard over the wall."

Marion shook her head.

"Should I go back and kick the daylights out of that little son of a bitch? I'd be happy to. What do you say?"

"How very sad," Marion said. "That poor boy will go through life never experiencing a miracle."

"Fuck him! What about me? Is that what I was doing at the wall, asking for a miracle?"

"What's wrong with that?"

"I don't believe in miracles."

"I'll tell you what I believe. I believe God heard your prayer and sent that boy to give you a Zen slap."

"Is that what you think that little prick gave me? A Zen slap?"

"Look at you. Your whole belief structure was shaken by that encounter. You went to the wall to pray, as you've prayed all your life and it never occurred to you to consider whether you have the right to petition your God. Now, for the first time, you're questioning the very foundations of your faith. That's what a Zen slap is. It's a punch to the heart and the brain. Without it, people go on pretending that what once worked for them will see them through again, even though they know it no longer does. They're stuck because they're afraid of change. That's where the Zen slap comes in. We would never get unstuck by ourselves, so something—call it the cosmos, call it God, call it the life force—provides the jolt we need to shake loose our rigid mindset and hopefully save our lives."

"So what is my rigid mindset? The fact that I don't believe in miracles?"

"You say you don't believe in miracles and therefore couldn't possibly ask for one, but that's precisely what you were doing at the wall and have done all your life. That nasty little Hasid simply made you confront the fact that you not only believe in miracles, you need them. Everybody does, particularly when their life is in crisis."

"Is my life in crisis now?"

"Look at me, Dan! I'm talking about killing myself to escape the pain. You say you can't live without me, but I can't go on like this! We've tried everything and nothing's working. You saw what happened to me yesterday. This miserable disease is only going to get worse. I'm convinced that this Zen slap is a gift from God telling us to shake ourselves free from the close-mindedness that keeps us going to doctors and hospitals that we both know can't help us."

"If this is a Zen slap, what's the message?"

"The same one I got yesterday from Doctor Ephrat."

"What's that?"

"A way to survive."

"What did he prescribe?"

"He didn't prescribe anything, not purposely, anyway. He did make it clear that medically, there was no acceptable way to treat lupus. That's when I asked about possible alternative treatments. He said he was not competent to comment on such things. Then I asked him point blank if he ever had a patient, or even heard of someone, who was healed of an incurable disease that couldn't be explained any way other than . . . a miracle. That's when he became visibly uncomfortable."

"I did notice that. What did he say?"

"He said he preferred not to talk about it, but I insisted. Almost apologetically, he finally said, 'Once I did see what you might call a miracle, but I must tell you that I do not believe in them. However, it is true. It did happen. *C'est vrai. C'est passe.* I saw with my own eyes.' When I pressed him for details, he said—and I'm translating word for word—'I have never spoken of this and I hope you will not seek advantage, but as you ask, I have no alternative but to tell you what I saw, precisely, with neither embellishment nor critique.'"

Dan looked at her skeptically.

"Didn't you get any of our conversation?" She asked.

"No. You were both talking too fast and it sounded like you were purposely leaving out a lot of consonants."

"The doctor had been treating a woman at his clinic in Paris for many years. Over time, she developed advanced neuropathic arthropathy, a disease of the bones, marked by resorption and deformity. She had suffered from severe arthritis for years but was able to lead a more or less normal life. When the disease became degenerative, her right ankle was severely contorted to the point where she could no longer walk and was confined to a wheelchair. There was nothing Doctor Ephrat could do for her. The only possible treatment was amputation of the diseased leg but he couldn't recommend it because chances of recovery for a woman her age and in her condition were slim to nil. One day, the woman's husband called and said a business associate of his from India told him about the magical cures he had witnessed at the Matrix Shrine of Resurrected Souls in the village of Petan, in Nepal.

He said he was going to accompany his wife to the shrine and asked for the doctor's blessing. As a man of science, Dr. Ephrat was appalled. He was convinced it was a hoax, but the X-rays he had taken over the years chronicled the progression of a malformation that would certainly lead to a painful end, probably in the very near future. It was a crisis of conscience for the doctor. In his eyes, such a pilgrimage was nothing more than a shameful delusion, but he understood it was not his decision to make. All he could do was offer his hope that she would find some respite from the agony of her affliction, but he never believed she would.

"A month later, the couple returned to Paris. Dr. Ephrat was amazed by what he saw on her X-rays. She still had slight residual pain but the progression of deformity not only halted, it had begun to reverse. One month later, without any additional medication or treatment, she was able to stand, and then walk a few paces at a time. She needed the support of a walker or her husband's arm, but no more wheelchairs. The doctor said he could not believe it at first. Such a rapid change in bone structure without surgery is unheard of, but there it was, on the X-rays. Compared to the ones he had taken over the past years, the change was astonishing. Soon she was able to walk with the support of a cane but the throbbing pain emanating from her ankle had all but disappeared. She still had arthritis, but there was no deformity, no ulceration, no abnormalities, whatsoever. When the doctor migrated to Israel, there was a lot of weeping. They were grateful for his help and thanked him profusely. Happy though he was with his patient's progress, there was no way he could credit medical intervention for her miraculous recovery."

Marion's uncharacteristic reserve over the next few days was both understandable and unnerving. Since her lupus attack and the mind-twisting encounter with the French doctor, Marion had very little to say. Instead, she devoted all her energy to exploring the web.

Shut out, Dan was confused and worried—and lonely.

"Have you ever heard of The Uncertainty Principle?" she asked.

"Can't say that I have."

"Copenhagen, 1930s? Matrix mechanics?"

"As you know, theoretical science is not my strong suit."

"Aristotle's definition of resurrected souls?"

Dan shook his head.

Her attention reverted to the computer.

"This wouldn't have something to do with Dr. Ephrat's unique experience with his aging, arthritic patient, would it?"

No response.

Dan didn't want to get into an argument. Actually, he did but deferred to her weakened condition. It took all the restraint he could muster not to render his opinion that the doctor was either a quack or seriously deluded. By the end of the week, Marion appeared to be getting her strength back. Her appetite was improving and Dan felt she might be ready to make the trip home. They'd been away far too long and worked much too hard. They confronted the most horrific physical and emotional challenge of their lives and survived, but who knows when the curse would strike again? Dan was convinced that what she needed was a long period of rest and recuperation in the Pacific Palisades.

Marion had a different idea.

{ Chapter Twenty-One }

"We're going to Nepal."

"Nepal?! What the f. . . .?!"

"Deal with it."

Dan felt smoke wafting out of his ears. The idea that Marion intended to travel three thousand miles to visit a Buddhist shrine in her condition was just whacky! Dan didn't question Doctor Ephrat's sincerity, but neither did he believe the story about the magical healing that allegedly took place at the Matrix Shrine of Resurrected Souls. Something was missing, either in the telling or the way events unfolded. What cannot be, cannot be, no matter who says otherwise. Dan certainly understood Marion's desperation to find remission, but fly halfway around the world to an ashram because you heard about a miraculous healing that allegedly took place in the Himalayas? This was Marion, after all, a rational mind that encompassed conundrums that would set off fireworks between Schopenhauer and Hegel.

Dan didn't have to say how strongly he opposed the idea. Marion read his face. "I'm aware of your dilemma, Dan, but right now, I need your total support, physical, emotional and spiritual. To do that, you must give up your goddamn cynicism and believe! I know you're capable of it. You were a great believer once. Now, call it up! Put on a *yarmulke,* blow a *shofar,* eat a bagel. Do whatever the hell you have to, but you must once again believe that there is a force for healing in the universe and that I will be cured of this horrible disease. Stop looking for the downside or you will create one. Is that what you want? Let's face it, Dan, one more episode like that and I'm gone! All I'm asking is that you believe with all your heart. Is that more difficult than it would be to live without me?"

"Life without you? Unthinkable! But you're asking me to *believe* that yoga can cure Lupus! How do I do that?"

"Stop trying to figure it out!" Marion's frustration was reaching a boiling point. "There is nothing logical about this. It is a leap of faith, like *Nachshon's.* Remember him? If he hadn't risked his life to demonstrate his faith, we'd all still be slaves in Egypt."

Dan was amazed that Marion remembered the obscure rabbinic version of what happened when Moses and the Israelites were stranded on the shores of the red sea.

"For a miracle to happen, you have to take that leap. I'm ready and I'm counting on you to take the leap with me."

LEAP OF FAITH. That sounded so foreign to Dan now, but it didn't always. He was once a firm believer. Even as a child, an inner fire drove him. Long before he read The Psalms, he saw the glory of God everywhere. "The torch of faith burns brightly within you, Daniel," Professor Abrams said when he heard him preach for the first time. "You are a true believer, a bearer of the light and a messenger of the Holy One, Blessed Be He."

Faith was the fire in his bosom.

When did it go out?

It started that Friday night years ago with the phone call from his sister-in-law Marge. When Dan asked how everybody was, Marge said in the most controlled voice she could marshal, "Are you sitting down?"

"What's going on?"

"Art's plane went down."

Dan couldn't find words.

Finally, petrified, he asked. "Is he going to be all right?"

"Art's dead."

Dan fell on the floor and wept. He pictured Sandra, his brother's five-year-old daughter, who was always hanging onto some part of her daddy whether he was sitting, walking or driving. He thought about Justin, the three-year-old who wore a superman cape and believed he was invincible, and Tess, who was only four-months-old. He'll never see them grow up. He'll never . . . *"There is no judge and no justice!"*

When Art was buried at Arlington, the honor guard fired several shots into the air. What Dan heard were the gates of heaven slamming shut and in that moment, he realized that the fire in his bosom had been quenched.

So after all these years, he is being asked not only to resurrect his crumpled faith, but devote it to a belief in the power of a shrine, an ashram, or some maharishi. How much good did that do John Lennon?

But all that ruminating was futile. What happened in Jerusalem could not be ignored. That wretched disease will attack again and very likely with even more fury. Shocked, terrified, numb, Dan heard himself think what he never imagined he could: *It appears . . . no, I believe . . . that our hope for a life free of misery dangles from a gossamer thread connecting us to a hippy fantasy!*

This was clearly Marion's journey, but where did *her* absolute certainty come from? It must have been sealed during that last phone call with Alan Marcus, her rheumatologist.

Several days after the lupus attack in Jerusalem, Marion called Alan in Los Angeles and they spoke for a long time. She told him she had seen a French doctor who told her about the miraculous shrine in Nepal.

"I'm thinking about going, Alan. What do you think?"

"In your heart of hearts how badly do you want to find remission?"

"With *all* my heart," Marion said. "How can you ask me that?"

"Do you *believe* in your heart of hearts that you *will* be healed?"

"I want to believe that, of course."

"That's not good enough. Every day, after treating an office full of patients, I spend hours at U.C.L.A. working with researchers, thinking inside and outside every box, exchanging ideas and notes with peers who are as devoted as I am. Ask me how I am able to do that day in and day out and there is only one answer: Because I believe with *all* my heart that we *will* find a way to eradicate this horrible disease. If I didn't believe that, I'd have to be crazy to live like this. I'm doing my part, Marion. You do yours. Believe with every breath, every fiber of your being that you will find respite and to get there, you must do whatever it takes. Beseech every power or force in the universe with every ounce of strength you can muster. Nothing that genuinely comes from the heart is foolish. Nothing is humiliating or beneath you."

THE SIXTEEN HOUR FLIGHT to Nepal included a three-hour layover in sweltering Bangkok but by the time they arrived in Kathmandu, the temperature had dropped precipitously. From the airport, Marion and Dan rode for nearly two hours in a cold, windowless taxi through rough roads teeming with fume-spouting motor scooters and rickety old buses before they reached Petan. Nestled amid the majestic snowcapped mountains, the remote village was strewn with rubble and remnants of buildings destroyed in recent earthquakes.

Hotel Paradise, the only standing building that survived the last quake was surprisingly comfortable. Exhausted and cold, Marion decided to forego dinner and went straight to bed. Despite his resentment, Dan was able to enjoy a delicious dinner of curry rice and chutney.

After a few hours of sleep, they were awakened before dawn by itinerant monks beating drums and clanging cymbals. The hotel found a taxi that took them to a large wooden enclosure, crowded with seriously sick people of all sizes, shapes and colors. The sign in Nepali and English read: Matrix Shrine of Resurrected Souls.

At the entrance, blind beggars sat in a row with wooden bowls in their laps. Marion had studied the protocol and was prepared with a pack of coins for which she received mumbles that she assumed were blessings. Several yards in, they joined a line of supplicants waiting to enter the grotto of the eight-armed Buddha. Some leaned on crutches, some lay on gurneys pushed by saffron robed monks, while others were carried in the arms or on the backs of relatives.

A pervading stench covered the huge crowd and despite a

light intermittent drizzle oozing out of a dark cloud, the air was so foul, Dan could hardly breathe. Could it be that the emaciated body on a gurney alongside him was already dead and decomposing? He took a handkerchief from his pocket and covered his nose. On his other side was a child in the arms of saffron robed monk. The boy's eyes bulged and the skin on his face was blueish and pealing. Dan had never seen such hideous distortions of the human form. For a second, he thought of *Nightmare,* a horror film he once made in which the special effects artist concocted gruesome-looking makeup for mutants, but they weren't nearly as horrific as the deformed shapes of *real* people slowly advancing towards the grotto, *really* believing that divine water flowing from the Buddha with eight arms would pass through their third eye and miraculously make them whole.

The cruel cynicism of the place made Dan feel like screaming.

Marion sensed it immediately and under her breath firmly said, "Snap out of it! I need you to be totally here. Meditate, count backwards, pray, but do something, goddamn it!" Dan held her hand as tightly as he could, trying to force himself to believe. He remembered a prayer for the sick from his rabbi's manual and began to recite it. *"Lord, God, merciful and gracious, send healing to Marion as you did for Hezekiah, King of Judah . . ."* The words curdled in his mouth.

Marion and Dan finally entered the dank, cold grotto where a gold statue of a Buddha with eight arms looked down a sheer stone wall at the line of pilgrims below. Two saffron cloaked monks sat cross-legged on a dirt floor in front of the Buddha. From behind the statue, rivulets of cold water poured down all eight arms, over a solid rock wall and into a gulley.

Each petitioner stood or knelt before Buddha, dipped his hand into the water, then touched the space on his forehead known as the third or inner eye, eight times. When Marion finally stood in front of the statue, she dipped her hand into the ice-cold water and touched her forehead eight times. She waited for something to happen. Nothing did. Impulsively, she pressed her hand against the cold, wet rock. Rivulets of freezing water from all eight arms of the statue poured down the wall onto her outstretched arm and drenched her woolen sweater. She closed her eyes, shivering as she mumbled a Hebrew prayer, *"sheh-hechy-anu, ve-kiya-ma-nu ve-higy-a-nu laz-man ha-zeh."* Then, she sneezed.

They didn't say a word on their way back to the hotel. Chilled and still wearing the sweater soaked with water from the grotto, Marion sneezed incessantly but said nothing.

That evening, they ordered a light dinner in the room. He ate. She couldn't. The constant dripping from her nose was agonizing and she was in a terrible funk. In the middle of the night, Marion got into a sneezing jag. Between the flow from her nose and the constant wheezing, she could barely breathe.

"The damn Matrix Shrine of Resurrected Souls gave me a fucking cold! Damn it, damn, damn, damn! I'm cursed. Everybody in the world goes to shrines to be healed and I get clobbered. Fuck it. Fuck it all."

Their flight home had to be delayed for two long miserable weeks until Marion's congestion subsided. Neither of them spoke about Nepal, the Shrine or anything related to the experience. Marion's dejection was deep and palpable. The disappointment, the embarrassment and shame of having allowed herself to be so deluded, was crushing. As if that wasn't enough, the remnants of her cold made the flight to Los Angeles a living hell. When the cabin pressure dropped in preparation for landing, her eardrums felt as though they were going to burst.

When they got home, Marion took a swig of Promethazine and checked her phone messages while Dan went into his study to slog through the huge pile of mail.

"Dan!" Marion shouted. When he entered the kitchen, Marion was listening to the accumulated messages.

"What's up?"

"Listen!"

"Where are you? I've been trying to reach you for weeks . . ."

"Who's that?"

"Alan Marcus. Listen."

". . . JAMA calls it the most important medical advance since penicillin. Call me as soon as you get this. Anytime, day or night."

They immediately called Alan, who couldn't restrain his excitement.

"It's here, Marion. A medication to treat lupus! Your worst nightmares are over!"

The news was so overwhelming that they couldn't process it all at once and they made Alan repeat it several times until they were sure they understood every detail.

"It's called Etacerdone, trade name Corbride. It's been in the works for years but was held up by a lawsuit that was finally settled . . ."

"Cut to the chase," Dan said. "Does this mean Marion will be completely cured? No more lupus? No more swollen joints? No more excruciating pain?"

"Yes, yes, yes and a couple of no's. First, the no: Technically, the underlying rheumatic disorder remains in your body, but it will be *neutered* and incapable of generating any of your debilitating symptoms. It's like having a deaf mute tenant living in the attic that you never hear and doesn't affect your life at all. Now for the yeses. The painful flairs are over. The short answer to all your questions is yes, this is a time for celebration."

Dan and Marion both cried.

"Thank God," Marion said.

"Thank God, indeed," Alan said.

Dan was stunned, unable to speak.

"There are some side effects, but nothing comparable to what you've been through. What this does is reset the immune system which will diminish your energy. You'll have to build a lot of rest into your schedule, but the importance of this new drug is that it—okay, I'll say the word—it *miraculously* eliminates the life-altering effects of lupus. I have been following the research for years and I know a miracle when I see one."

"So do I," Marion said tearfully.

Marion and Dan asked every question that popped into their heads. "When can she start? How long will it take before she finds relief?" They talked over one another on the speaker phone repeating questions, unable to hold back the tears.

"Hey, time out you guys. First things first. Dan, you will have to take training from a qualified technician in my office so that you can inject her twice weekly on the inner thigh. I asked for that job, but they turned me down. Seriously guys, I've put you on the list for the first batch of Corbride that comes down the line. That shouldn't be more than a few of weeks at most. It could take another six to seven before we see results but by then you *will* begin to feel better. A whole lot better! Reborn is not an exaggeration. I am obliged to tell you that even with all the miracle drugs in the world, as we grow older, our bodies become less and less friendly. There will come a point when you have to hang up your berets and riding crops and really call it quits. Until that time, go eat, drink, dance, make love and live happily for as many years as whoever you worship grants you."

Three months later, Marion's X-rays validated the total absence of her symptoms. She was soon feeling strong enough to take long hikes and with unbridled enthusiasm, explore art, read, reread, write. Marion was reborn, ready to resume her life, dancing!

Dan didn't wait five minutes to call the Hotel Regina on Rue St. Honore to reserve their *deuxieme maison*, suite 217, beginning the first week in May for three months with the hope of returning every year.

The night before they left for Paris, they drank champagne, smoked a *doobie* and reflected on the suffering she endured for so long. Marion credited the miracle of Corbride to The Matrix Shrine of Resurrected Souls. To her, the connection between her visit to the Shrine and the sudden availability of the new drug was obvious and it derived from one word: Faith. "Once you have that, everything else is . . . engineering."

"What about the cold you caught in the grotto?" Dan teased.

"Broaden your horizons,Rabbi. Think in terms of how your fellow theologians of the Christian persuasion would explain it. This Jew needed one final bit of suffering, one last stab in the ribs by that vindictive Roman soldier, before she could be resurrected."

PART EIGHT

Jubilation

{ Chapter Twenty-Two }

Dan and Rocky sat silently in the car on the side of the road while crowds of gaily-dressed celebrants wending their way to the many festivities, grew larger and louder.

Finally, Rocky spoke. "That's it? That's the great miracle of Nepal?

"You don't believe it?"

"What's to believe? That you went to Nepal? Of course I believe that, but what I don't see is the causal connection between Marion's experience at a shrine and the sudden discovery of a cure for lupus."

"The causal connection is the precise timing."

"But absent a provable scientific formula, you can't say that the timing is causal. Most likely, it's serendipitous."

"You don't know that."

Rocky shook his head. "I don't see how you or any rational person can accept that narrative. The cure for lupus must have been in the works for years. How could Marion possibly believe her faith had anything to do with the timing?"

"Ask Molly."

"I know what Molly believes," Rocky said. "She's convinced it's a miracle, but that's completely illogical, don't you see? If you believe a miracle *will* occur because you have faith, that implies predictability which is the foundation of science and faith is not scientific. If a scientist does X and Y, he can predict with absolute certainty, that the result will be Z every time. But faith is unverifiable and there is no way to prove that if you do X or Y, or both, a certain result will occur. To the contrary, ninety-nine percent of the time, we know it won't!"

"I agree there is an absence of logic, but that's beside the point," Dan said. "Marion's pursuit of miracles and I assume, Molly's too, goes into realms where science fears to tread."

"Like what?"

"Like death," Dan said. "To the scientist, death is the end. He believes that, not because he can prove it but because he can't disprove it. To the believer, death is a transition to some other consciousness and they don't see any need to prove it. They simply pursue what they call miracles to track the journey."

A blast of ear-splitting noise cut through their argument as a crowd of bizarrely dressed musicians circled Rocky's parked car, playing, singing and clapping hands to a riveting reggae beat.

Momentarily distracted, Rocky wanted to make sure he could be heard over the din. "But the *journey* as you call it . . ."

The music became so loud Dan and Rocky couldn't hear their own voices. A thunderous blare of trumpets emerged from the crowd, seemingly timed to blow holes in each of their incongruities.

Dan and Rocky were puzzled by the strange spectacle surrounding them. Unlike the festively attired celebrants back on the road, the band parading around their parked car was dressed in funereal garb. Following the musicians was a group of men in high hats and women with large black turbans, carrying white umbrellas. Leading the procession was a Grim Reaper, cloaked in a black hooded robe, with a long scythe slung over his shoulder.

As they circled Rocky's car, the brass section sounded a single long note, followed by wailing clarinets and the piercing clamor of drums. When the music stopped, all eyes turned to a group of young men approaching from across the road, carrying an open casket on their shoulders. The pallbearers stopped in front of the car and set down the coffin. Inside the pine box was someone wearing skeleton regalia and a death mask. The band came in strong and the crowd zigzagged from side to side, strutting around the coffin.

Abruptly, the music stopped again. Two fire eaters, one on each side of the coffin, spat huge flames upward that turned into billows of thick black smoke. Slowly the *corpse* stood up, engulfed in the dark cloud hanging ominously overhead. The crowd applauded as he slowly scrutinized each of the celebrants, waving and smiling broadly. When he looked at Dan sitting in the car, he pointed a finger and declaimed.

"De prophet Daniel revealed to us in de twelfth chapter, verse two of his holy book: *dose who sleep in de dust of de eart' will awaken dis day to eternal life.'* Daniel tell us *'on de day of de great Jubilee, we will all be set free, de livin' and de dead*. De time for resurrection is upon us."

"Hallelujah," the crowd roared.

Dan immediately recognized the magisterial voice behind the death mask. It was—it had to be—Abednego, his

Bible-quoting driver. The band picked up the beat and fire eaters spat flames that turned into large black clouds of smoke. The *corpse* sang and his chorus of mourners repeated each line. *"Dose who sleep in de dust of de eart; will arise . . ."*

Dan's eyes locked onto the death mask and the Hebrew text of Daniel 12:2 appeared to him like a burst of sunlight. *"Ye-she-ney afar yakitzu* . . . Those who sleep in the dust, *will* awaken."

The corpse, in Abednego's unique voice, repeated the Hebrew *"Ye-she-ney afar yakitzu . . ."*

Dan's brain waffled and he suddenly felt weightless. The corpse returned to its coffin and the entourage left as they came. The stain of dark smoke they left behind hung in the air and did not dissipate.

Perplexed by the strange appearance of a funeral procession and the curious sermon delivered by a *corpse,* quoting from the Hebrew Bible, Rocky started the car and inched slowly back onto the road. After driving in silence for a long stretch, Rocky said, *"Ye-she-ney afar yakitzu* . . . what do you think that means?"

"Daniel's prophecy is that those who sleep in the dust will awaken to eternal life."

"I understand the Hebrew. What I am asking is what does that mean to you?"

"Like much of the Bible, there is a hint of poetic truth that hopefully provides comfort for people in crisis."

"When Marion was approaching the end, did you find comfort in Daniel's prophecy or anywhere else in the Bible?"

"With Marion, the end didn't *approach*. It struck like a hurricane."

"But you saw it coming?"

"How does one see an immeasurable abstraction? It's like imagining negative infinity."

"So you never prepared yourself to deal with her ultimate demise?"

"Prepare? How does one do that? No sane person would contemplate that degree of misery. Occasionally, glimpses slipped through the firewalls and I was gripped with such dread I couldn't breathe. I knew that to be there for her, I would have to devise some mechanism to keep those demons at bay. Just staying alive during that time was difficult enough, but to contemplate what life would be like without her was the worst kind of self-flagellation. You dangle in the wind, waiting, hoping, crying silently and trying hard not to let your mind go to that place. But when the end finally does come, you find yourself with a heart broken into so many pieces your only wish is for that same liberation from suffering."

Dan was annoyed with himself for spewing pessimism and anger, like Job, railing against the order of life. It was the opposite of how he spoke to Marion where communication was instantaneous. Anything he wanted to convey was expressed in a few words without dramatic outbursts. They each knew what was in the other's heart . . . but that was the essence of being part of a *two*. A look, a word, a gesture is all they needed. They hadn't really talked very much during their last years but they communicated more intensely than ever before. It was their *twoness* that elevated life despite everything. Together, they were able to endure all the horrors of her terrible disease. On those occasions when she found remission, they danced to the setting sun on their balcony amid blue hydrangeas, violet pansies, yellow and red rose bushes and sang "Oh Happy Day" with the Edwin Hawkins Singers or lay cuddled together on their luxurious bed watching *2001: A Space Odyssey* or *Amadeus* or *Casablanca* or any one of the thousand DVDs Marion collected over the years. That was the loftiest form of *twoness*.

One might think that after all those blissful years there remained something . . . like *oneness*? No. *Twoness* is indivisible and when it's gone, the only thing left is *nothingness*.

As they drove through a crush of pedestrians, happy faces surrounded them and called out "Happy Jubilation Day!" Dan felt he was on a different planet from everyone else. It was like living in a French New Wave film, those searing depictions of existential aloneness in which the face of an isolated man is superimposed over busy crowds of strangers, each moving in a different direction towards someone or something familiar while the detached face looks on, unmoved, abandoned, like one shut out of the world everyone else lives in.

"Molly would have a more literal interpretation of Daniel's prophecy," Rocky said. "She believes with absolute certainty that highly evolved people do 'awaken from the dust' and move on to another 'plane' in some kind of post-human iteration."

"Marion believed that too."

"But you don't?" Rocky asked.

"I wish I could. I wish with all my heart . . . but to be perfectly honest, I would have to say, no."

"What do you believe?"

"I believe in love."

"But when the love of your life dies, what's left?"

"Nothing," Dan murmured.

"How do you face nothingness?"

"With nothing. There are no paths forward and you can't go back. It's not like you can return to where you were before you became half of the new whole. What butterfly can go back into a cocoon? Therapists tell you when you are bereaved, you must find the inner *you* and nurture it, but that's impossible. You can't pluck the yolk out of an egg once it's blended into an omelet. You had one whole life made of two interwoven components. When that is torn apart, what does the remnant look like? A dismembered leper. Even friends have only one thought when they see you: This guy gives me the creeps. He reminds me of how bad it's going to be for me. So what does a person do in the face of unrelenting anguish? Nothing. There is nothing anyone can do."

THEY RODE IN SILENCE ONCE AGAIN until they came to a particularly congested intersection. A group of musicians had assembled in the middle of the road, halting traffic. Rocky became more and more frustrated as he tried to maneuver through the boisterous crowd and threw his hands up in despair when two young men tried to attach a large placard to his car. It read: *in honor of Jubilation Day, all peoples invited to climb in and ride wid us.* The decibel level became deafening. Rocky got out and tried to explain through gesticulations—hearing was impossible—that the car had a diplomatic license plate and it was illegal to carry a poster of any kind. The boys either didn't understand or didn't want to and Rocky argued as they laughed.

A familiar face in the crowd waved wildly and pushed through the mob towards Dan as he sat alone in the car. Dan recognized him immediately. Abednego! Dan's first thought was, where is the coffin and the mourners?

That segued to, who the hell is Abednego, really? A Rasta chauffer with the junkiest car he ever saw? A ubiquitous Bible quoting character—in English and Hebrew!—who keeps popping up everywhere? Abednego came closer, holding a smoking silver chalice. When he reached the passenger side of the car, he took Dan's hand and shook it vigorously. Coming within inches of his face, he said something but the noise of the crowd and the amplified music made hearing impossible. Abednego took a long hit on the smoldering pipe and held his breath, then smiled broadly. A steady stream of smoke rolled out of his mouth and engulfed Dan. It was like a river of ganja flowing into Dan's face. Smiling, Abednego mouthed, "And a Happy Jubilation Day it is for you, my brother."

Dan's ganja-tinted brain vaulted through an endless garden of lilacs as he watched the slow motion blossoming of psychedelic flowers sprouting all around him in a sea of lavender. In the center was Marion's snorkel with a blue and white-dotted ping pong ball in the little cage on top, winding through the violet mist, coming closer and closer. Just as she was about to poke her head through the waves, he was hoisted upward with Marion in his arms! He was ecstatic as they sailed higher and higher above the earth. When they entered a cloud, she wasn't in his arms anymore but he felt her presence all around, circling him like she did in those dances they loved to improvise. Fun and sexy, it was always thrilling. In a magical moment, Marion reappeared in his arms and they laughed and sang in unison. Unencumbered by gravity, they flew majestically towards the sunset. Suddenly, the track went wildly dissonant and Dan was thrust back into the car.

HONK! HONK! Rocky pressed down on his horn, trying to maneuver through mobs of people dancing in front of him on the highway. Dan knew he was in a car, but couldn't remember why. He was on the road . . . the road to . . . where?

And where was Marion? His mind couldn't get traction. Was she still in that cloud? How can he get back there?

"Hi, Dan," a familiar voice said.

Dan twisted around to see where she was.

Nowhere! Empty backseat.

He was alone in the car with Rocky who was surgically navigating the traffic, but the voice was unmistakable. Didn't Rocky hear it? Judging from the intense look on his face, apparently not.

"Dan?"

There she is again!

"This is important," the voice said, "and I need your complete attention."

"Is it you, Marion?" he wanted to shout, but words wouldn't come. He was adrift and his heart screamed. "Where are you?"

"I don't have a lot of time, so I need you to LISTEN; *SHEMA!*"

Her voice had a reverb under the word "listen" and something illustrious sounding under *Shema,* like the music track from *Ben Hur.*

"I have to set you straight or you're going to screw everything up," she said with an uncharacteristically sharp edge. "What the hell were you saying to this sweet young guy who wants nothing more out of life than to have a blessed love affair with his *basherte,* just like us? Shouldn't you be encouraging him instead of 'life is nothingness, life is grief, life is pain?' When did you become a nihilist? You're Dan, for God's sake, the very incarnation of love. Because you're hurting, do you have to spread as much misery and despair as possible to everyone you touch?"

Dan winced.

She paused, then slowly, but resolutely, said, "I'm sorry, but what I'm about to say is going to hurt."

A seismic rumble rose from Dan's feet to his guilty heart. He was terrified of what she was going to say. He was now faced with the nightmare he had been trying to fend off since the day she died. As long as she lived, he never thought he fell short in his devotion to her. They spent their lives nourishing, comforting and encouraging one another and Marion constantly assured him that he had always done that brilliantly. Brilliantly, that is, until she was gone and no longer able to protect him from his searing self-criticism. With each passing day, his guilt grew. *Remember that screening when you argued with her in front of the whole crew? That was so humiliating!* He was in serious prosecutorial form whenever he accused himself. *And that other time you took her brother's side and accused her of . . . he couldn't remember what. How could you do that?* He felt like beating his breast like he did on Yom Kippur but that wouldn't come close to erasing his grievous sins. There were so many times he should have done better, should have said, should not have said, how much more he could have done, except those times when he overdid and made things worse. There were far too many sins of commission and omission to remember right now and he regretted them all, God how he regretted them. If only he could apologize, atone and . . . *wait a minute* . . . what was so important now that she was willing to hurt him deliberately which she never did before? Was it for all his shortcomings or one in particular?

"One in particular," Marion said. "Watching me endure that horrible disease all those years and witnessing the unspeakable agony of those poor souls at the shrine in Nepal, aren't you ashamed to carry on as though you are the only one who ever suffered?"

Dan was dumbstruck.

"If that cuts to your very core, that's good," she said, "because it's another Zen slap, which you badly need. What the hell is all this looking backward to yolks in omelets and butterflies trying to re-enter their cocoons? Look ahead, Dan. *Shiva* is over! We've got important work to do!"

Something marvelous just happened, but what was it? Dan's brain tried frantically to untwist. Then it hit. *We! Shiva is over but we . . . WE . . . Marion and me* . . . he began to tremble. *We've got important work to do!* Dan was giddy despite the stinging slap. *"We've got important work to do."* We! Marion and me. It's not over. He could barely keep from shouting aloud. There was the inescapable moment of panic when he realized that she had gone as easily as she came, but it was countered by the awareness of what this magical encounter meant. It wasn't the end, nor was it random. He was being enlisted to perform a holy mission. Like Jonah, he had been cranky and clumsy, but this was just what he needed, a stiff kick in the butt from God or a Zen slap from Marion to get him on the right path.

A loud BOOM shook the car.

"A celestial exclamation point," Dan thought at first, but when he saw Rocky struggling to control the unresponsive steering wheel and they staggered aimlessly across the road, it occurred to him that this was probably not the lingering echo of his cosmic thunderbolt, but a simple, mundane, very uncosmic tire blow-out.

The smiling onlookers were delighted. Seen through the prism of lilac-scented ganja, this was an exciting event. Dan tried to recreate the vision that nursed him back to life just moments ago. He couldn't, but he didn't feel abandoned. She would be back, because *they* had important work to do!

Rocky got out of the car, went to the trunk, picked up the jack, unbolted the spare and rolled it around to the side with the flat.

"Let me help," Dan said, getting out.

Rocky winked and smiled. "I've got it under control. We'll be on our way in a few minutes."

Watching Rocky, Dan felt very old. He looked on as this sinewy young man kneeled next to the deflated tire, pried off the hubcap, loosened the lug nuts, placed the jack under the frame and raised the car just enough to remove the flat so he could replace it with the spare.

He was absolutely right, Dan thought. Rocky definitely had it under control. Watching the young man proceed expeditiously through the same procedures he had performed so many times with his first junky cars back in Ohio was a moment of watching time moving inexorably forward, with him on the sidelines, observing.

Strains of a familiar song wafted toward them from across the road. It was a soft, pulsating rhythm, the kind that makes your body move before you know what you're moving to.

Drawn to the heady sounds, Dan found himself drifting across the road towards the cluster of handsome young people in jeans and baggy tri-color caps. At the center, was a Rasta with a huge head of long black dreadlocks, sitting on a wooden box, plucking a guitar strung around his shoulder.

Rocky watched from where he was changing tires and couldn't help smiling when he saw Dan swaying rhythmically to the music.

Continuing to strum, the guitarist bade Dan to come

closer. The crowd nudged him forward until he was directly opposite the Rasta.

"I love that song," Dan said.

"Me, too," the guitarist smiled. "What dey call you brother?"

"Dan."

"Dan?"

"As in Daniel."

The Rasta nodded, stopped playing and extended his hand.

"Dey call me Charon. Happy to know you, Brother Daniel."

Charon? Dan didn't see *that* coming. He shook his hand. "Did you say your name is Charon?"

"Dat's right. You heard dat name before? Not many have."

"Yes . . . yes, I have. It's a Greek name."

"If you know Greek, you know more dan me," he laughed. "You say you like dis song? Let's hear you sing it, mon." Charon plucked the strings but Dan was distracted.

"Go ahead, Daniel," the Rasta played the intro again, waiting for him to sing.

Familiar rhythms floated in and out of Dan's head, but he couldn't concentrate on the lyrics. Charon . . . that is what he said. The River Styx. Charon was the boatman!

Charon motioned for Dan to join in, but when he didn't, he started to sing by himself. The original lyrics were in French.

"Of course," Dan said. "Une Chanson d'Amour," from the movie *Béatitude Eternelle,* yet another version of the Orpheus story. Marion taught him the English lyrics and they danced to it a thousand Saturday afternoons on their terrace.

Charon offered him a hit from his spliff, barely missing a beat. Dan took it and inhaled deeply before handing it back.

The sweet taste of ganja in his mouth refreshed his

memory and the words came rushing back as Dan sang out, *"the song in my heart tells me that you will return and tomorrow we will be reunited as one."*

Charon plucked the melody and Dan sang harmony, just as he had with Marion. Amused, the kids laughed and cheered him on. When Charon came to the end of the verse, Dan sang out, *"We fly higher and higher on the wings of eternal bliss, forever one"*

Rocky put the flat tire in the trunk and slammed it shut. He was amused as he approached Dan, who was entranced by the music.

Charon played with dazzling skill and continued the riff into the next verse, which Dan couldn't remember, but his body was totally living it. When the song was over, the kids applauded and the guitarist smiled at Dan.

"Where you know dis from, Daniel?" Charon asked.

"The first time I heard that song, you were singing it in the movie."

"You saw me in a movie?" Charon mocked and someone started to giggle.

"Well, someone playing you . . ."

"What kind of movie is I playin' in?" Charon started to laugh.

"It's called *Beatitude Eternal,* Eternal Bliss. It's a beautiful love story based on the Greek myth."

"Say what?" The kids teased. "What you know about Greek stuff, Charon?" The crowd roared with laughter.

Dan wanted to say something, but what? Everybody was laughing and what could be better than that? He laughed, too. Charon continued to strum as another group of kids stopped to listen. One young boy, admiring his guitar, asked where he got it.

"Bought it wit' my last dollah," Charon said. "Dis guitar is my life and when I die, it gets buried right beside me."

The crowd chuckled.

"Whoa! That's not the line," Dan said. "You're supposed to say, 'Before I came along, this guitar was someone else's. After I'm gone, it will belong to whoever can play it, but right now, it's mine and I'm going to get all the music out of it that I can."

No longer smiling, Charon stopped playing. He looked suspiciously at Dan and said, "What you talkin 'bout mon? Dis guitar is mine. I paid good money for it. Ain't nobody ever gonna play it but 'cept me! Why you talk foolish? You t'ink you know me?"

"Well, only from the film," Dan said.

Charon laughed mockingly. "You know me from a film? You possessed, brother. You possessed."

Rocky tapped Dan on the shoulder. "The tire's changed," he said. "Time to move on."

A bus, adorned with streamers, paper lanterns and a large sign in gala letters that read "Happy Jubilation Day" somehow inched through the crowd and the doors whooshed open. Charon, followed by his entourage, got on board.

Back on the road, Dan sang softly as Rocky looked on.

"Can you turn up the volume?"

Dan sang out, baring his soul. *"Savor the sweet golden rays of autumn as we fly higher on the wings of eternal bliss."*

"Obviously that song has some special meaning for you."

"Don't all lovers have a song? Marion taught me the lyrics the first night we made love. I sang it to her as she walked down the aisle at our wedding. The last time we danced to it . . ." Dan's mind shot back to that moment when they were dancing and Marion suddenly asked, "What if I die before you, will you come and get me?"

At the time, he was unaware of the complexity of her question and answered as if he were being asked under the *chupah* to take Marion as his lawful wedded wife. Without thought, without reservation, the words stormed out of the depth of his soul: "Of course!"

His answer was correct, but he had no idea he was responding to a very different question, one that fulfilled the promise of *bashert* lovers: Will I come and get you? To the ends of the earth and beyond!

{ Chapter Twenty-Three }

CHARON . . . Charon, the boatman on the River Styx. Dan's brain was reeling. He didn't even notice that Rocky had taken an off-ramp. When the car turned onto a wide dirt path with deep potholes, the car began to bounce. Dan popped out of his reverie and looked around.

"Where are we?"

"Ochos Rios," Rocky said and pulled up to a huge three-story house. Gaily dressed people of all ages and sizes filled the lavish grounds. The atmosphere was festive and smiles were everywhere.

"Is this where Molly's Obeahman lives?"

"He and several dozen other people."

"Sounds like a commune," Dan said.

"No, just extended family . . . a very extended family."

Rocky parked between several cars and a bus—a familiar looking bus—adorned with streamers, paper lanterns and a large sign in gala letters that read "Happy Jubilation Day."

Rocky turned off the ignition and they got out. "Make yourself at home," he said and walked towards the house. "I'll see if Molly's arrived."

Dan strolled among cheerful people chatting, some sitting on improvised chairs in the shade. "Happy Jubilation Day," several older women waved and smiled.

"Same to you," Dan replied. Rising above the laughter and good cheer, he heard voices emerging from a group sitting in the shade of a tall cedar tree with a canopy of green glossy leaves. The song sounded familiar. *"Come and go with me to my father's house, to my father's house . . ."* another gospel song from his childhood in Ohio. *There'll be no cryin' there, there'll be no cryin' there. Come and go with me to my father's house, to my father's house."* Only cymbals and a piano were missing. How that church rocked every Sunday morning.

Dan approached the group. They were the same young people that boarded the bus, no mistaking them, and they were clustered around a guitarist—no mistaking him! It was Charon, but he wasn't playing. He was sitting next to a young boy who was barely bigger than the guitar. Charon held the instrument and placed the boy's fingers on the strings. "E," Charon gently coaxed him. He held his hand on the boy's left fingers. "Now strum with your right hand . . . .that's it." Charon encouraged the older kids to sing when they heard the strum.

Strum.

"Come and go with me to my father's house, to my father's house."

Charon shifted the boy's fingers. "B-7th," he said.

Strum. The note rang out and the group joined in. *"There'll be no cryin' there, there'll be no sighin' there."*

"Back to E," Charon moved the boy's fingers.

"Come and go with me to my father's house . . ."

After rehearsing a few verses, Charon said: "You know de chords." He took the guitar and placed it on the boy's knee. "Now you play it."

"Come and go with me to my father's house . . . to my father's house . . ." The boy strummed hesitatingly at first, but he got the chords right. The older kids encouraged him and soon he was in tune and on the beat. *"Come and go with me to my father's house, to my father's house.* By the second verse, the song was accompanied by clapping of hands and everyone joined in. *"There'll be no cryin' there, there'll be no sighin' there. Come and go with me to my father's house . . ."* Charon had the proud look of a teacher as he watched his young protégé.

When the song ended in a rousing crescendo, Dan went to Charon who smiled and extended his hand. "Good to see my brotha Daniel again." He winked. "De Great Book say Daniel is one of de true believers. No mightier power in de world den dat."

"It is true that my namesake was a believer. No doubt about that. It was the only thing that saved him from Nebuchadnezzar's fiery furnace, but that was a long time ago and I'm afraid something was lost in all the years that separate us."

"Time don't make t'ings worse. Dey make dem better. You see, Daniel de First passed his faith on to his chil'en. What did de next generations do? Dey improved on it by inventing music to accompany de love poem between God and man, which is all dat faith is. If de mon worries dat his faith may be failin', what he do? He open his mouth and sing de love song. His ears will hear it and his faith will come back like an echo, only stronger den ever and dat's what carries us tru dis life and beyond. You can believe me when I tell you dat."

"You would know because Charon is the boatman who ferries believing souls across the River Styx, if I remember my Greek."

"You do and you don't. Charon is not just a boatman. He is de bearer of music, widout which dere is no laughter and no love and widout dat, dere is no way to cross over," he winked and laughed.

"I can't tell you how happy I am to see you teaching young people to play your guitar," Dan said.

"Got to. De music is made of good stuff. Stuff of de spirit dat nourishes de soul. Music and love, dat be here forever. Not de human body. No, sir. De body is made of cheap stuff. It don't last. Your fingers get de arterites and your back always be hurtin' and even though your soul maybe risin', your body is sinkin'." He laughed and laughed. "You got to keep de love in de world even after your body gets rotten and starts to stink. Dat's why you teach de young ones how to make music. Den when dey gets old and de voice is too hoarse to sing, dey passes it on to de next batch." Charon fired up a spliff and took a long hit. When he exhaled, he spoke in gasps, not wanting to lose any of the happy linctus. He handed the super-joint to Dan who took a long hit and handed it back.

"Dat's de True Word," Charon said, "exactly like it was handed down from Moses to Joshua to Daniel to Charon to Jesus Christ and reinterpreted most splendidly by our beloved King, Emperor Haile Selassie, de first. Selassiai!" He raised his hand.

"Rastafarai!" Dan said as he high-fived him and they both laughed enthusiastically.

"Back there on the road," Dan said, "someone asked you about your guitar and you said it was yours alone and after you were gone, it would be buried alongside you. No one else would ever get to play it."

"Dat's because you made me out to be somebody in a movie. I live in de true world. Movies lie. De mon say a lot of t'ings to odder men in de movies, but dey just bluster and swagger. Don't mean nuttin. Ain't no trut' to what a man say in a movie."

"But in that movie, Orpheus said what you just said, that the music would go on forever. Just as the guitar came to you, so will it pass on to whoever carries the music to the next generation."

"Well, sometimes what men say in movies can be true. Just like in de real world, people can lie right to your face but some of it be true."

"So how do you know what's true and what isn't?"

Charon took another long hit. As he exhaled, he said "de trut' is in de music, but you got to learn de chords to play it." They both laughed and slapped hands again.

By then, the kid playing guitar sounded really good.

Dan saw Rocky standing at the entrance of the house and walked towards him. When the door opened, a magical figure emerged. *That magnificent, familiar white dress . . . was it . . . ?* Dan couldn't speak, he couldn't move.

"Dan!" she said, but the voice wasn't Marion. As she came closer, he saw that it was Molly, but her hair and face . . . everything about her was Marion, even the dress! He was still numb when she reached him and they embraced for a long time. Then, she pointed to Rocky and said "I see you met my Dan."

ROCKY'S CAR pulled up to a small café opposite a thick wall of mango trees. Molly and Dan got out. "When will you be back?" She asked.

"As soon as I replace the spare," Rocky said. "If your Obeahman gets here before me, give him a hug and ask him to wait. It shouldn't take long." Rocky blew a kiss and drove off. Molly put her arm in Dan's and led him inside.

The café was smaller than the one where they met last night but it too was packed. Molly found a table in the corner and sat down. Dan took the seat across from her, but she moved next to him.

"Your Obeahman is joining us . . . when?"

"Hard to say. He's a busy man, but he'll be here," Molly said.

They sat next to one another without saying anything for what seemed like a long time.

"I can't tell you how happy I am that you're here," Molly smiled and held his hand tight.

He felt blood rushing to his face. "Molly . . . Molly . . ." How to broach this? The words from last night jumped around in his head: *"There will be a wedding or there won't."* Dan needed to get his bearings. "So, when you go back to Israel . . . after you're married," he said, trying to sound casual. "Have you and Rocky decided where you'll be living?"

"No, but I lean toward Safed."

"Why? As I recall, all the action is in Tel Aviv. Safed is a pretty provincial town."

"My philosophy professor at Berkeley was a Jesuit," Molly said. "He told me what life was like in Safed. 'Every Friday afternoon,' he said, 'just before sunset you could feel sanctity in the air.' When he saw the faces of the devout, glowing as they rushed to the synagogue to greet the Sabbath Queen, he knew what James the Apostle must have looked like when he ran to tell the world about the great miracle of the resurrection."

"Is that how you felt when you were in Safed?"

"I haven't been there yet. I talked to Marion about it and she suggested I wait."

"When was that?"

"Just before Rocky and I came to Jamaica, about three weeks ago."

Three weeks ago? Marion spoke to Molly in Israel . . . just like she spoke to me on the road . . . ?

"Walk me back a little," Dan said. "What possessed you go to Israel in the first place?"

"It started with *the phone call.* When I heard about Marion, I went numb. My mind just blanked out. Before that, I had a life plan and everything made sense. Then, nothing did."

"Who called you?"

"My father. Not a paragon of grace but a man with a heart. 'She's gone, Molly dear,' he said. I didn't know what he was talking about at first. There was a moment of hideous silence. 'Marion's gone' he said. 'She died last night.' I couldn't speak. I fell on the floor and couldn't get up. I just lay there crying hysterically. My father's voice kept rolling around my head like a bowling ball knocking down every reason I had to stay alive. 'She's gone,' is what he said . . . just like that. Marion's *gone?!* I lay on the floor repeating that over and over again like a mantra. Gone. Marion's gone."

"Did Steve come to see you?"

"No. He wanted to in the worst way but there was no way I could be with anyone. The earth opened up and I was pulled down into a terrible dark place. Nothing made sense. Marion was the center of my life and now she's *gone?* I have no idea how long I lay on the floor in a fetal position, maybe a day, maybe two, but when I finally got up, I couldn't stop mumbling the word: Gone. Gone? Gone where? Why can't I go wherever she is? I was in a fog for the longest time. Nothing in my head . . . until I remembered that when we meditated, we would sometimes play a game Marion called virtual mind-travel. Do you remember that?"

"I remember finding the two of you in our bedroom, cackling like geese. You were both sitting on the floor in the dark, cross-legged, facing one another with your eyes closed and having so much fun, I never wanted to interrupt."

"That was our special meditation. Marion had devised a method of virtual travel that enabled us to visit any place, any time in the past or future. We started out with familiar stuff, like Caesar's funeral while Mark Antony was giving his eulogy."

"How did she do that?"

"I don't know the nuts and bolts but I was definitely with her when we passed through dozens of different planes."

"Planes?"

"Each plane is a cosmic confluence of time and space. In our meditations, we could go anywhere in any universe, bypassing time and unencumbered by distance."

"Rocky said you believed you could pass between the universe we live in and . . . others."

"Exactly. That was the key and my father, without understanding why he said it the way he did, used the operative word: *gone.* My mission was clear. Go and find her. I tried to mind travel the way we used to, but I was so eager, I had no patience to quiet my brain down enough to meditate, let alone visualize the colors. After a while, I started to get migraines and had to stop. I became desperate. How long can I go on like this? What do I have to do? Where should I go? One night, I sat cross-legged on the floor and all I could think about were the cramps in my calves and back, when the strangest thing happened. The hands on the wall clock melted and a gentle voice came to me.

"'Darling Molly, the time has come to resume our journey.'

"Suddenly, I felt myself travelling with Marion. I don't know how it happened but we were holding hands, gliding through the colors of the spectrum and flying high above the clouds, happier than I had ever been. When we advanced through the last color, violet, we were standing on Mount Sinai, opposite a burning bush. There was no Moses, no Israelites and no God, just us, surrounded by jagged rocks and a tall, thick bush that seemed to be on fire but wasn't giving off any heat. Marion walked through the fire, unharmed. She turned and smiled to me. Without fear, without hesitation, I walked towards the flaming bush and just as I reached it, Marion disappeared and I was suddenly thrust back to my room, sitting cross legged on the floor, feeling ethereal. Something marvelous had happened. I knew precisely where I would find her. Nothing was said. No words, no hints, no innuendoes, no reasons. I just knew where I had to go."

"That's when you went to Mount Sinai?"

"Yes."

"And you found Marion there?"

"There were times when I felt I was close, but it was more confusing than I imagined. I had been looking for Marion, but what I found was something I was totally unprepared for:

Marion's intermediary. As wondrous and thrilling as it was to find Rocky, it made everything more incomprehensible. Was this beautiful, kind young man going to lead me to Marion or was he there to replace her? Or . . . was this her way of leading me to my *bashert?* I had to sort it out. If Marion isn't on Mt. Sinai, where could I find her?"

"So, you traced Marion's steps and went to Nepal."

I took the first plane I could get, but what I found was even more confusing. The Matrix Shrine of Resurrected Souls, which she talked so much about, had been destroyed in a fire years before. Not knowing what to do, I camped out on the site. I meditated for hours every day absorbing all the punishment my body could take. It was excruciating. At the end of every day, I passed out, totally exhausted. One night I was lying on my straw mat for I don't know how long, sweating, trembling, without a thought in my head. Suddenly, I heard a voice. My heart was bursting. My time had come and I was sure I was going to receive my Zen slap.

"'Darling Molly,' Marion's voice reverberated through my soul. 'A Zen slap isn't the only way to break through. There are also Zen kisses.'"

Dan suddenly heard Marion talking through Molly and he was spellbound.

"Zen kisses . . . Zen kisses!" Molly said. "I felt my whole body ring like a thousand bells."

"What did you do?"

"I did the only thing I could do. I started to laugh. It was pure ecstasy and I had no control over it. It occurred to me that I hadn't laughed since before the *phone call,* but there I was, laughing again! Before I knew it, Marion and I were laughing together and I was happy, happy, happy! I was united with the source of my life through laughter—hers and mine, together! How simple. How beautiful. I received the Zen kiss and my life was affirmed through laughter."

Dan was on overload. His head rocked with Marion's voice as it flowed through Molly, alive, funny . . . Pieces of the cosmic puzzle wafted around his brain.

Molly is the catalyst! Molly was the one who brought me to the place of miracles, during a time of miracles when everything will be revealed. But it goes back further, much further, all the way to Guatemala and the curse of the Shaman . . . that was not a curse at all! It was a prophecy. "One lives and one dies but no llores *because the one who dies, lives, and both die and both live. No* llores, *no crying because the child remains."*

A song burst through the café as a truck carrying a reggae band slowly drove by. The amplified chorus rang out:

"Jubilation is here! Resurrection is near!

Love's never lost, only misplaced

She be in time, you be in space.

Jubilation is here! Resurrection is near!"

Entranced by the music, Molly's eyes closed and she sang, swaying to the beat. When the truck finally moved away and the noise drifted off, Molly was aglow. "Did you *get* that?" Molly said. "*Jubilation is here*. The Jubilee has arrived!"

"What am I supposed to *get?*"

"Dan, what does the Bible say about the Jubilee?"

"Once in fifty years . . . slaves are freed. What should I glean from that?"

"On the Day of the Great Jubilee, we are *offered* freedom," Molly said, "but the miracle doesn't happen until we throw off our own shackles. If we are not ready to free ourselves, we remain slaves for all time. It's spelled out clearly in Deuteronomy: '*I set before you this day the choice between between life and death.*' What does God command us to do?"

"Choose life."

"In the text, the Hebrew word for life is in the plural," Molly said. "Not *Chai,* life, but *Chaim,* lives. Why is that?"

"I can't say."

"I can and so can you, Dan. The Kabbalah makes it perfectly clear: Chose life twice . . . here . . . and beyond."

An attractive young waitress came over with a teapot and two cups. "I'm sorry," Dan said, "but we didn't . . ."

"Dat's fine. My fadder say, bring over de tea when you come."

"Your father? Don't tell me your father is . . . ?"

"Abednego," she smiled sweetly.

"Did he sire every pretty girl on this island?"

She thought for a moment then answered thoughtfully. "No . . . not every."

"Well, please thank your father for me."

"You tank him yourself. He be here soon," she said as she filled the cups with the fragrant, lilac tea.

Dan turned to Molly. "Did you know Abednego would be coming here?"

"Of course," she said.

Everything she said—like with Abednego, Charon, and Peacock Man—and everything spoken by anyone on this island, was in a language in which each word contained multiple enigmatic possibilities.

"Molly . . . Molly," Dan said, struggling to steady his mind that was listing from side to side. "Last night . . . I must admit I was a little fuzzy, but what I do remember is what you said about . . ." He felt at once foolish and hopeful like a child who can't quite believe in Santa Claus anymore but still wants to know what kind of gifts he brought. "Marion . . ." he started, but he had to figure how to follow through. "You said she was here waiting for me. I want so much to believe that . . . but I feel like I'm in a game that everybody knows how to play except me. How can I . . . what's the word, rejoin? What am I supposed to do?"

"Throw off your shackles. Open your heart and receive. At the preordained moment, the miracle *will* occur."

Dan didn't realize Molly's hands were still on his until he heard someone say, "Hi, honey!" Rocky stood at their table and kissed Molly on the neck. He reached for Dan's hand and asked "What should I call you, Dan? Pop? Dad? I've already got an *Abba*."

"They're all fine," Dan blushed. He was in the family! Sitting down next to Molly, Rocky asked, "Your *Obeahman* get here yet?" The way he said the word made it hard to read his meaning. Was he a fellow traveler or was he mocking?

"Not yet." Molly had acquired a calmness Dan often wished for back when she was a wired adolescent.

The waitress brought over another pot of tea and filled all three cups. Dan thought he had ingested enough mind-benders for the day, but when Rocky and Molly raised their cups to toast, he couldn't refuse.

Soon, Dan thought it was soon, but who could be sure? A horn honked above jubilant noises outside the café. Dan looked out and saw Abednego smiling and waving from his "machine." Beside him was Charon. When they got out of his junk-heap of a car, Abednego was dressed in a purple velvet robe wearing a crown-like hat and carrying a walking stick that looked like it was carved from the heart of a tree struck by lightning. Molly got up and waved.

"Elegant costume," Dan said. "It was nice of you to invite him."

"Dan," Molly said, "Abednego is our Obeahman."

"What?"

"I thought you knew."

"No . . . I didn't know." Dan was reeling and it wasn't just the tea. Molly's Obeahman just *found* him on the sidewalk in front of the airport when he was a rudderless refugee in an alien place?

Molly led a perplexed Dan, followed by Rocky, out to the car at the epicenter of a crowd that clustered around Abednego, showing the kind of respect they would a bishop or cardinal, but rather than kiss his ring, they laughed together as he greeted each of them by name.

Abednego embraced Molly and when he saw Rocky, he smiled broadly. "De Et'iopian!" He placed his hands on Rocky's shoulders and said to Dan.

"You remember King Solomon?"

"I do," Dan said, "but I can't say I knew him well."

"No, but dis man did," he said pointing to Rocky. "You got to remember our King Solomon, Brother Daniel. He was husband to de Queen of Sheba, and dis young man is de great, great, great, great-grandson reuniting de two mighty civilizations of Ethiopia and Judea." Turning to Rocky, "am I right?"

"I'm sure you are," Rocky said, "but my memory isn't all that good, either. I'm okay with the last two thousand years, but I get a little hazy beyond that."

Watching Rocky, Dan couldn't help but laugh. He had fallen in love with his son's humor . . . did he say, his son? He turned to Molly. "Does Rocky remind you of anybody?"

"Of course. He's you, Dan," Molly said. "I told you, Marion approves."

"Marion approves . . ." the words did pirouettes around his brain, leaping exuberantly over the remnants of fallen firewalls. Clouds disappeared and everything around him was

bathed in clear, soothing colors: bright red, lush green and a golden yellow Jamaican hue that only yesterday seemed tawdry and foreign, but was now radiant and familiar.

"Let's go inside, shall we?" Abednego extended a hand towards the café. Navigating through the throngs that were gathered around him, Abednego had a warm greeting and smile for virtually every woman. They all seemed to know him and Dan thought of what the waitress said in the café. "No, he didn't sire every pretty girl on the Island," but judging from the affectionate embraces from the crowd of women of all ages, he hadn't missed many.

At the entrance to the café, the group stopped. With a wink from Abednego, Charon pulled a violin out of his case and placed it under his chin. His fingers danced on the strings releasing a magical tune—somewhere between gypsy and reggae. The enlivened crowd clapped their hands and sang. Some danced, slowly at first, but as the pace of the music quickened, the movements became more spirited. The dance ended with an audacious bravado, fast chord crossings and rapid flourishes of the bow. Dan was amazed at Charon's virtuosity. This was one of the best violin performances he had ever witnessed.

After lengthy applause and mutual blessings, Abednego entered the café, followed by Charon, Molly, Rocky and Dan. Inside, the noise level dropped precipitously. Abednego led them to a small round table in a corner where they stood patiently until the waitress arrived with a tray of five cups. She carefully placed them in a perfect circle. Abednego kissed her dotingly on the cheek. "My wise, lovely . . . daughter," he said, trying to remember her name. "Ya-el," the girl smiled, kissed her dad and left.

Abednego picked up each cup and ceremoniously handed

one to Dan, Charon, Molly and Rocky, keeping the last one for himself. They raised their cups and downed the fragrant tea. Abednego returned his empty cup to its place at the head of the circle. The others placed their cups next to his in the precise order they were served. Dan, a little wobbly, tried to place his in the circle but he couldn't make it fit. Without a word, Molly expanded the circle to make room for Dan's cup. The benevolent smile that appeared on Abednego's face when he looked at Ya-el was now directed at Dan.

"Shall we begin our pilgrimage?"

{ Chapter Twenty-Four }

"*PILGRIMAGE?*" Dan blurted out "What pilgrimage?" He pleaded, looking first at Molly, then Abednego. "Where am I going . . . and how will I know when I get there? I don't even know where I am!"

"Can any mon ever know de end of his journey before he's begun?" Abednego said solemnly. "As to where you are," he turned to Molly. "Please recall for my brother dat very telling conversation you recently had wid Marion concerning der sojourn in Paris."

Molly took a moment, and then channeled Marion's voice.

"In our stately suite at the Hotel Regina, I was sitting on the embroidered divan, staring dreamily at the lush Tuilerie Gardens and beyond to the Eiffel Tower, decorated for the millennium with a thousand multi-colored crystals. The sun was slowly setting through a blaze of copper and pink clouds . . ."

Dan felt the room shake. The voice, the inflection, the rhythm was absolutely MARION! His heart was racing.

"The grandeur of the moment was overwhelming. I was holding a flute of Pommery in one hand and with my other I picked up the joint that had been beckoning to me from the ormolu table next to the window."

Where is this coming from?! Dan was unnerved. Marion's voice . . . the multi-colored crystals on the Eiffel Tower, the embroidered divan . . . the ormolu table! How could Molly know that?

"Dan, busy-busy, worrying about our finances, was hunched over his computer, looking unhappy."

Dan was aware that he was in Jamaica and only watching the scene of them in Paris as it was being reconstructed in the private screening room of his mind in synch with the sound track of Marion's voice from the past, speaking to him in the present . . . my God . . . the wonder of it all!

Molly continued. *"What the hell are you doing, Dan?"*

Her voice changed and she sounded exactly like Dan! *"I'm trying to figure out where we are. Between our share of foreign and residual TV sales from a reissue of Graduation Day . . . and one of our long term investments . . ."*

Molly returned to her natural voice and spoke directly to Dan. "Then, Marion came to you and stuck the joint in your mouth." Reverting to Marion's voice, she said *"Stop figuring! I'll tell you where we are. We're in Paris and the sun is setting over the Tuileries Gardens in a dazzling array of colors and contours that we may never see again! That's where we are, Dan. Here, you and me, together . . . now . . . and forever."*

Dan felt stunned, then exposed. Surprising himself, he started to laugh . . . and laugh! It was uncontrollable. He laughed until he had no more breath. His first Zen kiss.

Abednego placed his hand on Dan's chest. "I will tell you where you are at *dis* moment, my brother. You are approaching de Garden. Your eyes are opening and your ears are beginning to hear, but if you wish to enter, you must t'row off every one of de shackles dat restrains your spirit. Are you fully prepared to do dat?"

"I am!" Dan said . . . but inwardly, for a brief moment, he waited for a dagger of doubt to slip between his ribs. It did not!

Abednego removed his hand from Dan's chest and focused on the table of five cups. Without a word, he slowly removed two cups from the circle. The first was Rocky's . . . and the second was in front of Molly, who was visibly stunned. Turning to Dan, Abednego said "Go now. Revelation awaits you." He pointed to Charon. "The hour of *Neila* is approaching. Move!"

Charon pulled Dan out the door and into the crowd. Surrounded by high-spirited revelers, Dan looked over his shoulder and saw Molly, still inside the café, holding her empty cup in front of Abednego and arguing strenuously. It was impossible to hear what they were saying but Molly was clearly upset. Abednego appeared to be unyielding.

Suddenly Molly rushed out of the café followed by Rocky. With tears running down her face, she hugged Dan then disappeared into the crowd. Rocky followed, clearly troubled.

Abednego emerged from the café and took Dan by the arm. Without a word, he pulled him across the road to a forest of tall trees and dense foliage. Charon followed, his violin case slung over his shoulder. Dan tried to see where Molly went but she wasn't anywhere he looked.

Abednego pushed through the clusters of hanging vines and gnarled underbrush until he came to a narrow path. He set a robust pace with Charon right behind. Dan followed, but it was hard for him to navigate the rugged terrain. Getting winded, he leaned against what he thought was a tree. It wasn't. It was one of the many tall thin plants that sprouted overnight in the leafy forest. Dan tumbled to the ground.

"Keep up!" Abednego commanded without looking back.

"I'm doing the best I can," Dan said.

"Dat's not good enough!" Abednego rebuked. Not the jolly Islander anymore. As they advanced into the forest, sounds of revelers from the road gradually dimmed until they vanished and were replaced by bird calls, crickets and a range of unrecognizable insect screeches. Further down the narrow path, bordered on all sides by tall green, yellow and red vegetation, they began to hear the pummeling sound of cascading water that became louder as they burrowed into the heart of the tropical garden.

At the end of the path, they faced a waterfall roaring down a massive sheet of solid rock into a wide but shallow pond below. Abednego took a silver chalice out of the elaborate bag hanging from his left shoulder. "We made it," he said. Raising the chalice to his lips, he lit the tightly packed buds. Soon, all three were engulfed in a cloud of aromatic lilacs. Dan no longer felt tired. He was energized.

"If you could hike as well as you smoke, we would all have fewer anxieties," Abednego gently teased. Dan thought that was hilarious and roared with laughter. "I can't tell you how good it feels to laugh at myself." Soon all three were laughing joyously, triumphantly and with complete abandon. When the laughter abated, a mantle of hallowed silence settled on them.

Abednego entered the pond, bidding Charon and Dan to follow. The water was warm and the rapturous sun sat perilously atop the waterfall, ready to drop at any moment into the darkness beyond. Still in the shallows, Abednego raised his hands to the wall of rushing water and began to intone, with the cadence of a high priest: *"Tru trials and tribulations, tru death and transmigrations, on dis day of de great Jubilee, separated souls will be rejoined and your children will rejoice as in days of old."*

Abednego waded across the pond. Charon followed with Dan close behind. When they reached the base of the falls, Abednego rose from the pond and climbed behind the curtain of water to a dry space, about three feet in width, separating the cascading water and a massive wall of sheer rock. Charon entered the dry space with the violin case strung over his shoulder. The rock wall was punctuated by tiny crevices, like rungs of a ladder. Carefully sliding his feet into the small openings, Charon began to climb, one foot after the other. Abednego motioned for Dan to follow. Bewildered, Dan wasn't prepared to climb a rock cliff behind a waterfall, but when Abednego began to climb and reached for his hand, he knew there was nowhere to go but up. The gaps along the wall and the natural incline of the slope made for a possible, if not easy, climb.

Just below the crest, Abednego led the group out of the falls to a stone ledge at the end of a narrow path. Below was a pristine lake in a perfectly formed crater. Abednego, Charon and Dan descended to the edge of the lake where they stood in silence, embraced by pale rays of the full moon. Slowly, solemnly, Charon removed his violin from its case, raised it to his chin and began to play.

An ethereal melody that was as mystical as it was passionate swirled through the awesome silence. The sun had completely set and only the haunting glow of the moon and a galaxy of stars lit up the night.

As Charon played, the most enchanting thing happened. His violin drifted out of his hands, wafted over the water and continued to play. He stood with both hands in position but the instrument was twenty feet away, playing itself! Dan had no idea how that happened or why he didn't react to the strangeness of watching a violin float over water on its own power, emitting the most celestial sounds, but it seemed perfectly natural at the time. All he felt was his soul gliding on the spellbinding waves of the music when something even more amazing happened. A long, perfect harmonious chord arose from the violin and heralded the appearance of a tiny bright spot of light emerging from the distant shore.

Abednego pointed to an obscure image across the lake that was approaching and becoming larger. It was a wooden raft with a woman bathed in white light sitting in the center. Behind her, a hooded man pushed and guided the raft with a long pole. Dan's heart pounded as the image grew larger and the raft slowly advanced across the smooth surface of the lake towards the shore.

"It's her! It is . . . it really is MARION!" There she was . . . radiant . . . splendid . . . the most beautiful creature he had ever seen. Dan tried to race toward the water, but he couldn't move. Abednego stood behind him, firmly holding both his arms. "Let me go!" Dan shouted.

"She will come to you when you have fully liberated yourself and are ready to receive her," Abednego said in a soft, but commanding voice. "Circumcision of de heart has only just begun."

Circum . . . where did Dan hear that? Yes, it was that ride in the mango truck. He turned to Abednego, who was still holding him from behind, "I don't know what the hell circumcision of the heart is, but I'll do it. I'll do anything!"

Struggling to free himself, he called out "Marion! My love, my *basherte.*" He screamed as loud as he could, unable to free himself from Abednego's powerful grip.

As he wrestled, the music grew louder. Looking up, Dan saw the violin that had been wafting over the water coming closer to shore and behind it was the raft. Led by the music, Marion was coming to him! An otherworldly radiance emanated from her and when she looked directly at Dan, it was as though she were sending him a bridge of light that he could actually walk across. Dan pulled with all his strength, but Abednego's hands were firm. The passionate sounds of the violin nearly drove Dan mad as he struggled to join his beloved.

Slowly, almost imperceptibly, the violin floated back into Charon's hands and the music segued to "Chanson d'Amour"!

Marion's eyes focused on Dan and her luminous smile felt like a splash of starlight. Helpless and held back beyond his strength, he screamed again "Marion!"

She looked from Dan on the shore to someone sitting alongside her on the raft. Dan followed her gaze. Sitting next to her on the raft was . . . him! He looked around and saw that Abednego was still holding him, but there he was also on the raft, simultaneously! Two people and both of them were him! Behind him and Marion was the hooded boatman, holding onto the long pole.

"What are you waiting for, Dan?" she gently teased, looking into his eyes. "Still trying to figure out where you are?"

The sound of Marion's voice thrilled him to his core and he couldn't find words. Words? Forget words! Here she was, sitting right next to him. They were together at last! This wasn't another dream. He wasn't mistaking her for some stranger in a crowd. This was his Marion, the whole person, at once regal and vibrant, exciting, funny, sexy, beautiful. Dan was giddy. He reached for her . . . to touch her face, to kiss her, to hold her, but his hands wafted right through her, like a hologram.

"Marion, my dearest love, you are here, aren't you?"

"I am and so are you, my *bashert*."

Dan passed his hand through her again and again. It was the strangest experience of his life. "What's happening?"

She smiled. "If you couldn't understand quantum mechanics, you won't get this. Not yet, anyway."

"Parallel universes?"

"Close. It has more to do with ionized electrons but forget the technology for now. You will understand when you enter this realm but that requires complete circumcision of the heart. You've taken the first step and that's how you came this far, but there's more."

"Circumcision? That sounds terrible, but nothing is as painful as being without you. Whatever it is, I'll do it."

The boatman, still hooded, spoke. "That is not something you can do. It happens or it doesn't."

The intrusion of this new pain in the ass was irritating, even though his voice sounded familiar. "Look buddy," Dan said, "you just steer the raft."

Marion laughed.

"Who does this guy think he is?"

"He has been looking after me since I crossed over."

"Well, tell him to bugger off. I'm here now."

Marion motioned to the boatman and he drew back his hood. He was . . . Dan, a slightly younger version, but Dan, nonetheless.

Dan suddenly felt outgunned or at least outnumbered. "How many goddam parallel universes am I in?"

"You are in the best of all possible worlds, Dan," the young Dan said. "I am merely a form. Once you get here, I'm off to another program."

"I don't want to be in the best of all possible worlds," Dan said. "I just want to be in the one with the circumcised heart, the one Marion is in . . . and who the hell asked you?" Turning to Marion, he said "Just tell me how circumcision works where you are and I'll do the cutting myself."

She laughed. "Honey, it's the same word, and maybe the same intent, but circumcision of the heart is entirely different from what you're used to. There is no knife, no *mohel* and no egg salad canapés. It happens when it's your time."

"Please, God, let it be my time now. Oh, Marion, I've been ready for two years, seven months and nearly two weeks. How much more can I take? You once said the most important goal in life is to find your *bashert* because that is what enables you to give all your love. Since you left, there is no love. There is nothing."

"I know how awful it's been and asking you to be patient isn't easy for me, but it's the only way we can be rejoined. I wish I could edit your program. I wish that with all my heart, but I can't. No one can."

"What do I do? Just eat my liver and wait? I can't do that, especially now that I've seen you. I want to touch you, caress you, make love to you."

Marion laughed. No one in the world had that joyous life-affirming laugh that made Dan's heart soar. "Dan . . ." she said as she tried to stop laughing. "Make love?" She couldn't stop.

"What's so funny?"

"In the parallel universe we are currently in," Marion said, still laughing, "there is a *semblance* of feeling, but it doesn't come through the senses. It's more ethereal. In other words, at this stage I can identify deeply with your passion on an extra sensory level, but a blow job is out of the question."

Dan laughed so loud he heard his echo reverberate across the lake.

"You are the only one in the world who can make me explode with complete happiness."

"It's important for me to see that, Dan. I am aware of your suffering, just as you were of mine and I know how hard this has been for you. I can't tell you how sorry I am that you have to go through it, but you do."

"Why?"

"How do I explain this? It's not that it is what it is. More accurately, it isn't what it isn't. Think Aristotle or Maimonides. Negative attributes enable you to approach, but there is no way to actually elucidate in explicit terms because it is beyond perception. I know you're not fond of the word, but in the end it is a matter of *faith*. Like it or not, that is the only passage available to us."

"Passage to where? What's it like where you are?"

"Well, fortunately I'm not a virgin nor a Taliban, so I don't have to be in a harem of some lunatic suicide bomber along with seventy-two other idiots."

"Is it true, then, what the *Jihadis* say?"

"Dan, have you met me? I'm joking!"

She did it again! Marion is the only one who was able to constantly surprise him and he loved that so much about her.

"What I have to know," he said, "the terrible pain you suffered all those years, is that part completely over?"

"And not one septillionth of a second too soon, but I came to understand through the pain—mine *and* yours—that the foundation of the entire program is *balance*. Like entropic gravitation, the force that prevents planets from crashing into one another, cosmic balance is the mechanism that enables preordained lovers to reunite."

"I'm sorry honey, maybe I'm shy a few billion brain cells, but I don't see the connection."

"Look at us, Dan. Ours is a love story conceived in heaven. Two *bashert* lovers *surprisingly* find one another and live a life of perfect bliss. In time, just as the cosmos expands—each star and galaxy on its own trajectory—so too does each half of the blessed union evolve to the next stages of death, transmigration, resurrection and reunification but all in perfect balance and all preordained. Unfortunately for the suffering survivor, the only thing he can see is confusion and torment, but in the vast realm of parallel universes, there is a glorious climax to this Divine Spectacle. We *will* be reunited in *béatitute eternelle*."

"All I want is to dance with you until the end of time."

"That's exactly the point," Marion said.

"It's time to move on," the pain-in-the-ass young Dan with the guide pole said.

"You shut the fuck up!" the current Dan barked.

"Whoa!" said the young Dan. "When did we become such a grump?"

"We?! What we? There is no we. There's only Marion and me and we're not going anywhere!"

"Look, I'm with you, guy," the younger Dan said to Dan, "but my job is to look after Marion until you get here and it's time she returned."

"He's right, Dan," Marion said. "This has been wonderful but I have to leave you now and I have an important favor to ask."

"Anything!"

"It's Molly," Marion said solemnly. "She's allowed her priorities to drift. You recall I told you on our last visit that we have an important mission. Well, it's become more critical. Molly was so wounded by my passing that she thought reuniting with me should be her primary objective in life and that is when she veered off course. Neither Molly nor Rocky have yet learned the essential lesson that sustains *bashert* couples. '*. . . through trials and tribulations . . .*' their primary obligation must be to shield one another from every force that threatens the Divine Mandate that brought them together. They demonstrated that they can withstand any challenge from without, but when they turn against one another their holy covenant is in jeopardy. You and I are part of a cosmic chain that is reinforced as each link fulfills its destiny. Molly and Rocky are the next link but their love is as vulnerable as it is exalted. If we don't intervene, that could create an irreparable breach. To put it bluntly, their actions could have catastrophic implications."

The violin stopped playing abruptly and "Chanson d'Amour" was over. The boatman, his hood in place, quickly pushed on the pole and the raft began to glide back across the lake. As it drifted away, Dan was no longer on it. Before he knew what was happening, he was back on the shore, watching as Marion waved.

"Tell me, what can I do?" Dan yelled as loud as he could.

"Gan Eden Farloren!" she called out and was gone.

"Marion, come back. Please!" He screamed until he was hoarse.

"Gan Eden Farloren . . . ," Abednego said. "Paradise Lost? Does dat mean someting to you?"

"I'm afraid so."

PART NINE

Bashert

{ Chapter Twenty-Five }

RIIIIIING . . . RIIIIING . . . RIIIIING. Reaching around in the dark, Dan knocked something over. Riiiiiing . . . riiiiiing . . . whatever fell, it wasn't the phone. Riiiiiing . . . He turned on the table lamp behind his bed and groggily picked up the receiver.

"She's gone," a voice said.

Fragments of last night floated into his dazed brain . . . Marion, the raft . . .

"Molly's gone, Dan! You've got to help me."

"Rocky?"

It was still middle of the night when Dan came downstairs. He couldn't have slept more than a couple of hours. The festival ended at midnight and the lobby was practically empty except for a few bedraggled partiers finishing their nightcaps or saying goodnight to yawning friends. In a dark corner of the reception area, Rocky sat alone, his face in his hands.

"What's going on?" Dan said.

Rocky stood up and Dan embraced him. "She's gone, Dan. This time I'm afraid it's for good."

"What do you mean, she's gone? What happened?"

Rocky slid back into his chair. "I can't really say." His voice broke.

Dan sat next to him. "Talk to me, son."

"It's stupid," Rocky said sorrowfully. "An argument that never should have happened."

Their eyes met. Dan waited.

"When Abednego told her she would not be part of . . . the event, Molly blew a fuse. He explained that what was about to happen could only take place between the *bashert* lovers. He said there might be another encounter that could involve her, but that would have to happen at another time."

"Molly's face turned red and her hands began to shake. 'It isn't fair!' She screamed and burst into tears. 'You can't do this to me!" Abednego said he understood how distressed she was, but she had no choice other than to reconcile her ego with the strict guidelines of the process. 'You can't shut me out,' she said. 'It's not right.'"

"What did you say?" Dan asked quietly.

"Me? Nothing. What could I say? She was so upset she wouldn't even talk to me. When we got home, she fell onto her bed and wailed. She was completely irrational and said all kinds of things that made no sense. I tried every way I knew to calm her down. I told her that she wasn't being cut out, merely placed in whatever order her Obeahman thought was appropriate and since she trusted him . . . She sat up and stared at me, her face twisted in anger. 'Abednego betrayed me. Why are you taking his side?' I told her I'm not taking anybody's side!

"Clearly she was upset, but why take it out on me? I told

her to talk to Abednego when he gets back. I'm sure . . . something . . . I don't even remember what I said. I just wanted her to settle down. She looked at me like I was her worst enemy and spoke so softly I could barely hear, 'You don't know me at all. Never mind. I'll go myself.'"

"Go where?" Dan asked.

"I can't say for sure."

"You didn't ask?"

"I knew where she *wanted* to go, to the waterfall everybody talked about but only Abednego knew how to get there. I told her there was no way for her to find it by herself.

"Without even looking at me, she said disdainfully, 'If you loved me, I wouldn't have to go by myself.'

"I told her how ridiculous that was and yes, I blew my stack, okay? 'If I loved you?!' After all you put me through, running away to some ashram in the Himalayas without a word, making me so miserable, all I could think about was killing myself and now you want me to prove my love for you by running out in the middle of the night to look for some path in a forest neither of us could ever find? I told her to get some cosmic GPS. Maybe that way we could find the *alleged* waterfall."

"What did she say?"

"She said I was mocking everything she believed in."

"Weren't you?"

"No, not really, not intentionally anyway, but I was angry, too. I didn't mean to say it that way. It just came out. She left without even looking at me. I know the way I said it was wrong. If I could take it back, I'd swallow those words. It was a mistake, a simple, stupid mistake."

"What are you going to do?"

"I was hoping you could talk to her."

"Gan Eden Farloren . . ." the words drifted into Dan's brain and pushed everything else out. He looked around to see if SHE was there. SHE wasn't, but the voice was unmistakable.

"Do you love Molly?" Dan asked.

"I would die for her," Rocky said.

"She doesn't want you to die for her. She needs you to be on her side. She needs you to defend her, support her . . ."

"GAN EDEN FARLOREN! Get to the point," said the voice.

"Rocky, have you ever heard of *Gan Eden Farloren?*"

"What?"

"It's a Yiddish version of *Paradise Lost.*"

Rocky looked at him as though he were an alien from a distant planet.

"It's like no other film you've ever seen," Dan said. "On one hand, it's a love story about mice, but . . ."

"What the fuck, Dan?!"

"The mice are only a metaphor. The movie is about how people in love can let a thoughtless action by one partner and an equally reckless response, destroy a sublime union."

"If this is going to be a sermon or a pitch for a movie, spare me, please. I'm losing it here! Can't you see that?"

"It's not a pitch. It's a life lesson and one you badly need to learn or you're in deeper shit than you know."

"I'm trying to focus, Dan, and with respect, I don't know what the hell you're talking about."

"I'm talking about your lover's disappointment because you failed to fight for her and you felt underappreciated. You believed you were being unfairly blamed for something you had nothing to do with, so you countered by mocking her, but the point is that neither of you created the problem. It came crashing into your lives. Neither of you knew how to diminish the tension, so you reacted by attacking one another. The result is that she ran away. Can you blame her?"

"What was I supposed to do? I don't understand what she and her *Obeahman* are talking about half the time."

"Amazing," Dan said, "The grate beneath both of you heated up to the point where it was obliterating your love and you were both willing to let that happen!"

"I love Molly with all my heart, Dan. I'm lost without her. Lost."

"I believe you're both lost without one another."

"If I could just talk to her."

"What would you say?"

"I would explain that I love her and I'm not the one to blame for her unhappiness."

"You tried that, didn't you? How far did your *explanation* get you?"

"We're civilized people, for God's sake. If we can't rationally discuss our problems, we're savages."

"Rocky, Rocky, Rocky. Forget what you learned at M.I.T. Of course we're savages! We're Neanderthals, just a few millennia down the evolutionary pike, but the dominant instinct remains. A man must defend his mate, no matter what. When she feels threatened by anyone or anything, you'd better be on her side. Forget rational. Love, if it's real, is beyond that. There are no exceptions, no right or wrong, no limits and no consideration for anyone or anything else. When you fail to stand up for her, you destroy the one thing every woman since Eve is entitled to—complete trust in her man. When that's missing, everything dries up and dies. It's as simple and tragic as that."

"I can't let that happen."

"It may have already. You'd better get her back and soon. The longer you wait, the harder it's going to be to repair the damage."

"I would take her back in a second if I could, but what can I do?"

"What can you do? What has every man done to get his woman back after he's disappointed her and made her feel unworthy and unloved? Drop to your knees and tell her how wrong you were and how sorry you are and beg her to forgive you. Swear to stand by her forever and you'd better mean it or you'll lose the greatest gift life has to offer."

"I would in a second, I swear it. I would crawl at her feet if she would let me. I would defend her to the death, but she's gone, Dan. Gone!"

WHEN MOLLY'S TAXI drove through the open-air mall that surrounded The Moonlight Bay Resort, it felt haunted. A few straggling tourists stumbled past empty stores but the party was clearly over. When the cab pulled up to the hotel, she got out, dried her tears and entered.

The concierge dialed, then held a phone to his ear and smiled to Molly. After many unanswered rings, he hung up. "Apparently Mr. Sobol isn't in his room. Would you like to leave a message?"

Molly shook her head and left. The vast mall that was the hub of action earlier in the day was now eerily silent. Fumes from the fire eaters still wafted through the night air as Molly walked aimlessly past closed shops. Elaborately dressed mannequins flaunting their stylish wares silently challenged her. *Who gave you permission to be here? To be anywhere? You were left out, remember?*

Molly sat silently, miserably on a stone bench. Later, hard to say when, a hand approached out of the darkness and rested gently on her shoulder. Looking up, she saw Abednego standing in front of her, his face, the image of compassion. When he extended his hands, tears filled her eyes. Abednego gently raised her up and wrapped his arms around her. He held her lovingly, as he did with his own daughter earlier that day, until Molly was all cried out.

DRIVING IN THE DARK with only their headlights and the full moon to keep them on the road, Rocky and Dan made their way slowly. The massive crowds were gone, which made driving easier, but left them without anyone to ask if they were going the right way. After a few wrong turns, Rocky finally found the café where the pilgrimage with Abednego began.

"The path is somewhere through those trees across the road," was the best Dan could do. He led Rocky to a point in the wall of thick foliage that he thought might lead to the familiar path. It didn't. Rocky saw a narrow clearing and raced towards it. He called excitedly to Dan, who ran to join him. By the time he arrived, they both saw that the clearing led nowhere. Winded, Dan had to sit down but Rocky refused to rest. He raced through thick trees, over huge gnarled roots, desperately looking for some kind of path. Rocky thought he had finally found a trail that appeared to go further into the forest. Excited, he moved deeper and deeper through dense undergrowth, accompanied by loud sounds of crickets and night birds. By the time Dan joined Rocky, they were at the end of the trail. There were no diverging paths, only a dead end.

Suddenly . . ."Listen!" Rocky said.

Dan heard nothing except the night creatures of the forest.

"Cascading water! Don't you hear it?"

Dan shut his eyes and tried hard to concentrate. "I'm sorry," he said. I don't hear anything like that."

"Beyond those tall bushes!" Rocky shouted as he raced

briskly through the wall of plants and gnarled scrub into the heart of the forest. He was practically running through the spiny foliage that felt like so many needles, forging ahead to the source of the sound, while Dan did his best to keep up. Rocky was a good thirty yards ahead of Dan when he turned and waved both hands, frantically pointing to his ears. Dan tried hard to listen. It took a few moments, but he did hear something. It could be . . . it was . . . a waterfall! *If I can hear it, it must be close,* Dan thought. He ran through the brush and tripped several times on the knotted roots until he got to Rocky. That's when he saw it. Cascading water from the falls roared into the pond below, reflecting the full moon.

When they reached the pond, Dan waded in as he had before with Abednego. Rocky followed, but when they approached the falls, Rocky threw up his hands. "How does anybody climb up that?"

Through the roar of gushing water, Dan shouted and gesticulated that behind the surging tide was a dry area, and a wall of rock, but with fissures that serve as a ladder. Rocky sprang ahead and cautiously found his way behind the sheet of water to the massive dry rock. Dan followed. When Rocky found the gaps in the wall, he literally pulled Dan up. Just below the crest, Dan pointed to a stone ledge. Rocky found the way down a narrow path and carefully guided Dan to the lake below. When they arrived, Dan was totally exhausted and had to stop to catch his breath.

In the distance, two lone figures stood at the shore. Exotic strains of a distant violin, in rhythm with the dancing waves, created a dreamlike ballet.

At water's edge, Charon stood with his arms in position to play his violin, but the instrument was already wafting over the water. Rocky and Dan approached Abednedgo who was facing the lake, chanting aloud. *"Tru trials and tribulations, tru death and transmigrations . . ."*

When he completed his invocation, he turned and opened his arms.

"Welcome, my brothers, we been expectin' you. Wasn't too sure you would find us," he said to Dan, "but we had fait in de Et'iopian."

"Help me," Rocky said. "I love her . . . I need her . . . What can I do to bring her back?"

Abednego put both hands on Rocky's shoulders, whose eyes were filled with tears. Standing face to face, Abednego looked at the young man as Abraham must have stared at his son Isaac, aware that his mission carried the awesome mandate that God required and he could do nothing other than obey.

"Are you prepared to undergo complete circumcision of the heart?"

"I am."

"Without fear or doubt?"

"Without any fear or doubt!" Rocky's response was swift and firm. "Just tell me what to do."

"Follow. Listen. Obey. You cannot go to her. She will come to you at the appointed time."

Abednego stepped into the water. With his shawl over his head, he raised his arms with his fingers spread as the priestly *Cohanim* did in the Holy Temple on the Day of Atonement and waved them across the lake. When he completed his incantation, he signaled Rocky to join him. Without the slightest hesitation, Rocky strode into the dark depths. The previously calm water formed ripples around him slowing his pace but he continued to forge ahead. When he was in up to his waist, the swells became violent and he couldn't move.

Dan, feeling like a protective father for the first time in his life shouted to Abednego, "Stop! He'll drown!"

"He's still in de shallows, but it's good you noticed," Abednego said softly. "Very good indeed."

Advancing towards Rocky, Abednego raised his hand to Dan indicating that he should remain on shore. The violin hovering above the lake followed Abednego as he approached Rocky. The two men stood face to face without a word. He placed his hand on the young man's chest as the music, listing between somber and passionate, reflected the uncertain mood of the night. Rocky's eyes were wide as a child's, waiting for a magician to perform an amazing trick. Abednego's face was solid rock, betraying not the slightest hint of what might happen.

At the exact moment that Rocky felt his heart bursting, a small light appeared in the distance. The light grew brighter and the raft came closer. At its center, Marion shone in all her splendor. On her lap was Molly, engulfed in her light, laughing, happy and stretched across Marion in the pieta position she assumed when she was a child and Marion taught her everything she needed to know about life. Rocky's instinct was to race towards the raft, but Abednego raised his hand commanding him to stop. To Abednego's consternation, Rocky lurched ahead and swam with increased might against the turbulent water, crying out "Molly, wait, I'm coming!"

The music suddenly became dissonant and the violin sprang back into Charon's arms on shore. The raft came to an abrupt halt and Rocky made a lunge for it, but the boatman reacted quickly and reversed the forward motion. Horrified, watching the raft swiftly moving in the opposite direction, Rocky tried to swim towards it, but he was blocked by the intensity of the raging waters. He cried out to Abednego. "Stop them. Please . . . I have to bring her back."

In the twinkling of an eye, as Rocky's pleas drifted plaintively across the lake, the light disappeared and darkness once again hovered over the face of the deep.

"Gan Eden Farloren," Abednego whispered solemnly.

With eyes full of rage and sorrow, Rocky shrieked with the excruciating reverberations of the bereaved. "NO!"

Back on shore, Charon held his violin at his side. Next to him, Abednego stood facing the lake. Only Rocky was left in the water, flailing and weeping as he looked in vain for the raft that was no longer there. The unbearable echoes of his cries filled the night.

When he got back to shore, Rocky fell on the ground and wept until he had no more sounds left. Dan put his hand gently on his shoulder, but there was no comforting him.

"Let him be," Abednego murmured. "God counts repentant tears."

Suddenly, they heard a voice call out.

"Rocky?" It was Molly, standing on the shore, not far from them.

Rocky ran to her and held her so tight, Dan was afraid he might crush her. "Can you ever forgive me, Molly . . ." he began, but she interrupted him.

"There's no need to forgive, only to love one another completely and totally to the end of time. Did you ever hear of *Gan Eden Farloren?"*

They embraced for the longest time. Abednego smiled broadly. Turning to Dan, he said. "Circumcision of de heart is de key to parallel universes, and like Marion say, once de mon got dat, everyting else is just engineerin'."

{ Chapter Twenty-Six }

IT WAS A BRIGHT SUN-KISSED MORNING when Charon, driving Abednego's junk heap, dropped Dan off at the hotel. Jubilation Day was over and tourists headed for the airport in caravans of taxis and buses. There was a message at the desk. It was from Steve.

In his room, Dan placed a call and wonder of wonders, he got through.

"So . . . ?" Steve asked.

Dan's first reaction was to say I don't know where to begin, but instead, he simply said "It looks like the wedding's on."

"I can't tell you how . . ." Steve's voice cracked. "Call you back." Click.

Something wasn't right. Steve sounded distracted, not the forceful, positive commander who was always firmly in control and ten steps ahead of everybody else.

After a few minutes, the phone rang again. Dan picked up

immediately. "Are you okay? You sound like you're coming down with something."

"I'm fine," he said, then coughed. "I've just landed in Kingston. I'll be at the hotel as soon as I can. Listen, I'd appreciate it if you would talk to a friend of mine. It would mean a lot to me . . . ." His voice broke again and he hung up abruptly.

After a quick cup of Jamaican coffee that he made in the brewer in his room, Dan was in the lobby to meet Steve's friend, who called shortly after they spoke. He looked through the crowd of departing tourists and bustling hotel personnel and there she was. When he got to her, they embraced lightly.

"Dan, I'm so happy you agreed to see me," she said. It was Gabrielle and he began to think there must be more to this story since she was in the seat next to him on the plane from L.A. and Steve had given him his ticket, complete with seat assignment.

There was. A whole lot more.

After the perfunctory niceties, Dan said, "Obviously your coming to Jamaica had something to do with Steve."

"He told you about his divorce?"

"He did," Dan said.

"Did he say he was involved with another woman?"

"He did."

"Can we . . . ?" Gabrielle pointed to a quiet corner of the lobby.

Seated comfortably, each waited for the other to begin.

"So, where did you meet Steve?"

"On my couch."

"Excuse me?"

She laughed. "That's Steve's favorite joke. I've been his

psychotherapist for over two years and his lover for half that time."

"Two years? Where have I been all that time?"

"With the exception of his daughter, Steve loves you more than anyone in the world. He knew what you were going through and he was careful not to expose you to anything he wasn't sure you could handle . . . with one exception."

"What's that?"

"His baby's wedding. He needed a favor only you could provide. Didn't he tell you what would have happened if you refused?"

"He said he wouldn't be invited but I didn't take that seriously."

"I don't really think he did either, but that was a risk he couldn't afford to take. Even the remote possibility that he might be shut out was so upsetting, he became seriously depressed."

"Why was Molly so adamant about me conducting her wedding? We haven't seen each other in over two years."

"She didn't say, but it was obviously important to her."

"She could have called me directly. Why all the intrigue? "

Dan heard someone laugh. "Intrigue! I love it."

When Dan turned around, he saw that Abednego was standing behind him. Gabrielle smiled broadly, stood up and embraced Abednego. Pieces of the puzzle flew in from every direction. Until that moment, the entire episode in Jamaica had been about Marion, her parallel universes and their preordained encounter. Everything Dan had wished for, hoped and prayed for every day of the past two years of tear-drenched misery led to a glorious reunion with his *basherte*. How many more blessings could he receive?

"Dan," the familiar Voice rang in his ear. *"This can be a transformational event in your life," she said. "The question isn't how many more blessings* you *can receive. Think about it."*

A Zen kiss!

ABEDNEGO'S HEAP with Dan bouncing around in the back seat snorted its way to Rocky and Molly's stucco house, surrounded by lush gardens filled with fragrant flowers of every shape and color. The front porch was crowded with a large contingent of Rocky's family. The distinguished looking gentleman in a three-piece suit was his father, who cheerfully introduced himself to Dan and Abednego. His mother, an elegant woman who looked young enough to be one of Rocky's many handsome siblings, introduced them to all the aunts, uncles and cousins. The happy smiles they shared with Abednego became even broader when he spoke to the family in fluent Amharic. Dan never ceased to be amazed by his enigmatic friend's untold talents. When Rocky and Molly came onto the porch for the signing of the ornate Ketubah, the traditional Hebrew marriage contract that Dan had carefully prepared, the embraces were joyous and seemingly endless.

TOURISTS HAD ABANDONED THE HOTEL and the lobby was eerily quiet when Dan returned. "Did you see Molly?" Gabrielle asked.

"She looked ravishing."

"Did you tell her Steve's plane landed and he was on his way from Kingston?"

"I did. She said she would come by to say hello."

When Steve finally arrived, he embraced Dan and Gabrielle but said very little. Dan couldn't help but notice the dark rings around his eyes. He didn't remember Steve being that pallid when they were in Los Angeles, but at the time, Dan was unable to see anything beyond the gates of his own hell.

Time passed slowly as they sat in the empty lobby, waiting. Steve had the wan look of someone who had given up food—and possibly more. Dan tried to engage him in conversation but Steve had nothing to say, only trepidation which he wore like a mantle of ashes and sackcloth.

Gabrielle ordered coffee and rolls. It came and sat in front of them, untouched as they waited. When Molly arrived, followed by Rocky, Steve jumped to his feet, his heart thumping. His head drooped as Molly approached him, smiling. Standing face to face, words didn't come but tears flowed in a torrent down Steve's cheeks, something Dan had never witnessed in all the years he knew him. Steve tried to hold back, but couldn't. Molly's eyes moistened and she lifted her small hand—tiny, exactly like Marion's—and gently touched Steve's face. His tears rolled down her arm and Dan suddenly flashed on the wall of water at the shrine of resurrected souls, soaking Marion's sleeve. "I'm . . . sorry I wasn't a better . . ." Steve said. Molly wrapped both arms around his neck. "I didn't know how to be . . ." he said choking on his tears. "I'm so sorry about Simone . . . about everything I didn't . . ."

With tears in her eyes, Molly put her hand to his lips. "You're a good man, Dad and I love you." Steve tried to formulate words but a wail burst from the depths of his soul. They both wept as they clasped each other tightly.

Another Zen kiss!

Like a radiant pearl, the *chupah,* a wedding canopy of embroidered silk, rose from the center of the pool garden, resting on four sturdy legs carved in the shape of African lions.

Standing next to Dan, Abednego pointed to the images on the pillars supporting the canopy. "Dese African Lions were on de doors of de ark of de covenant. You remember our covenant wit' God, Daniel? He say dere would be light and dere was light. God say He would lead His people out of Egypt and it was so. He say He would deliver us from slavery to freedom. Dat taking longer dan we expected, but He's workin' on it." He laughed and Dan laughed with him.

Plaintive sounds of Charon's violin emerged from across the garden, prompting guests to be seated. Abednego placed his hand on Dan's shoulder and they proceeded to the rear of the nuptial carpet. Guests took their seats, holding rum-filled coconuts while trying to avoid the overly friendly peacocks strutting among white linen covered chairs. Steve's business associates were having a grand time with Rocky's relatives, richly attired in elephant sleeved brocade gowns and feather-beaded African headdresses, customary festive attire among Ethiopian Jews.

When the guests were seated, Charon began to play Pachelbel's "Canon in D" and a preternatural hush wafted through the garden.

Dan and Abednego walked together down the flower-strewn carpet and took their place under the *chupah.* Dan wore a traditional blue and white *Talit* that he hadn't donned in many years. Abednego also wore a *Talit,* but his was purple and gold. His yarmulke was shaped like a crown and he carried his walking stick like a scepter.

Next, Rocky, flanked by his father and mother, a handsome couple whose faces shone with pride, walked solemnly down the aisle. When he passed the contingent of his Israeli buddies, including the officious sergeant from the welcome desk at the Consulate, they let out a roar that reverberated throughout the garden.

At the base of the *chupah,* Rocky's parents took their places while he turned toward the gossamer covered archway at the rear. Charon put down the violin and picked up his guitar. He played a three-chord intro and the curtains parted, revealing Molly, who looked sublime. She stepped forward and took Steve's arm. With Charon's accompaniment on guitar, Rocky faced his bride and sang aloud, "Une Chanson d'Amour."

Under the canopy, standing next to Abednego, Dan heard someone singing along: *"Savor the golden rays of Autumn . . ."* It was MARION! Abednego was on Dan's left, but she stood, luminously on his right . . . singing!

"If you're trying to figure out where you are, Dan," Marion whispered, *"you're here with me, and our daughter is joining her* bashert *for all eternity, just like us. The cycle is complete."*

As Rocky sang, Marion and Dan harmonized, silently to everyone else but in full voice to one another. *"Once again—and for all time—reunited in love."*

When Molly arrived at the *chupah,* Steve embraced her then sat down in the front row beside Gabrielle. Hand in arm, Molly and Rocky stepped under the canopy, opposite Abednego and Dan. Marion glowed in mystical splendor as she stood face to face with Molly. Dan wasn't sure if anyone else could actually see Marion, but judging from the expression on Molly's face, it was clear that she did.

There was a long pause after the couple took their place under the canopy. The song ended and everyone waited for the ceremony to begin but the magic of that moment began to wane as people waited for someone to say something. The coughing and clearing of throats led to soft mumbling. Dan, too, waited for something to happen and he looked to Abednego for direction.

"Don't look at me, rabbi," Abednego said. "This is your turf."

Dan forgot entirely that he was there to conduct a wedding. With everything else that was going on—at the speed of light, it seemed—it never occurred to him to prepare a sermon. With all eyes on him, he turned to Marion and whispered. "What should I say?"

"Open your mouth. The words will come."

Standing next to his *basherte,* elevated by the radiance of their daughter and her beloved, Dan opened his mouth and the words did flow. "In the beginning," Dan heard himself say, "when the heavens, the earth and all the galaxies were put in place, God planted His greatest gift in the hearts of the first preordained couple, the gift of love everlasting and with it, the holy mandate that they unite—body and soul—and become one flesh, for this is the purpose of creation."

Rocky's foot came down on the glass like an exclamatory "Amen!" The audience shouted *"mazal tov!"* He held Molly in his arms as they savored a long, sweet, divinely blessed kiss.

"A Zen kiss," Dan said with a happy heart.

Waiting for a response from Marion that wasn't forthcoming, he turned to her . . . and with the reverberation of shattered glass still in his ears, he suddenly felt a shiver through his body. Marion was gone! Even her lustrous aura disappeared without a trace. Surrounded by deafening cries of *"mazal tov," "coo yah"* and a rash of exuberant Jamaican and Israeli benedictions, Dan was frozen in place as the awareness of what just happened came crashing down. How could he not have anticipated this? Marion's work was done! The mission was accomplished and she would not—could not—return again. The sting of that realization was unbearable.

Rocky and Molly walked joyously back up the aisle, to the accompaniment of applauding guests. Abednego looked at Dan and his ageless eyes saw everything that didn't need to be said. He went up the aisle alone, leaving Dan under the canopy in utter despair.

At dinner, the speeches were thankfully brief, except for the traditional roasting by army friends and Steve's tearful message of gratitude. Then came the dancing! The *freilach*-inspired music of the Reggae band energized the room. Molly was lifted up on a chair as everyone danced around her. Charon played his violin as if he had been raised in a *shtetl* and segued into a Reggae version of *Fiddler on the Roof.* Four of Rocky's strongest buddies, including Sergeant Mary Sunshine, lifted him up in a chair and the two groups did the longest circle dance in history. When they came down, Molly dragged Steve onto the floor and they danced. He was ecstatic. When he saw Dan, Steve threw one arm around him and kissed him sloppily, tearfully, on the face.

The dancing never stopped and the boisterous celebration made it seem that this wedding defied gravity and wafted in space. The Jamaicans mocked the Ethiopians' accents and vice versa. A cluster of Israelis, Rastas and friends of Steve circled the bride and groom in an endless hora line.

When Dan saw that the center of gravity was the dance floor, he quietly moved towards the exit and out to the parking lot. No sooner had he gotten into Rocky's car when he felt a heavy walking stick come to rest on his shoulder.

"Where are you now, my brother?" Abednego asked. "You know you cannot pass through the gate until you are called."

"Even God needs a Zen kiss every few millennia," Dan said.

"I ask you once again, my brother. Do you know where you are?"

"For the first time in two years, seven months and fourteen days, I know precisely where I am."

THE SUN WAS SETTING when Dan parked next to the roadside café. Leaving the car, he crossed the quiet road to the thick forest as darkness began to claim the night. Dan wondered for a brief moment if he would be able to find the path. He made a few wrong turns, but ultimately found it.

Dan followed the narrow trail, making his way through hanging vines and thick foliage as the night birds welcomed him with their song. Although he hadn't seriously considered the possibility that he might not find the secluded waterfall, he was reassured when he heard the percussive sounds of gushing water in the distance. When he reached the shallow pond at the base of the falls, he looked up. Awed by its primordial power, he watched as the last vestiges of bronze and rose-colored clouds slipped silently into the abyss. Dan kicked off his shoes and waded through the shallow pool. Without a thought in his head, he climbed out of the pond and found his way behind the sheet of cascading water. Feeling the wall of stone with his fingers, he found the gaps. Summoning every ounce of strength he had, Dan slowly pulled himself up.

From the stone ledge just below the crest, he found the narrow path. Barely able to catch his breath, Dan slowly made his way down to the meteor-shaped lake. An eerie calm hovered over the water. No waves, no ripples, no sounds. Dan strained to see a glimmer of light in the distance.

Nothing. Only the clear reflection of the full moon as it basked motionless on the face of the deep. Dan looked around the lake until his eyes hurt, but he saw no one. Hoping to hear Abednego's voice or Charon's violin, he examined the shore where they stood twice before, but they weren't there. No chanting, no silver chalice and no mellifluous accompaniments.

Sounds of the forest that accompanied Dan to this point became deathly silent and the only thing he heard was the voice of Abednego inside his own head. *"When circumcision of de heart is complete, preordained souls will be rejoined in celestial harmony."*

Dan walked slowly to the shore. Feeling neither courageous nor fearful, he entered the lake. The warm water soothed his feet. He didn't remember it that way, but it was comforting after the strenuous climb. The water gently lapped at his ankles as he looked out at the vast, still lake. How to read it? Was it his enemy, like Goliath, arrogantly challenging him to fight for his life . . . or a *mikveh,* a ritual immersion, graciously offering spiritual purity?

Dan moved slowly forward. When the water rose above his calves, it was even more comforting. He waded in further. The water seemed to welcome him as it rose above his knees and gently touched his thighs. As he was about to take another step, a thought sliced through his brain. What if . . . ? Maybe . . . ? No, NO NOOOO! He caught his mind mischievously trying to employ logic to sidetrack him from his destiny and he angrily shut it down. This was not a time for distracting calculations. There was no downside and no consequences to consider. That was over. The mission was clear and he surged ahead.

The water reached his waist. He took several more steps. The water passed his chest . . . and continued to rise. He stood motionless for a brief moment, then slowly stepped forward and felt the water touch his chin . . .

Accompanied by an exhilaration he had experienced only in Marion's embrace, he inhaled deeply, held his breath as long as he could and took the next step.

Then he exhaled. The water was still at his chin, but that's as high as it got. Dan held his breath again and took another step forward. An aurora borealis in the shape of a rainbow flashed through the sky then disappeared.

Dan exhaled again. The water was still at his chin! Perplexed, Dan walked backwards. The water dropped slightly, to his neck . . . but no farther. He moved his feet. They were underwater, but on solid ground.

Totally confused, Dan laughed aloud. What was he supposed to feel? Relieved? Disappointed? The apparent reality rendered all poetic possibilities moot. Nothing happened! "Marion! Marion, what do I do now?" He cried aloud.

"Blessed be life in all the worlds." A voice, riding the crest of a strong reverberating note, sang to him from across the lake. "Blessed be life in all the worlds . . ."

"Blessed be life in all the worlds . . ." The last verse at the end of the circumcision ceremony, Dan recalled.

From the corner of his eye, he saw . . . that is, he thought he saw . . . a small dot of light across the lake. With the water still at his neck, he looked up to see if Charon's violin was wafting overhead. It wasn't. He looked across the lake again, and there, in the distance, was an unmistakable dot of light. *How do I get from here to there?* Dan's legs were already tired. He tried to swim, but that didn't last long. As the shaman warned Marion, her husband is not a very good swimmer. The dot of light did seem to be growing larger. He couldn't be sure, nor could he help wondering: is it exhaustion? Is this a mirage? Suddenly, the voice grew louder . . . and without the reverb . . . familiar!

"I am my beloved's and my beloved is mine," their favorite verse from Song of Songs.

"Marion," he cried out. "I am my beloved's and my beloved is mine!" Dan's heart swelled as he watched the luminous dot grow in the distance. Struggling to reach it, Dan finally came close enough to see that it was . . . a raft. He called out again. *Ani l'dodi v'dodi li* . . . I am my beloved's and my beloved is mine."

The raft came closer and there was no doubt. "It is Marion," he assured himself. "She is here! Alone on the raft . . . alone? Who is steering it?"

No one was guiding the raft, but it continued to advance towards him. When it came within just a few feet, Dan saw that there was indeed someone on the raft with her . . . but it wasn't the boatman. It was . . . him. Dan was sitting next to Marion on her raft and her smile was radiant.

"Do you know where you are now, Dan?"

Confused, he looked out at the lake where he had been standing, but he wasn't there.

"Blessed be life in all the worlds," Marion said. "Circumcision of the heart is complete. *Mazel tov,* Dan. Don't you want to kiss me?"

He reached towards her but recalled that the last time he

tried, his hands went through her as though she were a hologram or cluster of ionized electrons.

His hands were inches from her face and . . . he touched her. He touched her! He felt her soft skin. It was real. Not a vector of light, but flesh! Like before. Like always. They kissed.

In the beginning, when the heavens, the earth and all the galaxies were put in place, God planted His greatest gift in the hearts of preordained souls, the gift of love everlasting and with it, the holy mandate that they unite—body and soul—and become one flesh, for this is the purpose of creation.

Marion wrapped her arms around Dan.

"Dansez-moi . . . dansez-moi à la fin de temps."

"Dance me," Marion said, "dance me to the end of time."

"Dance me, Marion," Dan said.

". . . dance me to the end of time."

All's well that doesn't end.

ACKNOWLEDGMENTS

Homage to Marion Freed—*sine qua non.*

Other outstanding women and men were essential to my completing this book and I take great pleasure in acknowledging their contributions.

My daughter, Polly Segal, a prominent singer and song writer whose encouragement and insights helped me commit to paper some of the most heart-wrenching and exhilarating events of my life with Marion.

Coming from the world of film, universally acknowledged as a communal endeavor, I had no idea how to manage scenes and dialogue in a novel where there is no music, soundtrack or special effects. The first to help me with that transition was Ziva Kwitney, a talented psychotherapist and writer. She showed me how to bring out the light from within, past the pain and onto the page.

Janice Lynde, award winning actress and best-selling author helped bring form and dimension to the characters who populate this book. Her wisdom, skill and tenacity helped me tell a fictional story that is entirely true.

After writing and rewriting for five years, I was left with a thousand disconnected pages. Fortunately, I didn't have to blow my brains out because I met Carl Lennertz, the wizard, who edits and guides companies and writers. Carl is the midwife who enabled me to give birth to this novel.

Meryl Moss and her team of talented artists and advocates created the bridge to bring this story out of my head and into the hearts of like-minded readers.

To all of you, I offer my respect and gratitude.

THE AUTHOR

Herb Freed has directed and produced over a dozen feature films, including *Graduation Day, Tomboy, Haunts* and *Child2Man*. He began his adult life as an ordained rabbi and eventually resigned his pulpit to become a movie director. Bashert is his first novel.